TRAVELING LIGHT

TALES OF THE MAGICAL GATES

NATANIA BARRON   MARIE BRENNAN

LINDSEY CARMICHAEL   MIKE CHEN   KATE ELLIOTT

VICTOR MANIBO   MARSHALL RYAN MARESCA

ROWENNA MILLER   CASS MORRIS   J.C. PILLARD

MICHAEL R. UNDERWOOD   VALERIE VALDES

Presented by

WORLDBUILDING FOR MASOCHISTS

Edited by

ROWENNA MILLER, CASS MORRIS, AND MARSHALL RYAN
MARESCA

CONTENTS

Brödel
Remor
FJALLINIR
Ullande
KOIDEV
SJALSTINAT
Gottinsholmikkaster
Reseinal
Hakelinak
Karsoffia

MIRRADEN
Midpoint
Lodge
GRIASTA
Saloein
Notalto
AL-NOTLIR
Brightyellow
Gann
Muste
Berit
Nalin
Alinno
AL'NAR
Al'inaset-kuu
Yaff'niq
Unnoa
INDEYA
DELTA
Huwk
Markets
Lolloelhfan
Telo-Sre-
Nava
nadi

FOREWORD

Back in 2019, I was thinking a lot about fantasy worldbuilding. In part I was doing so because I had been working on the world that my *Maradaine Saga* novels were set in since 1993, and while I was continuing to tweak it, I was also thinking a lot about the mistakes I had made due to youth and ignorance, and what sort of work it would take to build a new fantasy world that felt truly complete, real, and lived in. I wrote down a lot of ideas about the principles behind worldbuilding, created spreadsheets and tables, and kept thinking about how to do it *better*, even if— and perhaps regardless of whether— said *better* didn't necessarily translate to any marked improvement of the actual stories written in that world.

In other words, I was getting *weird* about worldbuilding.

But I was sure I was completely alone, even among the other fantasy writers I knew, about being *this weird* about it. Which was a strange thing to think, because fantasy writers are a demographic traditionally filled with overthinking weirdos. But I had convinced myself I was an outlier and no one else was like this. Until a few conversations on Twitter about the effects multiple moons would have on a world— calendars, tides, cultural references, idiomatic phrases (would someone be called a "lunatic"?)— snowballed into further and further delightful weirdness, and then a magic phrase dropped into the conversation.

"Y'all should start a podcast."

And that hung there for a moment. Should we start a podcast? A podcast about being especially weird and extra about fantasy world-building? Would anyone actually be interested in that? Despite not having any clue about the answer to that last question, Rowenna Miller, Alexandra Rowland, and I got started with putting together *Worldbuilding for Masochists,* and after recording a few episodes, we realized we were having a fun time *and* that people were having a great time listening to us, so we kept going with it. After about a year, life circumstances forced Alex to step away, and we brought in the fiercely brilliant Cass Morris, and when Rowenna had to drop out, the incredible Natania Barron stepped in.

One aspect of the podcast was creating a fantasy world on air, developing and adding to it as we went, so we could take principles we were talking about and put them to practice. Every time we had a guest on the show, we invited them to gift us with another little element to incorporate into the world. This became a delightful way to make a world that was filled with odd details and pockets of unexpected weirdness, and with each new gift, the world grew and changed.

And then, there was the gift from Kate Elliott.

In an episode about transportation systems, Kate gave us a gift that changed everything: a series of Gates that teleport people to places all over the world, but only living things. You can't bring armor or weapons or anything else through it. You emerge on the other side completely naked.

Thus, the Magical Nude Gates were born.

One thing we quickly realized was how such a thing would be a tentpole concept for a world. A world that had these, especially an extensive network of them would *have* to be, on some level, defined by them. A world where all sorts of cultures and peoples from every corner of the globe are able to reach each other by stepping through a Gate? And that it works in such a way that almost *demands* that conversation, diplomacy, and understanding come before war or aggression? What sort of world would that be? How would these Gates be used? What sort of cultural norms would arise? We were so excited to explore further into it.

So we decided we should write some stories in this world, and we should invite people to come play with us. We had so *many* brilliant minds joining us over the course of doing the podcast, I couldn't possibly single just a few out— all our guests have been amazing and brilliant, and there's no way we could fit stories from all of them in one anthology. So we put out a call for stories, and were blessed with some absolute gifts. Some from long time Friends of the Podcast, some from folks who had never been published before. All of them exploring beautiful, different facets of this one wild, interconnected world.

For me, it's been an absolute privilege working with these brilliant, creative writers over the past five years, and I'm thrilled I get to not only help put this collection in your hands, but to keep doing this work, building incredible and intricate worlds for us all to imagine ourselves in.

-Marshall Ryan Maresca

VIGNETTES FROM THE HILTHSTAD

CASS MORRIS

The door opened, and a naked man strolled through.

Freyda no longer even sighed when this occurred. People *ought* to know, when traveling to Fjallanir—and if they didn't do their research ahead of time, there were helpful little signs posted in every arrival chamber, in the traders' argot as well as a variety of the most common languages, for the convenience of those who, unlike Navigators and other such secret orders, did not bear tattoos with embedded translation charms.

It was Arjen's turn to deal with it, and he smoothly stepped from behind his desk and into the new arrival's path. "Your journey is honored, traveler." Ritual words of welcome, offered to all. "But you will wish to avail yourself of, at the very least, the robe provided in the arrival chamber—"

"Oh, no, I'm quite alright," the traveler said, waving Arjen off and trying to scoot around him. He spoke the argot with a Griastan accent, which rather explained his nonchalance about nudity.

"—and we do suggest taking advantage of the options available to you in the wardrobe chamber," Arjen continued, as though he had never been interrupted. "If you need assistance, I would be pleased to—"

"No, no, it's perfectly fine." The man laughed. "I'll find something out there eventually, I'm sure, if your people require it, but for now, I'm quite comfortable." He slipped around Arjen and made for the Hilthstad's front door.

Arjen and Freyda locked eyes briefly. They weren't *supposed* to let anyone out without taking down their name, origin, and other pertinent information.

But some people just had to find things out for themselves.

Freyda had only counted to six in her head when the door burst back open, and their wayward Griastan traveler lunged back in, slamming it behind him. "Moons above!" he gasped. "It's *freezing* out there!"

"Yes, honored traveler," Arjen said, to his credit without the lacing of sarcasm that Freyda would not have been able to keep from her own tongue. "If you'd care to step back into the wardrobe chamber, we can outfit you more than adequately."

The somewhat chagrined visitor accepted the offer this time, and Arjen accompanied him back through the door he had first burst through. Clucking her tongue, Freyda prepared an entry in the folio for him.

The Fjallaniri had a global reputation for being uptight, and perhaps it was not entirely undeserved, but much of that did stem from the unarguable reality of their climate.

> *Fifth hour, first quarter: Arriving*
> *Tregan Amani*
> *Nation of Origin: Griasta*
> *Point of Arrival: Tella Gate*
> *Purpose of Transit: "I just like to see new things"*
> *Intended Duration of Stay: 3 nights*
> *Intended Lodging: Haraval House, on concierge recommendation*
> *Notable features: dark hair, tanned skin, very large ears, large mole on left shoulder blade*
> *Processed by: Drëla Freyda Sandvik*

THE ULLANDE GATES WERE IMMACULATELY DESIGNED. WELL, NOT THE Gates *themselves*, so much. Those were relics, stone arches erected around each blurry portal. Not even all Fjallaniri could read the runes carved into them anymore—though Freyda had, naturally, taken a course prior to applying for her position.

No, it was the Hilthstad itself that she admired for its elegance. Ullande was home to several Gates, clustered together on a hillside. The nation of Fjallanir had a few more, scattered upriver, but this was the hub, just outside its largest city.

Around each Gate, the people of Fjallanir had constructed a small room, well-heated by a hypocaust drawing from underground hot springs. This was the arrival chamber, small and—it had to be stressed —*private*. Whether coming or going, a traveler had this space to themselves, to reorient and, if arriving, don the thoughtfully provided plush robe.

Stepping out of the arrival chamber, a traveler found themselves in the wardrobe chamber, stocked with an array of garments. Most were lace-up rather than buttoned, allowing for easy adjustment of size, particularly with the modesty panels tucked into a drawer. A traveler had—as a helpful notice, printed in tidy lettering and affixed to the wall, informed them—the option to borrow or buy. Most travelers opted to borrow, returning their selection as soon as they'd gotten out into Ullande and either purchased new clothing or located what sartorial arrangements they had made in advance. Very few failed to return what they borrowed, even if they left Ullande by some other method than the Gates; a mild suggestion that the garments were hexed against just such thievery may have encouraged honesty.

This chamber also had a small lavatory. The Fjallaniri had no custom of pre- or post-Gate evacuation, since they knew perfectly well that the Gates had no effect upon partially digested matter, but some cultures did, and they liked to be conscientious. The doors on either side could be locked, so if someone arrived swiftly after you, or intended to depart just after you'd arrived, embarrassments could be avoided— though it did mean that the Hilthstad attendants had to check the doors frequently, lest someone get trapped in an arrival chamber because the person before them had forgotten to flip the bolt back.

Around *all* the wardrobe chambers stood the customs hall, where Freyda and the other officials worked. It was impossible, unless one was really determined in matters of improvisational carpentry and demolition, to pass through unnoticed.

"No arrangements made, then?" Freyda asked their next guest, a small man from Ussuchnel huddling with his borrowed garments drawn quite close about himself, as though worried they might vanish without warning.

"N-No," he said, so quietly that Freyda strained to hear him. "I d-didn't have the chance to send word ahead."

Not unusual. Fjallanir was, without the Gates, not the easiest place to reach, requiring a long sea voyage from most other major population centers. Regular travelers might have partners here, ready to see to their needs, and diplomatic sorts tended to plan well in advance, allowing their letters to arrive before their bodies did. But for the rest, Fjallanir stood ready to provide.

Freyda smoothly supplied her usual spiel for such occasions. "Of course, honored traveler." She pulled a leaflet from the cubbyhole beneath her desktop and picked up a pen. "It would be my pleasure to direct you to one of our most reliable establishments." She hardly needed to look at the map to circle the three locations she knew had vacancies as of this morning. "These inns are much accustomed to providing for travelers from the gates. If you already have banking arrangements, they have affiliations with all the major worldwide financial institutions; if you have not, they have agents on-hand to assist you."

"Oh. Oh, I do." The man said it in a way that made it seem like it was a surprise to him. "I'm with Tepa International."

Freyda nodded, always pleased to have her expectations satisfied. Tepa was the common institution favored by travelers from his subcontinent. "Very good, honored traveler. In that case, I recommend deVerdt House. Their arrangement with Tepa International provides additional amenities, at no extra charge to your honored self."

The man looked so perplexed by the idea of costless comfort that Freyda had to wonder what, exactly, they did with their travelers in Ussuchnel.

Fifth hour, third quarter: Arriving
Durosh Timpessa
Nation of Origin: Ussuchnel
Point of Arrival: Soren Gate
Purpose of Transit: Negotiating trade agreement between
his local silk-production guild and Drëlen Merrack
venKessel's clothier house
Intended Duration of Stay: 5 nights "unless the negotia-
tion takes longer than expected"
Intended Lodging: deVerdt House, on concierge recom-
mendation
Notable features: Grey-dusted red hair, pale skin -
complexion a bit sallow, looks like you turned a
mouse into a human
Processed by: Drëla Freyda Sandvik

As Durosh Timpessa finally found the necessary temerity to step out of the Hilthstad, a figure well-known to its attendants stepped in.

Haviva venPress never waited until the wardrobe room to begin alleviating herself of burdens, and she *always* wore more than was necessary. "Freyda, *darling*!" she trilled, pulling at the laces of her sleeves. "Oh, I'm so glad it's you in today. Last time it was that young one, with the face." She gestured vaguely at her own. "Harald? Harand?"

"Harennd," Freyda supplied.

"That's the one." She removed her left sleeve and dropped it unceremoniously on the ground. It had so many beads and baubles that it clattered. "I hate to say it, my dear, I know you all work so *very* hard, but that one needs a *bit* more training in matters of sartorial conservation. I'm afraid my gown was *quite* wrinkled when I returned home."

Freyda inclined her head a touch. "I will ensure that everything is properly packed and stored for your return."

"You always do, dear, you *always* do."

"And where are you heading today, Damen venPress?"

"Anvar Gate. I'm for Volleningen, eventually, though of course I've multiple transfers ahead of me, and *one* of them—" She pulled at the laces of her right sleeve while she chattered. "It's through Qichel-wei, and you *know* how they are about their Gates."

"I'm afraid I've never had the pleasure of traveling there, Damen venPress."

"Oh, there's just always a *line*." The right sleeve joined its partner on the floor, and Haviva began pulling jeweled pins out of her cap. "They're so anxious about exceeding their Gates' capacity. And of course they give you a robe there, too, but it's a thin little thing, and it's never warm enough in their antechambers, and sometimes the wait is *hours*." She dropped the pins on Freyda's desk. "They'll give you water —there's a little natural spring right next to the Gates—but they don't offer any other refreshments, not even a *nibble*." Tugging loose her hat and snood, she placed them on top of the pins and shook loose a mane of silky dark hair. "Well, at least I'll be able to eat soon after I get to Volleningen. *Straight* to a party at the embassy, as soon as I've got my frock on."

Haviva kept a set of clothing in at least a dozen different Gated locations, so far as Freyda knew. Not all had wardrobe chambers, of course, but there was always *some* kind of arrangement one could make—at least if one had the combined financial and social clout of a venPress. Volleningen was, apparently, one such location.

Sometimes, Freyda wondered what it would be like, to live a life such as Damen venPress did. Oh, she had traveled, of course; it was required training for her position. She had taken in a concert in Al'tamer, visited family in Brelethrope, and been in the Republic of Ossetan during their equinoctial festival. But for someone who spent the bulk of her days mere steps from a Gate, she did not travel often enough to have the easy familiarity with it that Haviva venPress demonstrated, nor such conversance with the customs of the peoples on the other sides of those Gates.

'*But then,*' she thought, as the Damen swanned off, trailing accessories in her wake, '*we all have our roles to fulfill.*' And Freyda was, if she allowed herself some small pride, quite well-suited for her own.

<hr>

ARJEN STOOD READY FOR THE NEXT TRAVELER SO THAT FREYDA COULD fulfill her promise to Damen venPress. Once the woman had gone, Freyda picked up every piece of discarded clothing, every bit of jewelry, every hairpin strewn across the hall and both chambers. She took her time in the wardrobe chamber, ensuring that every item was stored properly and noted in the wardrobe log.

She took particular care with counting the jewelry, including an inscription on the back of one of the Damen's bracelets: *brighter than the untouchable sun,* the venPress family motto. She also noted, though did not write down, the precise number of lapis (four), carnelian (one), and topaz (two) stones embedded into the cuff.

Freyda unlocked a storage drawer, tucked it all away, and locked the drawer again. Then, reaching deep in her pocket, she pulled out a thin graphite pencil and a small commonplace book: the sort of thing nearly every Fjallaniri carried, to jot down quotes from plays, lyrics from songs, riddles and jests, new recipes—all the verbal detritus of their lives that might be worth remembering.

Flipping to a clean page, Freyda jotted down a series of symbols. To anyone else, they would have looked like she were working out moves for a game of sjakkë, but to Freyda, the code meant: *Damen venPress • Ullande • Republic of Ossetan • Berit • Qichel-wei • Volleningen,* along with the date and a few other tidbits from the Damen's dropped conversation.

For all that Damen venPress loved to chatter and could sound a full frivol, she knew to whom she spoke, when she spoke to Freyda Sandvik, and to whom Freyda reported. Her words, though effusive, were nonetheless carefully chosen. If Freyda had guessed her route correctly—and who would get from Ossetan to Qichel-wei by any path but the Envers road to Berit?—then Damen venPress would be traveling through a few locations of geopolitical interest, and she wanted Freyda aware of it.

Freyda was not always certain which pieces of information someone else might find worth knowing, but it paid, she had long since discovered, to be thorough.

> *Fifth hour, fourth quarter: Departing*
> *Damen Haviva venPress*
> *Nation of Origin: Fjallanir*
> *Point of Departure: Anvar Gate*
> *Purpose of Transit: Social occasion*
> *Intended Date of Return: 5th Curand, morning (note for*
> *whomever is on duty that day: it will absolutely not*
> *be before midday, no matter what she says)*
> *Notable features: see entry in Frequent Travelers Folio*
> *Processed by: Drëla Freyda Sandvik*

AT THE TOP OF THE SIXTH HOUR PAST SUNRISE, A MESSENGER ARRIVED at the Hilthstad—a girl with a coronet of tight black braids, face fiercely set in the lines of someone determined to do a good job. Judging by her age, she was likely new to her post and taking it quite seriously.

Freyda took the bundle of missives from the girl, gave her the expected coin for her trouble, and divided the stack between herself and Arjan for processing. Most were routine: diplomats and merchants arranging future travel, local inns and hotels confirming availability for unexpected arrivals, bills from the laundry, and so forth. Such things were compiled then added to the calendar, the folios, the ledgers.

Freyda's stack, however, included an envelope with her own initials on it and three small ticks radiating from the corner.

Without any external flicker of interest, Freyda popped the seal and read the brief, innocuous note within. Then she withdrew the other contents: a second envelope, with no lines of address, and an entirely blank seal. This, she slipped in her pocket before moving on to the next item in her pile.

THE NEXT MAN TO EMERGE FROM BRELE GATE HAD A ROBE TIED HASTILY but sufficiently about him, a salt-and-ginger grackle-tail beard, and a permanent expression of vague harassment. He approached Freyda's desk, scrubbing irritably at his hair.

Freyda lifted her pen and flipped to a fresh page in her folio. "Any luck this time, Sir Isaac?"

"No, dash it all." The man spoke Fjallaniri with a strong Thurane accent, high and sharp. "Would you believe it? All the way to the Srivashi Isles, and one of the westernmost at that, and there a dead end." He sighed, sweeping away his cap and scrubbing a hand through his bright hair. "What a waste."

"Still," Freyda said, smiling, for it was impossible not to like Sir Isaac, even with the element of the absurd about him, "the Srivashi Isles? Hard to complain about white sands, turquoise waters, and warm weather no matter the time of year."

"Hm? Oh, yes, I suppose."

Sir Isaac Permutus, Seeker of the Optimal Path, was in fierce if supremely unacknowledged competition with the Navigators. He, and a few like him, were convinced that the Gates could be reckoned mathematically and scientifically, not through the chaotic and haphazard experimental ways of the Navigators. And indeed, his society had made a few interesting discoveries.

He'd become a regular figure in Fjallanir, as he was, Freyda assumed, in most of the other major hubs, dashing back and forth from Gate to Gate, then following land and sea routes to locations where his calculations suggested new Gates might have formed or be in the process of forming.

Freyda knew her business and, while she jotted down the relevant information, asked the expected questions about the honored traveler's journey.

Never needing much in the way of encouragement to talk, Sir Isaac effused so much information that Arjen had to take the next two arrivals, out of Soren and Fiera Gates.

Sir Isaac's path had taken him first upriver to Brelethrope, then over the tundra to the remote port of Drangavik, a boat ride across the Bay of Ghosloekr to a Gate leading to an equatorial city called Zarranaq, and thence, apparently, to the Srivashi Isles, famed for their gorgeous sunsets.

It *would* be a coup for the Isles if a Gate should form there. Freyda imagined that, quite the opposite to Fjallanir, it was a place where spontaneous nudity would be both appropriate and comfortable, and that often meant a thriving tourist trade.

Alas, Sir Isaac returned disappointed.

With his arrival entry complete, Freyda moved to the departure column. "Are you back to Thurantil, or trying another vector?"

"Back home, I'm afraid," Sir Isaac sighed. "I must revisit my calculations, and of course all my books are there. Oh. Oh!" A dawning look of inspiration leavened his creased features. "Your library! The one at— at—dash it—the University of Southrend?"

"Southriver College, you mean?" Freyda supplied. Already, her hands moved swiftly, pulling open the third drawer down and withdrawing a requisition sheet.

"Yes, yes— Well, they *must* have a copy of Eunys Cottier's treatise on Kjastari's Recursive Sequence Theorem, yes? She was—*was* she Fjallaniri?"

"Manveyli," Freyda answered, "but she published here. Yes, I expect they would." In brisk, sharp penstrokes, Freyda filled in a few boxes. "If you'd like to have a copy shipped to you in Thurantil, Sir Isaac—"

"You're a treasure," the Seeker proclaimed, eagerly seizing the pen. His handwriting was haphazard, but Freyda could neaten it—or copy it to a fresh sheet entirely—before sending it to the college. "And if this leads to a discovery, I shall be sure to mention you in the monograph, Drëla Sandvik. I surely shall."

"I'll be happy enough just to read a copy, Sir Isaac, but I thank you for the thought."

Sixth hour, third quarter: Arriving
Sir Isaac Permutus

Nation of Origin: Thurantil
Point of Arrival: Brele Gate
Purpose of Transit: Scientific exploration
Intended Duration of Stay: Immediate transfer
Intended Lodging: N/A
Notable features: see entry in Frequent Travelers Folio
Processed by: Drëla Freyda Sandvik

Seventh hour, first quarter: Departing
Sir Isaac Permutus
Nation of Origin: Thurantil
Point of Departure: Thuran Gate
Purpose of Transit: Scientific exploration
Intended Date of Return: Undetermined
Notable features: see entry in Frequent Travelers Folio
Processed by: Drëla Freyda Sandvik

LATER THAT HOUR, THE CUSTOMS HALL WAS HOST TO AN ENTHUSIASTIC, if abbreviated, conference of medical knowledge.

One entered from the wardrobe chamber attached to Thuran Gate; the other was soon to depart in that direction. They met in the middle, providing information to Freyda and Arjan in between their gabbling to each other in words that, although Fjallanir in origin, might as well have been in T‡leshi, for all Freyda could understand them.

"—yes, and I'd be honored if you would examine the cranistaxial abnormalities in my patient suffering from Turvoid's Syndrome—"

"—of course you'll see in my notes, the progression of chrondosclerosis is much accelerated from what one might expect in a subject of this age—"

"—unresponsive to *traditional* treatments, but I've found an application of henwort and pulverized adakite to be peculiarly effective—"

Ullande was, in addition to its other notable attributes, home to a premier medical college, and as the Fjallaniri were ever in pursuit of knowledge, they arranged for frequent exchanges between its professionals and those at other eminent institutions.

Their respective nations had many reasons to be grateful for such peaceable transfer of learning from one society to another. For her part, however, Freyda wished they could focus their attention, for a few minutes at least, on the necessities of well-ordered transit.

Seventh hour, third quarter: Arriving
Doctor Sariah Callaghan
Nation of Origin: Embreigh Isle
Point of Origin: Thuran Gate
Purpose of Transit: Research exchange program
Intended Duration of Stay: Until 15th Urshand
Intended Lodging: Lütken House, University of Ullande
Notable features: Nearly black eyes, rosy skin, small
*   raised scar on back of right hand*
Processed by: Drëla Freyda Sandvik

Seventh hour, fourth quarter: Departing
Rector Dyri Daggheist
Nation of Origin: Fjallanir
Point of Departure: Thuran Gate
Purpose of Transit: Research exchange program
Intended Date of Return: 15th Urshand
Notable features: see entry in Frequent Travelers Folio
Processed by: Drëla Freyda Sandvik

THE KJARAN AND FIERA GATES RECEIVED TRAVELERS AT NEARLY THE same moment, so Arjan and Freyda were both kept busy. Arjan processed a taciturn man who spoke only a little of the traders' argot. From what she could overhear, he seemed to have made several stops, hopping along a chain of Gates until he reached his prior location in the Indeya Delta, and was now only vaguely aware that he was in Fjallanir. Their clothing was alien enough to him that he'd put the breeches on backwards and wrapped the sleeves around his torso like a sash.

While Arjan gently redirected the stranger's sartorial efforts and patiently attempted to communicate, Freyda was having nearly the opposite problem: a Fjallaniri woman who quite simply did not stop talking.

Drëla Sunfritha Ottarsi, Freyda learned quite against her will, was living now in Al'notlir because her father had been a trade negotiator there some years ago, and she'd met a lovely woman, Polisenna, a baker with a pet ocelot named Trobar, and settled down with her, and now their shop specialized in both Al'notliri delicacies *and* Fjallaniri treats, because wouldn't you know it, the Al'notliri had never had Frisian-style goat cheese pastries, but now that they'd got the taste for fennel and caraway, they couldn't get enough of them, so the shop was doing *quite* well, you should see the lines in the morning, but Polisenna would have to manage on her own for a little while, because Sunfritha's sister Sibbe, older by a few years and expecting her first child soon, well, their mother had passed a few years back, and they'd a passel of uncles but no aunts among them, and Bridgewater District had very good midwives of course, but all the same, Sunfritha thought she really ought to come and stay for the birth and a bit after, for the moral support if nothing else, and to keep Sibbe's house tidy, and if she'd timed it right, that would mean Polisenna would have to manage the shop on her own for three months or thereabouts, though of course Sunfritha *could* pop back over if needed, but sometimes it was hard to get back, the Al'notliri could be stingy with their Gate passes if you caught a customs agent in a bad mood or who didn't think you were dressed well enough, not that that *mattered*, not like anyone on the other side would see what you'd been wearing, but they could be a touch snooty about such things, in Sunfritha's opinion, *not* that you'd catch her saying anything about that in Polisenna's hearing, have to keep the peace, after all, and really Sunfritha quite liked her new home even if it still wasn't *home-home*, you understand.

Freyda dutifully extracted from this ceaseless monologue the information she needed for the folio, hoping all the while that Sunfritha would not pass out from lack of respiration.

> *Seventh hour, fourth quarter: Arriving*
> *Drëla Sunfritha Ottarsi*
> *Nation of Origin: Fjallanir*
> *Point of Arrival: Kjaran gate*
> *Purpose of Transit: visiting family (sister is expectant*
> *   mother)*
> *Intended Duration of Stay: 3 months "or thereabouts"*
> *Intended Lodging: with family, Bridgewater District*
> *Notable features: red cheeks, prominent hairline peak,*
> *   violet-brown skin, loquacious*
> *Processed by: Drëla Freyda Sandvik*

At the eighth hour, Arjan's shift ended, and he traded places with Drële Hadrian Barimen, leaving Freyda to welcome another regular traveler.

Orvokki-Juhván had been in the Youth Council in his earlier years, and while he could no longer serve as a legislator, had stayed within the broader apparatus of civil service. Fjallaniri government generated quite a lot of paperwork, and so it required quite a lot of bureaucrats to keep it all straight and verified.

Juhván habitually wore the faded heather shade of purple common to Vadkanger, the last major town before the Trüle River became unnavigable to all but the shallowest of skiffs. He had not lived there in decades and had lost every trace of his upland accent, thoroughly trained out of him by Ullande education, but he remained proud of his remote heritage. Faded heather had long been sneered at by wealthier, city-bred Fjallaniri as a peasant's color, but Juhván had been such a charismatic Council member that there'd been quite a vogue for it in his heyday, and now it could certainly be worn with no embarrassment.

"Your journey is honored, traveler," Freyda said, wearing more of a smile than her usual pleasant-but-placid expression, for she had always liked Orvokki-Juhván—and, delivering Damen venPress's message to him meant she could check another item off of the day's to-do list. "We only received notice of your intended departure this morning. What trouble sends you abroad on such short notice?"

As she spoke, Freyda splayed four fingers out against the edge of her folio and drummed them lightly. Juhván's eyes flicked down only briefly as he sighed, scrubbing his corkscrew-curly hair.

"A dispute between two of our financiers about the exchange rate for the Hashimae li." The weariness in his voice suggested he'd been enduring the debate for too long. "They changed their coinage again."

"Again?"

"They've had three sovereigns in two years, and each one takes it in their head to reissue currency. You'd think slapping their own heads on the coins would be quite enough, but no, now they've gone and changed the denominations."

Her eyes still on Juhván—for the topic *was* fascinating—Freyda swapped the four fingers at the edge of the folio for a single one, stretching down the page. Again, the slight dart of Juhván's gaze; again, he continued speaking with no more acknowledgement than that.

"Now our people aren't certain if a shō is half of a sleu or twice one, let alone what the little triangular nei—triangular coins, I ask you, whose sterling idea was that?—are meant to represent, so I've got to go all the way to Hashima to sort it out."

Finally, two fingers at the edge of the page. Juhván rapped his knuckles on his side of the desk, and Freyda relaxed her hand to a normal position. "How long do you think that will take?"

"Well, my Hashimae is better than our financiers', so I hope to commit a chart to memory swiftly. Back tomorrow, perhaps, but I may decide to linger a day, make it worth my while by taking in one of their light-and-shadow shows."

"Oh, those are supposed to be lovely. I've always wanted to see one." Freyda's pen moved in quick strokes across the page.

"Did you not catch the performance of that traveling troupe that came through, oh, four or five years ago?"

Freyda shook her head. "I'm afraid not. I was filling in for an attendant in Brelethrope that whole autumn."

Juhván shuddered. "Miserable time to be in Brelethrope."

"I was very glad to return home, I can tell you that much."

"And so shall I be. Do you need anything else from me?"

"No, honored traveler, your usual information is always on file."

"Of course, of course. Well, if I do see a show, I'll tell you all about it when I get back." He was already moving away from her before he finished talking, waving over his shoulder as he went into the Kjaran Gate's wardrobe chamber.

Freyda didn't have the slightest clue what the numbers meant. That was not her purpose. Haviva venPress's purpose was to send a message, and Orvokki-Juhván's was to retrieve it. Freyda was merely the conduit.

In truth, she was not certain that either Haviva or Juhván knew the meaning of 4-1-2, either—though she suspected both were deeper in the Agency's secrets than she was. They both had a certain degree of theatrical talent, able to conceal their depths beneath alternate personas: Haviva, the frivolous socialite; Juhván, the much-harried bureaucrat.

Freyda, alas, had never been able to seem anything other than what she was: a fair-haired, delta-born, academy-bred woman with a perpetually solemn face and a demeanor that nature intended to match.

But she was, also, a clerk, and a tremendously talented one, with a mind keenly trained in matters of organization and a tongue capable of speaking a dozen languages. *That* gave her value—and purpose.

Eighth hour, first quarter: Departing
Orvokki-Juhván
Nation of Origin: Fjallanir
Point of Departure: Kjaran Gate
Purpose of Transit: bureaucratic necessity

Intended Date of Return: tomorrow or the day after
Notable features: see entry in Frequent Travelers Folio
Processed by: Drëla Freyda Sandvik

A LITTLE AFTER THE BELLS OF THE NEARBY STAVKIRKE STRUCK THE ninth hour, Freyda ran a finger down the ledger of expected arrivals, saw the name she was looking for, then called out to Hadrian, "I'm going to go tidy the wardrobe rooms."

Hadrian nodded vaguely, eyes fixed on a copy of the Frequent Travelers Folio. He was still relatively new to the job, but he had already figured out the advantages of being able to recognize the regulars and know a little something about them.

Freyda checked the locks and tidied all the Gates, starting at the rightmost edge of the arc of doors. First Kjaran, then Brele, then Tella, then Thuran. Fifth was Anvar. Hadrian was no longer even glancing up when Freyda ducked out of one chamber and into the next.

In the arrival chamber of Anvar Gate, she pulled one of the robes out and hung it in front of the others. She tied a red belt about it in an emil-knot. Then, she withdrew the sealed envelope from her pocket and tucked it securely in the deep pocket of the robe.

Then, she finished her tidying in Anvar's wardrobe room and moved on to Soren.

THE NEXT GUEST TO ARRIVE IN ANVAR GATE WAS DELEN VIVIAN Meijer, returning from Manveylithe by way of the Republic of Ossetan. A diplomat of some note, the good Delen served in the Middle Council and was known by the people of Ullande to have a keen eye for public well-being.

They'd dressed in one of the plain round gowns available in the wardrobe, with the front laces hitched in an emil-knot. Their iron-gray hair was swept up under a tall black toque. As they approached, they were still fussing with their hairpins.

"I do love the robes you have here," they said, and Freyda recognized it for the acknowledgment that it was: envelope received. "So soft and cozy. Sometimes I think about just throwing on one of those over some stockings and breeches, rather than bothering with the gown."

Freyda gave a small smile. "It would certainly be a fashion statement."

Vivian laughed. "I'd love to see the looks on the other Councilmembers' faces if I wore it into the Chaerford, or swanning about Sjöquist House."

Freyda's lips quirked up a touch. "No, I don't think it's quite appropriate for Glister Square."

"More's the pity. All this travel I do, I don't mind telling you, sometimes I envy the fashion available to those in warmer climes. Still, having something like these robes for home would be a pleasure."

"They're made for us by the seamsters on Greive Street," Freyda offered. "They never will tell me where they get their fabric from, or if they use something special to treat it. Secrets of the trade, and all that. But I'm sure they'd be delighted to make you something custom."

Vivian's shoulders lifted and fell in a sigh of pleasure. "You're a summerberry, Drëla Sandvik, an absolute summerberry."

"I only try to serve our honored travelers, Delen Meijer, with all the hospitality I can."

<hr>

Ninth hour, second quarter: Arriving
Delen Vivian Meijer
Nation of Origin: Manveylithe
Point of Arrival: Anvar Gate
Purpose of Transit: returning home from diplomatic
*   errand*
Notable features: see entry in Frequent Travelers Folio

FREYDA'S FINAL HONORED TRAVELER OF THE DAY, A GIRL OF AROUND twenty, poked her head out of the Tella Gate chamber. She spoke Zhibvan, not the usual Griastan, with a certain muzzy-headedness that suggested she had quite thoroughly enjoyed whatever she'd been doing before wandering through the Gate. Tragically, Freyda had only small conversation in Zhibvan, and Hadrian none at all, but gestural language went further than many people might have assumed.

The girl had ivory-pale skin, the brightest red hair Freyda had ever seen, and apparently no modesty whatsoever, for she was wandering around the wardrobe room entirely nude. Freyda didn't know much about the Queendom of Zhibva, but from the look of the girl's sunburns, it was not in a tropical climate.

Whoever she was, she had enough sense to know she couldn't stroll out of the Hilthstad bare-assed to the world, but Fjallaniri clothing clearly flummoxed her.

Within a few moments, Freyda had her looking respectable in a lawn chemise, spring green kirtle, amber-brown sleeves and underskirt, and butter yellow snood and cap. With warm woolen stockings, solid buckle shoes, and a cloak, she felt confident that the girl wouldn't freeze while she figured out where she was and what she was doing.

Whether the girl understood that the clothing was on loan, Freyda wasn't fully certain, but she also sent her, with a clearly marked map, to Haraval House, where they were used to dealing with such translational embarrassments.

———

Ninth hour, fourth quarter: Arriving
Evawe Okpara Okdima
Nation of Origin: Queendom of Zhibva
Point of Arrival: Tella gate
Purpose of Transit: tourism, presumably
Intended Duration of Stay: undetermined
Intended Lodging: Haraval House, on concierge recom-
    mendation (insistence, really)
Notable features: eyes almost golden, ivory-pale skin,

> *cherry-red hair, patch of moles on left forearm very
> like the constellation Grilke*

A FEW DAYS LATER, FREYDA ALLOWED HERSELF THE INDULGENCE OF A lie-in on her rest day. Outsiders often assumed the Fjallaniri *had* no days of rest, for certainly their public services were always in operation, as were their schools, houses of worship, and entertainment venues. In fact, they were quite strict about the necessity of respite. Carefully managing schedules to allow for it was not, really, that hard, when an establishment was fully and properly staffed.

Freyda's income was quite enough for lodgings in a respectable house, with meals included and a cleaning service twice a week. She had a bedroom, washroom, and study all to herself, and if the commute to the Hilthstad was on the long side, that was well worth being far enough outside the Gates' dampening range that the house was able to have magical niceties like rooms with heat effusing from the walls.

On her way to breakfast, she stopped by the mail cubbies in the foyer. Two envelopes awaited her: one a letter from her cousin, down in the delta, and one from the Agency for the Assessment and Curation of Necessary Resources. Her cousin's letter she pocketed for later; Dee considered it their solemn duty to report all the extended Sandvik family's internecine quarrels in great detail. This made their letters worth savoring, but Freyda had to be in the right frame of mind before she could devote herself to appreciating the drama.

The other envelope, she opened.

The Agency for the Assessment and Curation of Necessary Resources had many functions. Publicly, it acted as an overseeing monitor for various economy-oriented Bureaus, Departments, and Commissions in their dealings with private firms, trade delegations, and foreign embassages, ensuring that all deals and transactions were conducted ethically, as well as passing reports on to the Tripartite Council about which of such deals and transactions would most benefit the Fjallaniri people.

Less publicly, it dealt with resources of rather a less tangible nature, but no less vital to the nation's continued health and stability. It assessed information; it curated the actions such information led to. If the information was gathered under peculiar circumstances, or if the curation required rapid decisive action—well, then it was for the best that the Agency could operate with such efficiency, unburdened by the scrutiny of public debate.

Freyda's letter from the Agency was perfectly bland, a formulaic composition just like a thousand others sent by the Fjallaniri bureaucracy every day, confirming that an honorarium in a specific amount had been deposited into her account with Ställen Trust.

Freyda did not do anything so dramatic as toss the letter into a fire after reading it; she tucked it in her pocket along with the letter from Dee, and when she went back upstairs, she would file it with the rest, to be duly reported on her tax forms in a few months' time.

Two younger girls shared the other flat on her floor, and they were both in the dining room when Freyda came down for breakfast. As she helped herself from the sideboard, they chattered amiably, neither deliberately including nor excluding her from their conversation. They were both incurable gossips, eagerly trading information they picked up in their respective positions as a milliner's assistant and a hotel pastry chef. It never mattered if they actually *knew* the people involved; anything would do, for the sake of a good story.

Freyda only marveled that neither of them had yet figured out the possible pecuniary advantages of their natural information-gathering skills. Perhaps she would have to pass their names along the next time she had the opportunity to speak with a recruiter. Then again, perhaps not. Multiple connections in one lodging-house might be an unacceptable risk.

"...well, *I* heard the poor man dropped dead in the middle of the soup course!"

"No, no, it was in the fish, I'm sure of it."

"Soup's much funnier."

"Well, I doubt the deceased gentleman chose his moment to best satisfy your sense of humor, Lin."

"I didn't *mean* that, I only meant that was maybe why I heard it that way. You know how these things change in the telling."

"Havoc! Can you imagine! Such a thing happening in Glister Square, of all places."

"Must've been a terrible shock to Denen and Damen Sjöquist."

Freyda had reason to be grateful for her naturally inexpressive face. What sort of instructions *had* been in Delen Meijer's letter? Or, perhaps more pertinently, what had the "poor man" been doing that had required such thorough curation?

Freyda set her plates down, but before sitting, she picked up the newspaper hanging over the rod in the corner. As the girls' chatter moved on to an upcoming society wedding that one of them was making the sweetwreaths for, Freyda's eyes flitted over the headlines.

An election in Kjaraval. Troop movements near the Qichel-wei/Kailani border—and Freyda knew she had been right to make note of Damen venPress's travel path. An outbreak of redpox in Touranil, which had neighboring nations considering closing their borders and Gate. Another internecine quarrel in Hashima—which explained the rapidity with which Juhván had been on the move. The usual summary of debates in the Tripartite Council and a brief on upcoming legislation —some of it the natural extension of the Agency's work, both public and subtle.

By the time her smoked ham and flat biscuits were consumed, Freyda had read all that interested her. She folded the paper neatly, hung it back over the rod on her way out of the room, and put all the possible configurations of information and speculation out of her mind.

It was, after all, her day off.

DEAD MAN'S MAP

MARIE BRENNAN

I f it weren't for the sudden, panicked scramble to quarters, the encounter would almost have been funny.

The *Ruffian Queen* had dropped most of her sail as she approached the shore of Nalin, coasting on a steady breeze around its southern headland. Her crew were singing a rousing shanty about the welcoming lads and lasses that were most certainly *not* going to be awaiting them in the uninhabited cove on the headland's far side. The sun shone down like a gentle blessing, not too hot, the sky decorated with just enough puffs of cloud to look like some sentimental artist's painting.

Then something hove into view around the headland that, though white, was *not* a cloud. It was another ship, coming out of that self-same cove the *Ruffian Queen* was headed for.

Erilith saw it as soon as her lookout did and had her scope to her eye even as the call came down. What were the odds, two ships practically tripping over each other near an island this obscure?

Low. But a lot higher if the other ship was—

She didn't have to see the whole stern to recognize those lines, the stupidly ostentatious framing around the windows of the captain's cabin. It was a wonder the *Stormwater Moon* didn't sink, with those new carvings weighing down its ass.

"Beat to quarters!"

The words were out of Erilith's mouth before she could think once, let alone twice. She had no desire to take them back, though. Not because it would make her look indecisive in front of her crew. Not because the *Ruffian Queen* had achieved nothing but fruitless hunting for going on three months now.

Because it was the *Stormwater Moon.* And that meant Iretne was on board.

Erilith couldn't spare any time to scan the other vessel's deck for her former lover. The drums had begun rapping out the double-time call that sent the crew flying to the lines and the guns, their bawdy shanty shifting seamlessly into the *Ruffian Queen's* battle song. Its fierce chorus rang out across the waves; if the *Stormwater Moon* was replying in kind, Erilith couldn't hear it yet.

No, they were too busy bolting. More white bloomed up the *Moon's* masts, the other ship hastily making additional sail and tacking in an attempt to get away.

"You just try," Erilith muttered through her teeth. Too much of their prey lately had seen the *Queen* coming and rabbited over the horizon before she could set a new bearing and close with them. Oh, she'd taken a few ships, but those all proved to have very little of value on board to begin with. The single one that might have been a tasty prize had been so heavily armed, Erilith had been forced to hole up for emergency repairs before they could even make it here, to Nalin.

Where her crew were supposed to have the time and leisure to make the rest of the repairs. The *Ruffian Queen* wasn't exactly in prime shape for battle. But—the *Stormwater Moon.*

And Iretne. Who by now would have recognized the *Queen,* and Erilith could imagine all too well her reaction. It would look a lot like her pitying, insincere smile the day their captain died and Iretne decided to disrespect his wishes about Erilith taking command after him. "You're just not aggressive enough," Iretne had said cheerfully as she put Erilith over the side after the mutiny. "Whenever you want something, you back off too soon. You do it in battle, and you do it in bed, and you did it here today."

It wasn't to prove Iretne wrong that Erilith was going after the *Stormwater Moon* now. Her crew needed a prize; otherwise, they might begin to desert. But…it wasn't *not* to prove her wrong, either.

Erilith rapped out orders, and sailors swarmed up the rigging to spread additional canvas. She feared it would be too little, too late: of the two vessels, the *Moon* had the shallower draft, and at this tide she might risk the narrow passage between Nalin and the smaller, nameless islet to its south. The *Queen* would have to navigate around, losing precious time.

But the *Moon* didn't make for that gap. She broke for open sea instead…which for Iretne was an uncharacteristic mistake.

Or she can't for some reason, Erilith thought. *Or it's a trap.*

Wood clapped all along the sides of the *Queen* as the gunports snapped open. "Bow chasers free to fire when ready," Erilith said crisply, and her first mate relayed the order forward. A moment later, the guns spoke. The *Moon's* spanker flapped abruptly, and from the burst of splinters below the sail, Erilith guessed a lucky shot had struck its boom. She made a mental note to reward whichever gun crew was responsible; their good aim had cut down on the other ship's maneuverability.

And now the chase was on. Not a sheer test of speed, like the ones the *Queen* had persistently lost in recent months; the islands in this region made the winds too unpredictable for that. Instead it was intricate tacking, dodging shoals and lee shores where they might run aground— and *that* was the kind of contest Erilith and Iretne both relished.

But something was wrong aboard the *Moon*. Even accounting for the broken boom, she simply wasn't moving with the kind of agility and confidence Erilith expected. Passing into the mouth of a wider strait, Erilith saw an opportunity. Bringing the *Queen* up so she presented her port side to the *Moon* provoked an exchange of guns, one her own ship could ill afford in its present state…but it also crowded the other vessel downwind. And when the *Moon* suddenly juddered, her way slowing, Erilith knew her gambit had worked. They'd scraped their hull along the submerged rocks there, springing gods knew how many leaks.

It would be a mistake to think that was the end of them, though. The *Queen* took additional beating as she came around and closed for boarding, every impact making Erilith grit her teeth at the thought of her poor, beleaguered ship. She could see the *Moon's* crew lining up on deck, cutlasses in hand, and from the crow's nests of both vessels the crossbows were doing their best to thin the ranks before hand-to-hand combat began.

Then the gap between them narrowed enough, and, bellowing the chorus of battle, the *Ruffian Queen's* sailors launched themselves across to the other ship.

The melody soon gave way to shouts and percussive steel. Erilith's own boots thudded down on the deck of the *Stormwater Moon,* and she immediately drove aft through the chaos, seeking the helm. By the rules of engagement, if she could get her hand on the ship's wheel, the crew would have to surrender.

Iretne, though…she might well fight to the death before she let Erilith get within breathing distance of that goal. *You back off too soon.* No one had ever accused Iretne of doing the same.

Except that as Erilith kicked a sailor out of her way and flung herself up the ladder to the poop deck, she saw no sign of her former lover.

Only Monthus, who had sided with Iretne in the mutiny five years ago, and who now flung down his cutlass in disgust at the sight of Erilith. "Ah, fuck," he growled. "Fate's spoken; I know when to shut up and listen. The *Stormwater Moon* is yours."

WHEN THE EXPLANATION FINALLY CAME, ERILITH DIDN'T KNOW whether to laugh or scream in frustration.

Iretne had popped out. Not on purpose, of course; it was one of the few things she feared, vanishing from existence without warning, even though people who popped out always came back eventually. The phenomenon unnerved her—she hated the idea of being at the mercy of things she couldn't control, even though that's what the sea *was*—and Erilith had very considerately not laughed when Iretne admitted her fear.

Her absence left the crew of the *Stormwater Moon* without a captain. Monthus was more loyal than Iretne deserved, Erilith thought with no small amount of venom: elevated to temporary command by her absence, he'd put in at the cove for a few days to see if she would pop back into her cabin. But when she remained stubbornly missing, he'd seen no choice but to go on with whatever plan the two of them had discussed before her disappearance.

A good decision on his part...right up until he cleared the headland and saw the *Ruffian Queen* bearing down on him.

"Of course it had to be you," he muttered, smacking his heel against the deck of the captain's cabin like he meant to kick through the boards. Monthus was stocky enough that Erilith couldn't discount the possibility. "Bad enough I lost Iretne's ship while she's gone. I had to lose it to *you.*"

Her disappearance explained the *Stormwater Moon's* poor performance during the chase. Monthus didn't have Iretne's deft hand and iron nerve; he didn't dare try to take the ship through the passage that might have let him lose Erilith at the start, couldn't carve a tight enough course through the islets to shed his pursuer. And that enraged Erilith, because she'd finally had a chance to avenge her loss from five years ago, to regain face and prove to her ex-lover that she could go for something and win...only to find Iretne wasn't even *there.*

She couldn't decide whether she hoped that Iretne would pop back in right now, there in her cabin, to see what had become of her ship while she was gone, or that Iretne would pop back in exactly where she'd been when she left, some feet above the open water, and have to race the sharks to shore.

They weren't supposed to ever meet again. Like two hostile cats staking out territory to minimize their fights, they'd divided the waters of the Al'notliri Islands between them. Iretne muscled her way into control of the more lucrative areas, and Erilith made do with the rest.

Why had the *Stormwater Moon* been here in the first place?

Before she could ask Monthus that, a knock came at the door. Erilith yanked it open and found her first mate, Sedivor, outside. "You've taken stock of the cargo?"

Behind her, Monthus barked out a sudden, wild laugh. That combined with the look on Sedivor's face added up to a sum Erilith couldn't read but didn't like. "Aye," the mate said uneasily. "Some

Griastan sculpture, Fjallaniri dyestuffs, a whole lot of Terrekish wood-block prints . . ."

"Rules of engagement," Monthus said, sounding far too vindictively pleased. "*Stormwater Moon's* cargo is all yours. *All* of it."

Erilith's jaw tensed. "What else?"

Sedivor stepped back. "I think it's better if you come see."

A NAVIGATOR.

A *dead* Navigator.

Standing behind a stack of crates in the hold like the sailors preferred not to have to look at him. Erilith didn't entirely blame them; it was unnerving to have an animated corpse on board. Not that this one was particularly animated—he just stood facing slightly to starboard, lifeless eyes unblinking. Waiting.

This one had been pale even before he died, and now the overlapping circles tattooed to the side of his neck, the Gate symbol of the Navigators, stood out like a bruise. Erilith had seen enough corpses in her time, though, that she wasn't squeamish about touching them. Reaching out, she turned the body around so it faced aft.

As soon as she let go, it shuffled back around to its previous heading.

She stormed back to the captain's cabin. "You're transporting a dead Navigator?"

Monthus shrugged. "It's custom. Gotta help the dead get home."

"How did you wind up with a dead Navigator in the first place? Where did you find him?"

"Jinamy," Monthus said, which was far from a complete answer.

But he didn't owe her answers, did he? She'd laid formal claim to the cargo of the *Stormwater Moon,* and that included the corpse in the hold. Monthus was right; you were supposed to help the dead get home. The dyestuffs and woodblock prints Erilith could sell wherever she pleased—those didn't have to go to their original destinations—but dumping the corpse on some random island...that would be borderline blasphemous.

A blasphemy somebody had probably already committed. Necromancy wasn't an Al'notliri practice, any more than Navigators generally were; someone else must have animated this one, somewhere else in the world where magic like that worked. And animated him to go *home*, apparently, given his persistence in facing a certain way. But why go to that effort, then abandon him in a place that was certainly not his home?

Far too many places lay in the general direction the dead Navigator was facing. For all Erilith knew, she'd have to sail halfway around the world to get him where he belonged. She indulged in a brief, spiteful fantasy wherein Iretne had somehow known she'd encounter the *Ruffian Queen* and had arranged to pop out just in time to stick Erilith with this problem—never mind that popping out didn't work that way at all.

When Erilith closed her eyes, she saw again the rowboat coming in from the vessel offshore. One man working the oars, and one sitting on the bench. Erilith, a mere eight years old, hadn't recognized how unnaturally motionless that second man was; she'd only recognized her father, come home at last.

For the last time.

She opened her eyes. Someone had once gone far out of their way to bring her dead father back where he belonged. Someone, somewhere, might be waiting for this dead Navigator to return.

And if Iretne of all people could be gracious enough to help, Erilith herself would not do less.

She shut the door on Monthus's malicious chuckle and called to her first mate. "We taking the *Stormwater Moon* for our own?" Sedivor asked.

Once upon a time, Erilith would have answered yes before he could even voice the question. After the mutiny, she'd spent a solid year dreaming about proving Iretne wrong, taking back the ship that should have been hers. Now…

Now, Iretne had made it *her* ship instead. Stupid carvings on the stern and all. And more importantly, the *Ruffian Queen* had become Erilith's. She knew every line and spar of that vessel, like they were extensions of her own body.

Claiming the *Moon* for her own would leave the *Queen* to Sedivor.

But Erilith knew him, too; he was happier as a loyal first mate than he would ever be as a captain.

"No," Erilith said. "I've made my point, even if Iretne wasn't here to see it. Take the cargo, the powder, and the shot—anything good from their galley, while you're at it—and cut them loose. We're done with the *Stormwater Moon*."

ARGUABLY, THERE WAS NO SUCH THING AS BEING RUDE TO AN ANIMATED corpse. Still, it felt impolite to shove this one in the hold the way Iretne had done—and yet, he couldn't be left standing around in any old place, not when the mere sight of him made even seasoned hands before the mast trip over their own feet with unease.

Still, Erilith wished she could have come up with a better solution than putting him in her own cabin.

She sat, chin propped on her knuckles, and glared at the dead man. Reo, the ship's ocelot, nosed warily at the ragged cuff of the man's trousers and yowled quietly, a strangled sound low in his throat. "I agree," Erilith said wearily, clicking her fingers in a summons Reo naturally ignored. "But what else am I supposed to do?"

Rising, she stared out her stern windows, at the forested shore of Nalin. Much as she wanted the dead Navigator off her ship as soon as possible, it would be foolhardy to put out to sea again without effecting a few more repairs first. And without giving her crew something of a rest, too. The thin crescent of the beach swarmed with people, some clustered around the portable forge, some carrying water from the inland spring, some very obviously trying to look busy so they could stay out in the fresh air a while longer.

Fresh air. The magic that animated the Navigator kept him from rotting, too, but Erilith's imagination refused to stop manufacturing a whiff of carrion for her to enjoy.

She turned back to him, scowling. "This would all be simpler if you could tell me where you're trying to go. And how you wound up on Jinamy. And who's responsible for putting me—you—*both* of us in this mess."

He stood, unblinking and silent.

Pale skin, black hair, hooked nose—but she couldn't assume his appearance said anything about where he'd come from or where he considered home. His clothing was a mishmash of styles, typical for a Navigator. No help there. Nothing in his pockets, either…or if there had been, Iretne had already taken it, and it wasn't eye-catching enough for Erilith to have recognized it as important while looting the *Stormwater Moon*.

Erilith sucked her teeth. Dead bodies didn't bother her, but she hadn't really considered what it would be like to have one standing in her cabin for however long it took to get him home. They were decidedly more unnerving when vertical.

Reo bolted when she opened the door, tail waving like a flag of surrender. Erilith found her quartermaster and got him to supply her with a length of sailcloth; back in her cabin, she approached the dead Navigator, intending to drape him with the heavy canvas and see if that was any better.

Then she stopped, frowning.

In the hold of the *Stormwater Moon*, it had been too dark to look closely at the man, and during the transfer over to the *Ruffian Queen* she'd been too focused on chivvying him into heading in a different direction from the one he wanted. But now she could see that his shirt had been cut open, and then its loose tails roughly shoved back into the waistband of his trousers. *Very* loosely, as if whoever did it had been reluctant to touch the man.

Like the whole enterprise had taken place after he was dead.

Erilith dropped the canvas at her feet and reached for the corpse. "You, uh, don't mind, right? I'm just wondering if you might have a clue under there."

He made no reply, of course. But she felt better for asking—if a touch ridiculous, too.

As delicately as she could, Erilith tugged the fabric of his shirt out and exposed the pallid skin of his chest.

Al'notliri to the bone, Erilith didn't have much use for Navigators. Even the name felt like an insult: *real* navigation meant learning the ways of wind and current, depths and shore. It meant mathematics to understand the movements of the stars, sharp observation to know where one's ship fit into that dance. It took skill and years of training to be a good navigator of that sort.

Whereas *this* sort of Navigator didn't need anything more than a friend with some sharpened needles and a bottle of ink. Like the others of his kind Erilith had seen, he had a map of the Gate network tattooed across his chest and probably onto his back, an intricate, spidering network branching from node to node. Labels delicately etched below the nodes named off cities, islands, other landmarks—though without the additional commentary some Navigators liked to add, trivial details about restaurants and beautiful scenery.

Had someone cut his shirt open just to look at the map? But that was pointless. The locations of the Gates were well-known. Unless…could he have a record of an unknown Gate somewhere on him?

If so, Erilith was hardly going to be the one to spot it. The Gates had their uses, maybe, but for most practical purposes, you still needed ships and other mundane forms of transportation. She had no particular desire to teleport anywhere if it meant showing up completely naked, bereft of everything that might be useful to her on the other side. As a result, while some people pored over maps of the Gates—usually ones written on objects instead of humans, but not always—and dreamed of where they might go, Erilith only knew the locations of the more famous Gates, and the ones in the Al'notliri Islands.

Which did not include the label tucked under the dead Navigator's left collarbone.

Curiosity and surprise overcoming her standoffishness, Erilith leaned closer to look. There absolutely was *not* a Gate on Miunte—at least, not that she remembered. There was one on Berit, though, just to the south, which wasn't included in his map.

Carelessness? It hardly seemed likely. Navigators were a cult; they took the mapping of the Gates as a holy duty. But it was true that Gates sometimes vanished from where they'd been, or formed in new locations. Maybe this was an old map? Though Erilith had never heard of a Gate having been on Miunte. And this Navigator, if Erilith was any judge, couldn't be older than thirty.

Unless he'd been standing around dead for a *lot* longer than she'd assumed.

Her gaze swept across his chest, and the more she saw, the more confused she became. It didn't take an expert in Gate mapping to recognize how wrong everything was. The Gates Erilith had heard of weren't marked; others were in locations she knew for sure didn't have them in reality. When she stripped off the Navigator's ruined shirt and his coat, she found the map extended across his back, and so did its errors.

"What the hell is this?" she demanded, despite knowing he wouldn't answer. "Are you not a real Navigator? Just some impostor? But... why?" She could understand Navigators marking themselves with the Gate map, even if she thought the whole enterprise fairly pointless. A *fake* map? That was pointless to the point of incomprehensibility.

Unless it served some other purpose entirely. And as much as she disliked it, Erilith didn't think she could answer that question herself.

So she would have to find someone who could.

Tugging the dead man's coat and shirt back on, she said, "I'm sorry, whoever you are. Getting you home is going to take just a little while longer."

ERILITH'S CREW WERE *FAR* TOO EXCITED WHEN SHE TOLD THEM THEY were sailing for Griasta. "We're not going to Snail-Lick Island!" she bellowed over the delighted shouts, which promptly sank to disappointed grumbles. "We're going to Rinalre. They may not have hallucinogenic snails, but they'll buy the woodblock prints for a good price, and you all can enjoy a proper shore leave for a few days."

She wanted to leave it at that, but a handful among her crew were clever enough that they'd notice which direction they *weren't* going. "And I can ask a few questions about our dead passenger before we ferry him home. Might even find a ship heading that way who will be happy to take him for us."

"Something wrong with him, captain?" the bosun asked.

Maybe, Erilith thought. "No," she said. "Just a little mystery I want to clear up before we get him off our hands."

This time of year, the winds to Griasta blew strong and steady. They made good time, with not much foul weather to trouble them, and the only bad thing was that Erilith couldn't make up her mind whether it was worse to have the dead man standing in her cabin without the sail-cloth over him or with it. She kept placing and removing the drape, and neither option was good.

But it wasn't hard to find a Navigator—a living one—in Rinalre. Griastans rarely chose that life for themselves, but they used the Gates so often to go sightseeing around the world that they made members of the cult very welcome in their lands. Discreet questioning earned Erilith a few odd looks, since everything from her accent to her coat proclaimed her Al'notliri…but it also earned her the name and location of a Navigator she could speak to.

This turned out to be a Pyel individual named Ahcir. They were old and wrinkled and barely came up to Erilith's sternum, but she hoped that —the age, not the lack of height—meant they knew enough to answer her question.

Ahcir's eyes might be half-hidden under the collapsing cliffs of their brows, but the gaze that came through was still sharp. "How many of the Gates did you say are wrong?"

Erilith shrugged. "I have no way of telling. All the ones I know about, but that's admittedly not many."

She felt good about her choice of person to question when Ahcir refrained from making a snide comment about her ignorance. Al'notliri didn't respect Navigators, and many Navigators therefore disrespected them right back. Erilith added, "Could it be fake? I mean—yes, obviously it could. Anybody can tattoo themself with anything they like. What I mean is, if he's a genuine Navigator, would there be some reason he'd mark himself with an incorrect map?"

The shake of Ahcir's head was the most decisive movement she'd yet seen them make. "No. No genuine Navigator would blaspheme like that. I don't merely mean that anyone who would do such a thing is by definition no genuine Navigator; I mean that I cannot conceive of any member of our order doing such a thing. It would defy our entire purpose." They leaned over to peer past Erilith and said, "You didn't bring him?"

"It would have been too difficult to persuade him to leave the ship and come here," Erilith said, gesturing around. Ahcir currently dwelt in one of the many hostels scattered in an arc around Rinalre's Gate. The whole area buzzed with travelers, some of them still wearing the robes and sandals they'd been given when they came through. Erilith could imagine what would happen if she tried to shepherd a corpse through their midst, and it wasn't pretty.

She dug in her coat pocket. "I did bring a list of the Gate names—"

But Ahcir shook their head. "No, the names alone won't be enough. I need to see the network, how they connect to each other."

Fair as that was, it left the two of them in a bind. Drag a dead man through crowds of drunken people looking for a party, or…

Grudgingly, Erilith said, "He's on my ship. You can come look at his map there."

The heavy curtain of their fallen brows twitched in a valiant attempt to lift, but once again, Ahcir forwent the chance to make a comment. Al'notliri captains like Erilith tended not to enjoy having Navigators on their ships. She'd already taken on board a dead one, though; what was a living person compared to that?

"Let me gather a few supplies," Ahcir said and shuffled slowly away.

***

AT AHCIR'S PACE, WHICH WOULD HAVE SHAMED ONE OF GRIASTA'S hallucinogenic snails, it took long enough to return to the *Ruffian Queen* that Erilith had plenty of time to question why she'd gotten herself involved in all of this to begin with. She didn't have to look under the dead man's shirt. She didn't have to come to Rinalre, instead of just sailing him to his final rest. Hell, she didn't have to chase down the *Stormwater Moon* in the first place.

No. That part she had to do. But the rest…

You back off too soon.

Not this time, she didn't. Her curiosity was up, and if she didn't do her best to satisfy it, the lack would nag at her from now until the end of time.

It was a good thing Erilith's cabin was at the level of the main deck; she didn't think Ahcir could have managed a ladder. Even the plank laid from gunwale to pier was challenge enough that at several points Erilith feared the ancient Navigator would tip over into the drink. But finally they reached the cabin, and Erilith removed sailcloth and shirt alike to reveal the dead man's tattoos.

Ahcir took their time, shuffling in a leisurely circle around him. When they finished the circuit, Erilith asked, "Well? Does any of that make sense to you? Or is he a fake?"

In an uncannily precise echo of their movement earlier, Ahcir shook their head again. "No. This man is—was—a real Navigator."

Intrigued despite herself, Erilith asked, "How can you tell?"

But Ahcir didn't answer. Very slowly, they began to drag at the small flat-topped chest in which Erilith kept her private stock of tea. When Erilith realized what they intended, she picked the chest up and set it in front of the dead man. Ahcir accepted a steadying hand as they stepped up onto the chest's sturdy lid, and then at their instruction, Erilith turned the corpse one quarter-turn at a time, while Ahcir copied the fake map onto the paper they'd brought with them.

She bit her tongue through this whole process, but when it was done, she couldn't hold back the question any longer. "So what's the story behind this map? Is it fake? Very old?"

Ahcir began to roll up the paper. "Old? In Fjallanir they'd be most able to answer that question. People there want to record the knowledge of the Navigators."

It was impossible to tell from Ahcir's tone whether they thought such records were a good idea or not. But it hardly mattered. "I'm not sailing to Fjallanir," Erilith said. "I'm already going a long way to get this fellow home, and that would be even more of a detour than this was. But you don't think it's fake?"

The old Navigator lurched down off the chest before Erilith could help and began shuffling toward the door. They got halfway there before Erilith realized they had no intention of answering the question. It only took her three strides to reach the door and station herself in front of it, and unless Ahcir had some weapon or magic trick hidden inside their loose tunic, Erilith was as immovable an obstacle as the Rocks of Dorr.

"You know something," she said, quiet and level. "Something you're not telling me."

Ahcir peered up at her, all tufty brows from this angle. "We don't owe you our secrets, Al'notliri."

Ah, there it was at last: the contempt of the Navigator. Under normal circumstances, Erilith would have let it pass; after all, she didn't care what these cultists thought of her. But she had one of their former comrades in her cabin, along with a growing sense that she'd stumbled into something far larger than one dead man.

A fake map after all? A Navigator somehow gone rogue, and Ahcir didn't want her to know? Otherwise there was no reason not to dismiss it as a foolish bit of decoration. Or possibly old, though Ahcir hadn't confirmed that. Or—

Like a storm wind slapping out of a mild sky, Erilith remembered her own thoughts when she'd first seen that misplaced Al'notliri Gate. That existing Gates sometimes vanished . . . and new ones sometimes appeared.

Her hands, braced on either side of the door, went slack. "There's no way to know. Is there? If *all* those Gates are new—I mean, if they're ones that will exist in the future—how could you tell? Navigators don't have any way of knowing a new Gate is about to form, do they?"

Ahcir's mouth vanished into its wrinkles, and for a few heartbeats, Erilith thought they would refuse to answer again. That the two of them would stand there, staring at one another, until somebody got bored enough to give up.

Then the ancient Navigator spoke.

"One of the Gates marked on him does exist," they said, gesturing at the dead man, silent and eternally patient. "I heard of it only a few days ago. In Clepoc. Very new."

The man's tattoos were *not* new. They had the faded look of marks that had been on him for years.

It didn't prove the whole idea. It could be coincidence. Or the grain of truth that made an otherwise elaborate lie look real.

Erilith couldn't quite bring herself to believe that.

Her gaze went to the dead Navigator, marked with a map of the world as it was not...but as it might be.

A world in which the network of Gates was *radically* different. Countries that thrived on the contact with distant locations would find themselves cut off. Lands that currently stood isolated would become hubs. Some of them would welcome it, leveraging their newfound status to gain power on the international stage; others would loathe the influx that brought.

One way or another, the world would change.

"It doesn't happen that often, right?" Erilith said, hearing the unsteadiness in her own voice like it belonged to a stranger. "Even if this is what it might be—decades, surely. Centuries. One Gate at a time."

Ahcir's shoulders lifted far more easily than their brows did. "Maybe."

And maybe not.

Erilith looked at the rolled-up copy in the old Navigator's hand. "What are you going to do with that?"

"We are Navigators," Ahcir said simply. "We keep the knowledge of the Gates."

"Keep? Or spread?"

She couldn't decide which would be worse: to share this news, or to hide it away. People might do a lot of stupid things if they thought they knew the future, even if they didn't know when that future would arrive. Or if it was even real. On the other hand, if this happened fast, and they were caught unawares…

"I think you should help this fellow get home," Ahcir said. And this time, when they shuffled toward the door, Erilith stepped out of their way.

ERILITH DIDN'T THINK THE DEAD MAN WAS HEADING HOME.

Maybe he really had lived on the tropical island he led the *Ruffian Queen* to—an island that, from what Erilith could tell, had no inhabitants at the moment. It might have some in the future, though; if she was reading the map marked on his skin correctly, this place would eventually be called Hily, and it would have not one but *two* Gates.

She ordered her crew to stay on board and lowered the dead Navigator in the ship's longboat. Then she rowed him to shore, as someone had once rowed her father, decades ago.

On the beach, he climbed awkwardly out of the boat and started walking. Erilith followed, several paces behind, one hand on her pistol in case it was needed. But that soon fell away, as the corpse took an appallingly direct route up the island's forested slope and Erilith needed both hands to scramble over the rugged terrain. If anyone showed up to threaten her, they could wait until she caught her breath first.

There was no one. Just trees, underbrush, and a steep slope that terminated in a ridge where Erilith stopped and stared.

In front of her, the ground dropped away again, but now there were no trees. The barren soil and stone ahead formed a broad bowl, and inside that bowl…

The dead man kept walking. She let him go.

She lost sight of him in the steam and foul smoke that wafted through the crater. At one point there was a flare of brightness, which might have been something going up in flames. But no sound.

After she'd waited long enough, Erilith turned and began her descent, back along the trail of trampled grass and broken branches that marked the way she and the dead man had come.

The whole trip took long enough that dusk was closing in by the time she reached the shore. Tired, sweaty, wishing she could strip off and swim in the waves but wanting much more to be far from this island, Erilith rowed herself back across to the *Ruffian Queen.*

Sedivor greeted her as she came over the rail. "He got home okay?" her first mate asked dubiously. "There are people here to give him a funeral?"

"Cremation, I think," Erilith said shortly. "We can set sail."

"Shouldn't we wait for mor—"

"No."

He took it with good grace, recognizing her mood. "Think we can get clear of the reef before dark, all right. Where to?"

It was a fine question. They still had other cargo to sell. Other ships to chase.

Someone, Erilith thought, *cut that man's shirt open. Someone saw that map.*

Someone who might have made a copy—and who wouldn't feel whatever ethical burden Ahcir had about the right way to handle that information. Information that had sent a dead man into the crater of a volcano rather than leave his skin where other people might find it.

Erilith straightened her shoulders. "By now Iretne will have popped back in. Might have even gotten back to her ship. Set sail for Al'notlir. We're going to hunt down the *Stormwater Moon*."

THROWING MUSES

MIKE CHEN

For me, things started the way they always do with musicians and artists: by being a fan.

I was a big enough fan of the Rolling Moonstones to know that the four musicians in front of me just happened to be imposters. They looked the part, from their tunics to their hair to their specific models of instruments, and they sounded close enough, so much so that the front row of screaming teenagers failed to notice as the two lutes paused for twelve consecutive solo drum beats while two voices merged in song.

But I knew. I knew from the way their harmonies landed just slightly out of sync with each other, beats lasting a little too long or a little too short. Almost-but-not-quite imitators proved common when minstrel bands got as popular as the Moonstones, leading to all sorts of strange occurrences, from fans using the Magical Nude Gate to follow them across shows worldwide to the first ever fan convention last year, complete with mass sing-alongs and an all-day concert featuring multiple fake Moonstones. On that day, every band acknowledged that they pretended to be the real thing; in this case, deception lured fans in. And it seemed like only I picked up on the truth, since I'd seen the Moonstones about twenty times in the past three years, which meant that their details were seared into my brain: every string pluck, every vocal harmony, every clever word.

I stood, left of center to the stage, close to the faux version of Kay, the second lute but lead vocalist. Next to Kay stood Donnel, another lute player who sang vocal harmonies. Then Syzo, the drummer, and Lang, the flute player, all commanding the stage with individual presences that created something greater than the sum of its parts.

Just…not as great as the real thing.

The clarity of knowing this performance lacked authenticity sank in, enough for me to turn and head toward the exit.

And with that move, I left my own dreams of stardom.

Not dreams of being a musician. A musician meant performing, which meant getting in front of people and risking public embarrassment for the sake of applause. In that case, I was happy to remain a fan. I wanted to observe.

Really, observing was what I did best. It brought out the best in my talents, an ability to take in every detail playing out in front of me, along with an intuition for understanding the motivations at play.

Such skills helped me sidestep both a lifetime of both danger *and* humiliation, both as a kid and now as a young adult. If you can see the signs of violence about to erupt into the Red Shoes Riots two years ago, then you can be smart enough to turn the other way instead of rush toward it. If you can hear the village school's worst bully jingling coins in his pocket, you can know how to avoid the market until far later in the day.

Watch. Observe. And in recent years, I added reporting to that skillset.

Because, when you're slight of frame and somewhat lacking in the confidence department, writing is a very, very easy skill to perfect.

Still, in this situation, the fake Moonstones did stall my dreams once again. Of course, my goal wasn't to sing songs and play the lute in front of adoring followers. No, I wanted to *report* about it. Journalism, real quality journalism, covering happenings here in Al'notlir and beyond. After all, word spread fast thanks to the Magical Nude Gate, plus I told the world's most powerful, influential stories and asked the hard-hitting questions about what was happening or who was involved, even if events were as dull as Alnot'lir's political summits. News was still news, and I was trained to cover it.

The only issue, really, was that no one read any of it. At least, not yet.

I stood outside the stone walls of the small Sun Racket Theater, Brightyellow's only option for live entertainment. The echoes of notes and harmonies still carried through the propped-open door. Several late stragglers hustled inside, one digging through a bag while cursing about having misplaced his ticket.

For me, though, I did what I always did:

I wrote.

In my bound notebook, I opened at where the bookmark ribbon left off—an entry documenting the last imposter band I'd seen, four musicians who claimed to be the Rolling Moonstones but simply *weren't*. Like the band currently playing, they were good; they hit their notes and looked the part, but something just felt *off*.

One year ago, though, legit Moonstones shows stopped, sparking these faux minstrels to fill the void, like their popularity grew inversely with their willingness to perform. Did the Moonstones hire imposters in their place? Or did opportunistic musicians simply see a chance to earn some coin from a very eager crowd? More importantly, who *were* the Moonstones, really? They never spoke to journalists, and their biographies remained more rumor than fact. And what caused the sudden shifts in their schedule?

I continued scribbling notes, my brain already forming ways to combine the narrative of these imposters with the strange recent activity of the Moonstones and their as-yet-undefined real history, all with the goal of eventually telling the true story of the world's most popular traveling act.

Thirty or forty minutes must have passed, my pen constantly dipping into the small inkwell I'd carefully packed. My left palm smeared and dried as I moved so quickly—using shorthand to capture all of the ideas that fired off in my brain—that I barely noticed the pale, unblinking woman approach, her striking blue eyes drawing a contrast to a dark brown cloak and worn boots.

That was, until she approached me. As she came closer, the intensity of her gaze kind of became unavoidable. I shifted, angling this way or turning that way, trying to look as inconspicuous as possible, because for all of my experience reading people and situations, I got nothing from this woman. Something bubbled underneath, because a purpose clearly lived in her whole body, a sense of motivation integrating into her every move.

But for what, exactly? That in itself remained unclear. Her focus proved relentless, and *that* proved unnerving, especially when she approached in small, methodical steps.

"Are you writing about the band?" the woman finally asked.

I tried ignoring her, like I was just so wrapped up in my words that I couldn't possibly hear her or feel her piercing glare. But she inched closer, then repeated the question. "Are you writing about the band?

"I'm, uh," I said, my mind scrambling for ways to end this very odd confrontation. I supposed I could just run, but I needed to get the flow of ideas fully onto paper before they disappeared forever. "I'm taking notes."

"Are you a journalist?"

That was an odd question to ask a stranger. And also, one I pondered myself—could I call myself that? Though I'd pictured *by Steve Gau'regi* in print countless times, the truth was that other than carefully making handwritten copies of my articles for distribution—and, to be fair, a few bits of local summaries for the town crier to shout about—I didn't have a big portfolio. I did, however, make ends meet by delivering news sheets and sometimes inserting those handwritten copies in there. Someone, somewhere on my delivery route had seen that byline before, which kind of worked in this situation.

"I am, in fact," I said, hoping this strange woman did not notice the waver in my proclamation.

"Anything interesting today?" She pointed to the theater, then at my notebook. "You're using a lot of ink for a simple concert. What can you tell me that others miss?"

On one hand, this woman asked a lot of weird questions. But on the other hand, she wanted to know more—she wanted to know what I'd seen, what my own unique insights as an observer were.

No, not as an observer—as a *journalist*. I mean, she'd used that word.

"Here's a secret," I said, leaning in close and lowering my voice. I pointed in the theater and considered the power of my words. "That's not the real Rolling Moonstones."

I expected to be laughed off. Or face a wall of defensive rebuttal. Or something in between, a theoretical reaction that would have set my credibility back with at least one person. Inside, I started cursing my ego for giving it all away, especially for someone who probably wouldn't even believe what I saw in the first place.

Instead, though, the right side of the woman's mouth tilted upward. Not a giant grin, not even a toothy smile, just a simple bit of amusement slipping out. "That's a very astute observation. Which details drove you to that conclusion?" she asked. I could have taken the words personally, but the very fact that she selected those particular words…

Well, they seemed as methodical as my own. And that tied a thin line of trust between us.

For now.

Or maybe I just wanted to show off my knowledge to someone who finally listened. That part was nice. "If you listen to the timing of their harmonies, they're just a little off. Consistently. Kay always holds a half a beat too long. Donnel always comes in too early. Otherwise, they're an exact facsimile, note for note, but they're *too* exact. The Moonstones play with their music a little bit more, I dunno, joy. There's a looseness they have. It makes these little special moments that you only notice if you see them over and over."

Some fans would have dismissed my thoughts as conspiracy. Others might have been offended. This woman, though, nodded as I spoke, the intensity of her eyes softening and the sides of her mouth showing a tiny hint of curling up. "You know what?" she finally asked with a nod, "I think you've got quite the eye. And ear. And I'm in complete agreement with you. I do know for a fact that the Moonstones, the real Moonstones, not these fakes or the other ones you've noted." —she reached out a pale finger and tapped the side of my notebook— "They've got a show in a few days. Honeychain Theatre, in Notalto."

"Really? How do you know?" The questions came out as a reflex, though my mind hung a bit on the fact that the whole tapping-the-notebook thing was very odd. "Is this a secret gig? Is that why their gig schedule has been so strange lately?"

She answered by holding up a piece of paper. I squinted, looking at the writing on it. Rather than the usual pooling and smudges of ink, the writing appeared charred onto the very fibers of the paper. And was that a hint of burning odor?

"Not secret," she said, placing the paper on the side of the theater. Somehow, it stuck, despite none of the usual goo that came with paste. "But a significant gig. I get the feeling you're in this for more than a show. You want the full story behind this band? Come around behind the theater. Two hours before showtime."

"Wait, what do you mean? You didn't even tell me your name or—" I started, when suddenly the Sun Racket's doors opened. Voices surrounded me, giddy fans leaving the venue, at least until one person caught sight of the poster and the crowd started swarming it with pointed fingers like I wasn't even there.

I HATED TRAVELING BY THE MAGICAL NUDE GATE.

Some people didn't care. They jumped in and ran out like a deer dashing through a field, and that was that. They apparently didn't care for practicalities like tiny rocks that poked at the bottom of your feet, or the sheer windchill factor.

Or, if you're a professional, not having any of your tools with you.

And while regular Gate travelers signified their lines of credit to the immediate banking booths and barter stations with tattoos, I never made enough to even establish that, Gate or no Gate. I couldn't exactly jump through naked without any means of documenting this once-in-a-lifetime (I hoped) opportunity. Instead, despite the discomfort and smelliness of it all, I spent far too much on a late-night ferry to Notalto, followed by a horse rental to get into the university district. Too much, as in dipping into my reserves with payday still eight days away.

But with dawn creeping over the horizon and sweat-soaked clothes clinging against my skin, I considered if maybe I should have just chosen the MNG and improvised afterwards. Its shimmering glow shined like a beacon over the hill, and as my horse pushed further up the small hill before heading to the valley just outside of Notalto's university district, I saw more than just the Gate.

People gathered around it.

Not naked people—these weren't just travelers. No, a closer look saw three groups surrounding the gate. First, the incoming unclothed people, many of whom seemed to be of the carefree variety, sprinting off to meet their friends or families that greeted them with coverings in waiting.

But then on one side, a group simply *sat*. A few even carried signs. I squinted, and though the low light of dawn made it hard to read, it looked like one carried letters in large yellow paint against a wood sheet:

We love the Moonstones.

Those were fans, camping out at the Gate just in case the Moonstones happened to use it. Which made no sense to me, given that they needed lutes and drums and other instruments, but such was the nature of a fan—things didn't always make sense, and sometimes you just bet on a hopeful chance encounter more than anything else.

On the other side of those fans, though, sat a small booth with a different sign:

Best Rolling Moonstones shirts for your coin!

Several shirts hung off the booth's frame, each with the exact four moons in series painted across the chest—different colors available.

Those vendors probably weren't expecting the actual Moonstones to come through. But based on the line of naked people at the booth, they knew that some fans would be traveling this way.

I shook my head, kicking my horse to dash into the district. With the first beams of sun hitting the horizon, ten hours remained before I needed to meet the mystery woman at the back of the theater. Which meant time for food, bath, and some sleep. I glanced back at all those milling about, buying and selling, talking and laughing…

Because of the Moonstones.

Every visitor, every fan, every vendor: the Gate gave me everything I needed. My fingers flexed over the horse reins, tightening my grip with a fortitude as I thought about this chance ahead—my chance. I was going to tell the world about the Rolling Moonstones. And the ones congregating around the MNG—waiting for a miracle chance, traveling to a show, buying merchandise—they were the ones who wanted to hear it.

I FOUND AN INN WITH THE ESSENTIALS: FOOD, BED, A PLACE TO CLEAN up, and most importantly, within walking distance to the gig. The bath even provided good acoustics to croon Moonstones songs to myself, a little indulgence as I prepared for the day ahead. Perhaps some magic user had the ability to carry all of these lyrics and tunes as an on-demand reference; the rest of us relied on simple memory, a refresher course before going down to Honeychain Theatre. Cleaned from travel and with some sleep under my belt, I sat down at a corner table of the inn's ground-floor pub and reviewed my notes.

Bad plan. Sitting and thinking about my theories invited the doubts in. What if this was a scam? What if this was yet another imposter band? A gig would certainly happen tonight, but what made this one "significant"? Or was that woman simply trying to sell tickets?

The questions swirled, though I kept returning to one thought: she asked me to come early, to go to behind the venue. Fans filled the pub's tables, some singing as they sloshed drinks and others chattering away about their favorite minstrel or song. Some of them even bemoaned not seeing the Moonstones at the Gate.

"We must have missed them."

"But how? We would have seen! It's not like you can hide when you arrive."

"Maybe they each arrived separately in disguise?"

"I would recognize Donnel anywhere. Anywhere."

No one but me prepped for a back-alley meetup with a promoter or manager or whoever that strange woman was.

This had to be something. I nodded to myself, taking more than my share of spicy baked shrimp off the bar, complimentary appetizers from the island's plentiful haul. I may have been about to break the world's biggest entertainment story, but I was still pretty piss-poor. After reviewing my notes for the fourth time, I left all I could afford—a single coin—and grabbed my things, checking one last time for pens and inkwells.

The front of the theater bustled with activity, patrons coming and going, some lining up already to try and grab the best seats. Food vendors walked up and down the lines, snacks available on skewers or in bags, and one small group even led a sing-along of songs to pass the time. I walked down the long side alley, a stretch between buildings filled with leftover equipment and barrels.

But at the Honeychain's backdoor? Nothing.

Two hours before showtime exactly and no mystery woman. No stacks of lutes and drums. Not even theater staff preparing for the night's show. Just rats fussing over a dropped piece of bread.

In that moment, I realized I'd been had.

Of course I'd been had. All those things I told myself about how observation and intuition prevented danger and humiliation? None of them saved me. A flush came to my cheeks, frustration surfacing as I really, really focused on the money I'd spent to get here. I'd wanted my big journalism break so badly that I took a really weird woman at her word, just because her sheet of paper smelled like it was burning.

I was a writer, sure. In the technical sense, as in I wrote words. But a journalist?

Maybe not.

"Come on, Steve," I muttered to myself, my brain now in a full spiral of all the silly things I'd done to *feel* published. I mean, I'd inserted my handwritten notes into local newspapers? Who did that? How did that count for anything? And now I was stuck in Notalto, barely any coin left, and with a job to get back to except I was an island away. Oh, and no one even knew I was *here* because this big break was so secretive, so filled with potential that I hadn't wanted to—

"What are you doing here?"

A voice. Finally. Except this wasn't the woman from yesterday. No, this voice was male. And gruff. And clearly agitated.

"Oh. Hello," I said, straining to find some professionalism for my tone. "I'm, uh, Steve. I'm meeting someone here. I'm a journalist covering—"

"Everyone has to wait out front. Talent and staff only."

Out front.

It would be easier to give up, walk away. I didn't even have tickets for the show, but I could listen from outside. Or I could try to scrounge my way home, hoping that no one would notice.

The easy way.

Except I *was* here. I'd already invested so much. A real journalist wouldn't give up like this. Even if the woman had tricked me, I could still come up with an angle about the world's most popular band, maybe even about how fans traveled to see them. That had to mean something to someone. I offered my best professional smile, despite my shaky breath. "Sorry, lemme try that again. My name's Steve Gau'regi. I'm a journalist. You might have seen my work in the *Brightyellow Times*." The man didn't exactly seem thrilled, but at least he listened without violence. "I'm doing a story on the Moonstones and I was told to meet—"

"Again. You're not talent. You're not staff. You can't be here," he said, and *now* his voice—and his demeanor—turned threatening.

"So, I'm not technically part of the band, but I *am* here to document—"

"I'm giving you one last chance to leave peacefully. Otherwise, those rats will be nibbling on you instead of that bread."

On cue, the rats both paused from their snacks to give me a glance that may have translated to "don't be stupid, you've lost." My big break or keeping my limbs intact?

But I didn't have any money or place to stay. When you're all out of options, gamble big, even with some truth-stretching. "Listen, I'm part of the band's management. Go ahead and—"

"I don't have time for this," the man said. His fingers balled into a fist, and as he coiled his arm back to swing, my taste for gambling suddenly disappeared.

My eyes squeezed shut, though I held my bag tight. My face could heal, but I couldn't lose what little notes I had about the Moonstones.

But the blow never came. I opened one eye, then the other, only to see the man paused, his fist about six inches from my face. His mouth sat ajar, his eyes wide. His chest still rose with breath, so he wasn't exactly frozen, but something had clearly stopped him.

I moved one foot to the left, clearing the trajectory of his fist, then noticed another figure lurking. The approaching dusk cast shadows from both the theater and the adjacent building, leaving the person in hooded silhouette until they came closer.

"Relax your arm." I knew that voice. And as the person approached, the features under the hood became more distinct, confirming my suspicion. "Go inside."

It was the mystery woman. And her command wasn't addressed to me. Instead, the burly man did as he was told, walking into the theater's back door, leaving us alone.

"You came," she said, eyes now locked on me.

"I did," I said, though it came out more like a question than I wanted. I cleared my throat, then tried again. "Traveled all night."

"You must be tired." She extended a finger at the door, then flicked her wrist. A second passed before the door crept open on its own. "Would you like to sit down?"

This was the moment that curiosity started to tiptoe into concern. I was here to write about a band—one that clearly would be performing tonight—*not* get involved with a sorcerer and whatever her goals happened to be.

Sorcery would also explain the burned text on the paper.

"Um…"

"You wanted to tell the story of the Rolling Moonstones, didn't you? You wanted an exclusive that could put your words in front of eyes all over Al'notlir and beyond?" Her gaze shifted to me, a piercing look that held every muscle in my body still. Was this a trick of her magic? Or was she just really, really intense?

Seconds ago, I had asked myself to choose between my big break or getting my face smashed in by an angry guard's flying fist. Was dealing with this woman's magic going to be any better or worse than that?

"How do I know this isn't some sort of trick?" I asked, my voice slow and calm, and even though I presented a question, an honest answer did seem pretty unlikely considering this woman could open doors with the flick of her wrist.

"Everything is a trick. That's the way the world works," she said, her head tilted.

A sorcerer *and* a philosopher. Not the usual combination for someone promoting live entertainment.

"You have a choice right now. Leave here and enjoy the show or step inside and change your life."

My bag weighed on my shoulder, and suddenly I realized just how many words sat in that notebook. In fact, how many words had I written about *everything*? And how many of those words actually got read by someone else? The same panic spiral from just moments ago reappeared, only amplified as words and fears echoed off each other. If I gave up now, I'd be left with nothing.

Except if this woman was trying to scam me, the joke would be on her—I had nothing. And if an opportunity presented itself, I had to take it. Even if weird magic got involved.

"Alright. Let's go backstage," I said, taking my first step. In an instant, the woman materialized in front of me, leading the way. I pretended *not* to be shocked or impressed. "Where are the Moonstones? How do they get ready backstage?"

"They're resting. Performing can take a lot out of you," she said. We walked through the dark backstage area, and with each step forward, surrounding staff froze in action, pausing in mid-sweep of a broom or tying backstage ropes.

We moved through one long back corridor, eventually hitting a closed door, a small wooden sign with the words 'Talent - No Admittance' carved into it.

"Are you ready?" she asked. I pulled out my notebook, but she held up a hand and shook her head. "You won't need that. Not now." The woman knocked twice on the door, then opened it.

We stepped inside a dim room with only a single candelabra for illumination and meager furnishings: a table, some chairs, and a bowl of surprisingly ripe fruit given the season.

No band, though.

"Are they warming up?" I asked, nerves too obvious in my voice. The woman didn't answer, the door slamming shut behind me.

"What is your name?" she said, walking over to the far side of the room. By now, my eyes had adjusted, and I could see that she stood next to four lumps on the floor, a bed-sized blanket draped over each.

"Steve," I said, stepping closer. "Steve Gau'regi."

The woman knelt down and uttered quick, rhythmic words under her breath.

Then she pulled the first blanket.

Underneath was a small bed—or a cot, at least. But on the cot lay a single man, someone who in all ways seemed unremarkable: medium height, medium build, medium hair, light brown skin. Except his eyes. A green swirl floated around his eyes.

One by one, she pulled the other blankets, all to reveal men with similar magical bindings around their eyes as they lay prone.

And one empty cot.

On the far side, the green cloud flickered duller than the rest, a translucence to it that failed to match the brilliance of the other two.

"Damn," the woman said, and she immediately knelt down, whispering under her breath. The color shimmered but failed to hold, prompting her words to accelerate, the same intensity in her glare now coloring her voice.

Now my panic took over. I turned on my heel and took this distraction as my opportunity to get out before I turned into whatever *that* was. I might have had nothing, but having nothing at least meant I was alive, and I certainly liked being alive. That last cot had to be marked for me.

"We don't have time," she said, a quick look up before her hands hovered over the man's head. "The performance starts too soon."

I turned the door handle, only to find it locked—not in a metal rattling way, but a suddenly solid block thanks to some sorcerer's will. "I came to document the Rolling Moonstones. Not *this*," I said, pounding on the door.

"Don't you see? This *is* the Moonstones. Look," she said, an anxiety to her voice not there minutes ago. "I will give you everything you ever wanted. But I don't have time to explain. I need your help, and I need you to lie down on that empty cot *right now.* Will you do it?" As soon as the question got out, she turned to the cots and whispered a spell. The green halos sparked before growing in brightness. "I will fulfill your dreams, but you must choose. Otherwise this all falls apart. And I can't go back."

The green halos grew now, spreading to cover each person's head, then their whole body. "You are a fan," she said. "You know these songs. You can sing them. You know what makes the Moonstones real, why the imposters are who they are. I need your help."

The first man jolted, his arms bent at the elbows. But rather than this being some sort of rigor mortis, his left fingers formed into lute chords. And his right…the hand moved up and down, as if it were strumming invisible strings. Was this the real story behind the Moonstones?

"Alright," I said, setting my bag down and lying on the cot. "I suppose—"

I didn't get to finish my sentence. Instead, the woman stood over me, fingers tented and arms outstretched. I heard unintelligible incantations for just a few seconds before a flash of green hit me and my eyes shut.

SUDDENLY, I WAS STANDING ON THE SIDE OF THE STAGE, A LUTE SLUNG over my shoulder. Sort of. Though I clearly stood on the wooden planks of the side stage, I felt no ground beneath my feet, no air across my face, no sweat forming on my brow.

An observer in my own body. Or was it even my body?

No, it's not. But focus on the moment.

The woman's voice poked through, a conversation taking place solely in my thoughts. I tried to turn my head to see the people standing beside me, but my neck refused to budge. In fact, I couldn't order my legs to walk. I couldn't pull the lute off my shoulder. I couldn't look anywhere except straight ahead.

And straight ahead, the curtains drew back halfway to reveal a man on stage, his words starting to become audible. "...you've waited patiently and now they're here, Notalto's favorite band—the Rolling Moonstones!"

Applause erupted. In a way that I couldn't possibly explain, it was as if joy and cheering sparkled in both colors and sound. I watched through this body, somehow seeing and hearing everything that was happening. The lanterns burned around the stage, pulling the audience's focus our way. And their stares were intense, but not like the woman's. Theirs glowed with delight, screams projecting from open mouths.

As for me? I *knew* these songs. I knew them well, more than the words but the exact melodies. I'd even sung them to myself during my bath earlier. So hearing them come out of this voice, seeing the fans reacting, it pulled me further into this, whatever this was. The sense of floating gradually faded, grounding the whole experience into something that transcended physical space.

Though I didn't control the body, each foot tap echoed through my senses, every strum rippling across my nerves. The tension of the lute's strings pressed against my fingers, the mix of pressure and tension that only came with playing a stringed instrument.

Being here, *experiencing* this, my sense of self integrated into the body, and when the body sang, I sang too. I didn't know if anyone could hear it, but I didn't care. I was on stage, somehow, not *just* with the Rolling Moonstones but in their boots, and I was going to sing.

Then the woman spoke again, her voice interrupting my own inner melodies.

Yes, join in. Use your fandom. Embrace it. Sing it. Be inspired by it. Bring your joy, and make it your own.

I still didn't understand what was happening or why, but I went with it. For the next hour, I sang as if I was in a bathtub rather than onstage in front of screaming fans. Every word, every lilt, every note, when it came out, certainly sounded better than I ever did. We did song after song— "Strange Angels," "Fish From the Sky," "Two Steps Counted Backwards"—like the most brilliant fever dream. And when it finally ended, the four Moonstones stood together, hands clasped in bow after bow, an endless wave of applause that I never wanted to leave.

I WOKE UP TO FIND MYSELF ALONE ON THE COT. TO MY RIGHT, THE other three cots—and thus, the other three people—were gone, only bare stone floor remaining.

I blinked several times, my mind awash with a fever dream of images and sounds. Was that all real? Or did I just sleep through the gig?

In fact, did I miss the Moonstones…and my big break?

I sat up fast, and right as I did, a hammer smashed into the side of my head. At least it felt that way, a throb so intense that I fell back to the cot.

"You're awake." That voice—it was the mystery woman. She rushed into view, and now I saw that she waited in the other corner of a room, a cup of tea resting on a table.

"Take your time. You're going to feel exhausted. I know I am. The spell to throw the muse is not easy. But it's worth it. Here." She dashed back and grabbed the tea. "You're a little dehydrated. This takes a lot out of people."

"Did you drug me?" I said, taking the mug, and given everything that happened, I considered *not* drinking it.

"No. You wanted to see the Rolling Moonstones. That's who they were. They're a projection of me." She knelt down, and for the first time, I saw the details in her face. More than the intense eyes, but thin lips, round cheeks, and pale skin, all framed by short blonde hair.

And a smile. A weary, small smile, one that felt far from malicious or manipulative.

"My name is Herstin Krish. I come from a long family line of sorcerers. We Krishes are born into a hidden sorcery school in the south of Al'notlir, in a region beyond the mist. It's who we are. It's in our blood." Herstin brushed the light hair out of her face before looking up. "Except I didn't want that. Which did not go over well."

"What did you do?" I asked, sitting up enough to have a sip of luke-warm tea.

"They were my parents," she said with a shrug. "I had to listen to them. I went to school, I learned how to control magic, I helped people. I'm quite good at healing magic, actually." She laughed, then sprinkled her fingers over me.

A quick flash of orange filled my eyes, and then the headache, while not gone, went down way faster than any cup of tea would have done.

"But I just wanted to play music. I filled my nights learning the lute, drums, horns. Learning to sing. I could control magic since the day I was born, but it took years for me to learn to control my voice. And I wrote lyrics. "Fish From the Sky"…I've heard how people interpret it as a political rally against classism, but it's very personal. It's about how the most powerful magic isn't enough to make me happy."

That explained so much. Except for one contradiction: in this moment, Herstin looked happy.

"I started performing in pubs at night. No one knew who I was. These same songs, except just me on stage with a lute. No one cared." She laughed, a hearty chuckle that filled the small room. "Oh, no one cared. Most people didn't look up from their drinks. But part of it was me. I have terrible stage fright. No magic can overcome that. At least not for *me*. But them?" She pointed to the space where the three cots were. "One night, I discovered a projection spell. *Throwing*. It put my personal muse into a physical form—the voice, the instruments, even the performer I wanted to see. And with that, I *could* go on stage. But the problem, as you can see, is that it's really draining. So I needed help. And these songs I wrote, I wanted more than just one lute, one voice. I imagined a whole *band*." She pointed to the spots where the cots had been. "They were musicians I knew. Each of them was capable of playing instruments and singing. With them being the source of the spell, their energy could project the performance I wanted. *That* is the Rolling Moonstones. Those imposters copy me, but they aren't the same thing. There's no inspiration."

Magic to encapsulate a person's inner muse. Such a concept sounded both impossible and also the most logical thing in the world. "But why me?"

"Ah. Well…" Herstin rolled her eyes with twisted lips. "You know artists. They just want to do their own thing. The fourth cot was for Perry. He was the base energy for the vocals. Throwing works better when you have a passion for what you're doing. But Perry, he thought he could write better songs, be better on his own. He wanted a solo career." Herstin shook her head, a bemused laugh as she looked down.

"So you want me to tell the world that the Moonstones are just magic?"

"No. There are too many imposters now. I can't compete with them constantly." She sipped her tea, her face lighting up like it was the greatest tea in the world. "And I'm tired of the race. I just want to sing my songs again now without the gears of everything turning. If people want to enjoy imposters, at least let it be known that they're not the real thing because the real thing is *no more*." Now she turned, the intense stare returning and fully locked on me. "I want you to end the Moonstones. However you see fit."

HERSTIN KEPT HER WORD. THIS WAS THE BIG BREAK TO END ALL BIG breaks. This was a career-defining leap into the spotlight, a story that would make my journalistic career. The goal was simple: to announce that the Rolling Moonstones were ending, that the others were imposters, and for me to provide the exact details about how and why people could identify the imposters for themselves.

That gave my career a start. But one year later, things really took off.

I knew this, simply based on the amount of people in the audience. Unlike that night under Herstin's spell, these people were here to listen to me read from a book.

My book, in fact. I held up a copy of *The Complete Story of the Rolling Moonstones* as I looked at the small building that housed Notalto's public library. Most of the archives behind me held maps, medical texts, historical documentation of wars and politics. But my book?

That's why the line went out the door, why people filled every available seat. Copies for sale lay stacked behind me, and before I started signing any books, I asked for questions.

"How did you finally discover who the Moonstones were?"

The truth was that I discovered them through writing. Herstin gave me full authority to make up the history of each Moonstone, from their childhoods to their musical training to their unlikely coming together to form the world's most popular band. My book, in essence, was a work of fiction, taking little bits of Herstin's own life experiences and desires and weaving them into an engaging tale fit for public consumption.

"I actually only met the Moonstones once," I said, then I pointed toward the Honeychain Theatre I visited a year ago. "Right over there, at Honeychain, actually. It was quite an experience. And after, I talked with their manager. She's the person I worked with the most."

All of that was true. The three people who rested on cots while Herstin used a projection spell to throw their collective energy on stage, their names all made it into the real deal. As for the singer, well, I named him Steve.

Steve was, after all, Al'notlir's most common male name.

"How do we know everyone else is an imposter?"

"Oh, well, it's actually easy. The details I give," I said, holding up the book, "they can all be corroborated by theater staff, longtime fans, people who followed the band from city to city. Their manager has retired as well. She told me it was time for her to move on to different things. But if you find her, she'll vouch for everything in the book." I offered a quick polite laugh, as much for myself as for my captive audience. "I'm just very grateful they all trusted in me enough to tell their story."

"Do you believe they're really retired?" a voice called out. "Like they're not coming back?"

I looked up, a shift in movement catching my eye, and between the candlelight and the sunlight beaming in from the windows, I saw a familiar hood. Even at this distance, her intense blue eyes stood out, though beneath that her grin carried a warmth that wasn't there when we first met.

"Yeah," I said, a certainty lacing my words. "They're retired."

Two hours later, I managed to make it through all of the audience questions and nearly all of the customers. The funny thing was that these people didn't just want to buy the book or get the author's signature; nearly every customer shared their own story of how a Moonstones song was played at their wedding or how they sang one as a lullaby to their baby or how one of their concerts was the best night of their lives.

I nodded to all of these tales, not because I tried to shuffle the fans away, but because I understood. If the Moonstones were nothing more than a hobby or a frivolous way for me to earn some bylines, then I wouldn't have spent hour after hour learning their songs, attending their shows, discovering the idiosyncrasies of their melodies and performances.

I started out as a fan. And I was still a fan. Writing a book about them—the book, to close the door on their career—hadn't changed that.

With only a handful of people remaining in line, Herstin finally came up, hood still draped over her head, though her own lute was slung over her shoulder.

"You didn't have to wait," I said. "I think you of all people could skip the line."

"Oh," she said, looking over the library, including the once-tall stack of books that now had dwindled to a scant few, "I'm just enjoying the nostalgia."

I reached down into the stack, grabbing one of the few books left, but then she put up a hand. "It's okay. I don't need a copy."

"That is true," I said, looking at the last stragglers in line. They had no idea who Herstin was or what she did.

Though really, she probably preferred it that way.

"Well, then, I'm glad you came to see this." I took the book in my hands and opened it to the first page, a mostly blank sheet with just the title and my name on it. *To Herstin,* I wrote, *thanks for everything,* and then I signed my name beneath. "I'll keep this one for you whenever you're ready."

"Maybe. Someday. But for now, you know what would be fantastic?" She reached into her coat pocket now and pulled out a single sheet of paper, an address and a time written across the top. The words appeared burned into the fibers, accompanied by a familiar smell. "I'm doing a gig at this pub. All new songs, just by me. If you're free tonight."

An original Herstin Krish gig? In an intimate venue? With no magic involved?

That sounded like the hottest ticket in the land. Even if no one realized it. At least not yet.

I took the sheet, then wrapped my hands around Herstin's. "I can't wait."

MUSIC TO YOUR EARS

J.C. PILLARD

Vesper did not expect to be summoned by Mother Ingrid that morning. She'd been living under the witch's roof for nearly a year, and in all that time, Mother Ingrid had never asked her for anything. The witch had other girls for that—actual apprentices striving to grow wise in the ways of magic. Vesper wasn't one of those, nor had she become friendly with any of them. She kept to herself, and Mother Ingrid let her.

So it was a surprise when the knock came, the door to her small room opening and revealing Asha's angular face. The girl was perhaps twelve but had the seriousness of someone three times her age.

"Mother wants you," she said.

Vesper frowned. "What for?"

"Don't know. A man came this morning, though, and he's still with her."

Anxiety spiked through Vesper as she followed Asha out, though she did her best not to show it. It couldn't be anyone looking for her. No one knew where she was. And no one would have cared to look anyway.

MOTHER INGRID WAS IN HER BOTANICARY. WHEN SHE'D FIRST ARRIVED, Vesper had tried to explain to the older woman that the room—with its glassed-in walls and lush vegetation—was a greenhouse, but the witch had wrinkled her nose.

"I built it," she said, "so I get to name it." And that was that.

The witch looked up when Asha opened the door. She was a round woman—Vesper thought she looked like a whole note on a page of music. Wisps of silver-gray hair framed a thoughtful face, and she wore a heavy apron over her practical gardening clothes.

Behind her sat a man. He half-turned as they entered, and Vesper was relieved to realize that she didn't know him. He looked about her age, with an aquiline nose and deep-set eyes, taut now with pain. Below his neck, his citrine-colored skin disappeared beneath a haze of lines and text, a tattooed map flowing over his body.

"Good," the witch said. "You're here. Leave us, Asha."

The young apprentice bowed and left, closing the door behind her. Vesper swallowed.

"You asked to see me, Mother."

"I did. This," she said, gesturing to the man, "is Evalus."

Evalus gave a weak smile, waving with one tattooed hand. The other he kept cradled in his lap.

"Fair winds, Navigator," Vesper said, inclining her head.

"I wouldn't have summoned you," Mother Ingrid continued, "but you're the only Al'notliri here. I need you to read something for me."

Gingerly, she picked up a wrapped object from amongst the gardening tools on a nearby table, handing it to Vesper. The Navigator tensed when she touched it but didn't say anything. Carefully, Vesper unwrapped it. And nearly dropped it.

"This is an Al'notliri composer's death mask," she stammered. And not just any composer, she realized when she saw the name carved into it. It was for Cristina Agnici, famed privateer and musical genius. The mask was heavy in her hands, showing the woman's pinched face. Swirling text ran over the back side, interspersed with images of clouds and waves.

Mother Ingrid's mouth tightened. "Can you read it?"

"Umm, yes." Vesper swallowed, eyes tracing the text. "I—It's a curse, I think. 'I sing of death's sweet melody / To any who my slumber breaks / Unless they find a remedy / In the perfect music they must make—'" She broke off, turning the mask over. "I—I'm sorry, I don't see any music. Was there something else with the mask, perhaps? A manuscript, or—"

"What about this?"

Though threaded with pain, the Navigator's voice was sonorous, putting Vesper in mind of a cello. Wincing, he held up the arm he'd been cradling. Below his elbow, the black ink of his tattoos was subsumed by a different darkness entirely. Tendrils of rot grew up from his fingers, forming vertical lines along his forearm with sickly spots of decay pocked along them. Nausea filled her gut, but Vesper refused to look away. She traced her eyes over the black splotches, making sense of the pattern.

"That's musical notation," she whispered. The necrotic lines formed a staff for the round bodies of notes to dance along. She traced her finger over the main melody, playing it in her head. It was a dirge, one she wasn't familiar with. "It's not complete, though. This is just the opening theme."

"What instrument is it for?" the witch asked.

Vesper followed the staff to its beginning. As she saw the clef, everything in her tightened painfully, violin strings about to snap. She forced herself to relax, to straighten and look at Mother Ingrid.

"It's for stormorgan," she said, keeping her voice level. "It's a particular Al'notliri instrument. I've never heard of one anywhere in the world except the archipelago."

Evalus let out a groan. "Fantastic. You may as well let me die."

Mother Ingrid frowned. "Stop griping. This is your own cursed fault for stealing from a grave."

"I didn't know it was a grave!"

"And I didn't know you were a self-pitying fool," the witch snapped. "I've slowed its spreading. Now we just have to play it."

"It has to be played perfectly," Evalus said, exasperation in his tone. "And I have to go to Al'notlir to even find the damned instrument."

Vesper tuned them out, eyes tracing over the melody again, playing the fragment in her head. They wouldn't be able to play it at all if they didn't figure out the rest of the song before it finished writing itself onto his body. She wasn't a healer, but she could see well enough the ruin it would make of him if allowed to spread.

"You need a composer," Vesper said, interrupting the ongoing argument. "Someone who can complete it."

Mother Ingrid's eyes narrowed. "You can read it. Can you finish it?"

"No," Vesper said quickly. "No, I can't, but—" She broke off. The old anxiety, buried for the past ten months, vibrated through her body like a crescendo. Bile crawled up her throat as she thought of the concert hall, Gustavo's cruel eyes just waiting for her to make a mistake—

"Vesper?" Mother Ingrid's voice cracked the memory. "What's the matter, girl?"

Vesper sucked in a breath, focusing on the room, grounding herself as best she could. She didn't want to go back there. But a man would die if she did not.

"I know a composer who can help," she forced herself to say. She looked at Evalus, watching him cradle that necrotic music in his lap, and swallowed the ash that had fallen on her tongue.

"I can find you someone to play this," she said. And she tried not to wince when he smiled.

THE GOOD THING ABOUT TRAVELING WITH A NAVIGATOR WAS THAT THE Gate jumps were more streamlined. Mostly.

"It's just a brief stint next to a volcano," Evalus was saying cheerily as they hopped off the cart they'd picked up from the docks. "And it cuts out three jumps."

"I really think the original plan is better," Vesper said, eyeing the building that enclosed their first Gate. It was constructed of pale wood, with large windows to catch the ocean breeze. Mother Ingrid's house was in a chain of islands, and they'd taken the ferry over from her atoll to Uanoa, the largest island and the one that housed the nearest Gate. The smells of salt and sandalwood mixed in Vesper's nose, and she breathed deeply, steadying her nerves.

"It's just a *little* volcano."

"I know you're eager to get there," Vesper said, "and for good reason. But I also don't want to fall into a lake of magma."

Evalus grumbled but didn't push it. Instead, he asked, "How did you come to be at Ingrid's house? You're not an apprentice, far as I can tell."

She glanced at him. She'd never heard anyone refer to the witch simply as 'Ingrid,' but maybe the rules were different with Navigators. "Mother Ingrid helps all sorts."

"Sure, but most of the time they don't stay very long." He pushed up the canvas flap that led into the building, gesturing for her to duck inside. "And you seem to have been there for a while."

"I needed a place to stay. That's all."

An attendant bustled up as they entered, bowing and showing them to the mid-chamber. Cubbies lined the walls, a handful occupied with clothing and other belongings. The attendant left them alone to disrobe.

"She's my aunt, you know," Evalus said casually. He was halfway undressed, gingerly maneuvering around his cursed arm. The piece played in Vesper's mind every time she looked at it, so she tried not to look at it too often.

Pausing in her own undress, Vesper finally processed his words. "Wait. Mother Ingrid is—"

"My aunt, yeah." He sat to take off his boots. "Da was a Navigator like me, and his sister is a witch. Guess odd professions run in the family. Anyway, when he passed a few years ago, she tracked me down and told me that if I didn't check in regularly, she'd flay me alive. Need my skin, 'cause it's got my map, so now I check in regularly."

Her nephew. Vesper folded her pants into a cubby thoughtfully. Strangely, she'd never thought of Mother Ingrid as having a family. She'd always assumed the witch was as unmoored as she was. What would it be like, she wondered, to have someone looking out for you?

Evalus suddenly hissed in pain, and she realized he'd jostled his arm trying to get his left shoe off. Hurrying over, she knelt and began untying the laces for him.

"She's a good aunt," she murmured. "When we come back, you'll have to stay for tea." She sat back on her heels and held out his boot. Going through Gates often enough inured you to nudity, but she still kept her eyes carefully trained on his face and not on his muscled torso or elegant tattoos.

Evalus took the boot with a laugh. "If we find someone to play this in time, I'd love to."

THEY PASSED THROUGH EIGHT GATES ALL TOLD. IT SHOULD HAVE BEEN eleven, but Vesper relented about the volcano when she noted the music spreading. It crept higher on Evalus's arm, passing the elbow and sprinkling his bicep with necrotic quarter and eighth notes. She knew Mother Ingrid had done something to make it progress slower, but she had no idea how long they had before it would be too late.

The sight of it made her stomach writhe with shame, especially when Evalus—cheerful, bright Evalus—seemed determined to ignore the curse as much as possible. They were moving quickly, but he always made sure to point out the sights, showing her stunning waterfalls and dragging her out of bed early just to see a candy-colored sunrise over the mountains in Griasta. When they stayed at taverns between Gates, he'd remain in the common room late into the evenings, talking congenially with the other travelers. Once, they even met another Navigator who was returning from Ullande in Fjallanir.

"They're building a new art gallery," the Navigator—a woman named Saba—told them dreamily. The ink of her map was the brassy gold of a polished trumpet. They sat together in the brightly lit common room of a tavern near a vast marsh. Outside, gentle rain pattered against the windows, and the wind gusted through the trees. It would be a chilly trip to the Gate tomorrow.

Vesper took a sip of her drink, reveling in the warm flavors sliding over her tongue. Normally, she would have slipped off to their rented room by now, but the Navigators had been talking so animatedly that she found herself rooted to the spot, entranced by stories of caribou runs and bubbling hot springs. She'd never been to Fjallanir—she couldn't imagine what a place so cold was like.

Saba let out a sigh, resting her cheek against her hand. "Where are you two headed?"

"Notalto," Vesper replied.

"Finally taking him to meet the family, eh?" Saba asked, arching an eyebrow.

Vesper felt her face heat with embarrassment. "Oh, no, it's not—we're not—"

"Vesper here is just saving my life," Evalus said easily. He gestured to his other arm. "Got myself a rather nasty curse. But Ves knows someone who can fix it."

He smiled at her, white teeth flashing, and Vesper wanted to crumple at the trust in his gaze. But she forced herself to smile back, wrapping her hands around her drink to keep them from tapping out a nervous melody on the table.

THE NECROTIC MUSIC HAD REACHED EVALUS'S SHOULDER BY THE TIME they came to the last Gate, rendering it impossible for him to undress on his own. Vesper had helped him at the past couple of Gates, sliding his jacket and boots off and trying very hard not to notice how muscular his back was. Here, though, they'd been given a private room with an attendant—a perk of being a Navigator, apparently.

"So," Evalus said as the attendant unbuttoned his shirt. "Notalto. Do you actually have family there?"

Vesper stiffened, halfway through taking off her own shirt. She'd been avoiding thinking about it, turning her mind every which way but to the city.

"It's just, the way you talk about it makes it sound like home, and—"

"We're going to see my uncle," she said, pulling her top off. "He should be able to help."

"Is he a musician?"

"He's a composer."

Evalus didn't say anything else until they were alone, waiting to be called to the Gate. They were both wrapped in blankets for modesty, though Evalus had let his slip down to his waist. He laid his good hand on her shoulder.

"Yes," he said softly. "You know you can trust me, right?"

She winced. "It's not about that."

"Feels like it is."

"Look," she said, facing him. "I didn't leave on the best of terms. But my uncle loves a challenge. I know he'll help."

"If you say so," he said uncertainly.

Vesper opened her mouth to say—what? That she knew this would save him? That she was sure she could convince her uncle to help them? She had a plan, but she had no idea if it would work.

She was saved from having to reply by the door opening. A robed attendant inclined his head, gesturing for them to follow him. It was time.

NOTALTO WAS JUST AS VESPER REMEMBERED. SHIPS FILLED THE WATER around the city, with canals crisscrossing various neighborhoods like veins. Large palazzos lined open piazzas, and people strolled along the streets in linen pants and cotton gowns, taking in the sea breeze and chatting amongst themselves.

And everywhere, everywhere, there was music.

A knot formed in Vesper's throat as they walked, listening to the competing strains of a hundred different tunes tangling in the open air. A rowdy shanty spilled from a nearby tavern. On a street corner, a violinist played a plaintive tune. A string quartet performed for a small crowd in one of the piazzas, their music sending enchanted blooms of light into the air. Vesper winced when she saw it, torn between pain and joy. The music of Al'notlir had always been magical.

Beside her, Evalus hummed, bobbing his head to whatever tune was loudest. The keepers at the Gate had given him a sling for his arm, keeping it held against his chest. Vesper couldn't help anxiously looking at his shoulder, where black lines of music were starting to peek out from beneath his shirt collar.

"All right, where to?" he asked. "I'll admit, I'm not overly familiar with Notalto."

"My uncle works at the Conservatory. From here, I'd suggest we take a gondola."

The gondolier they found punted them out into the rippling waters of the canals. As they went, Vesper tried to close herself off from the music, but it swelled in her ears, sending a gnawing in the pit of her stomach. She wasn't sure if the feeling was hunger or nausea.

They eased around a corner, and the Conservatory rose up from the palazzos like a serpent rearing out of the sea. A wide dome, encrusted with gold barnacles, sat atop a long building pocked with arched windows. A few students with instrument cases slung over their shoulders hurried along the dock as the gondolier pulled up. Vesper took a deep breath as she gazed at the building, memories of years spent there bubbling in her brain.

She led Evalus inside and up a flight of stairs. Like the city beyond, the Conservatory was much as she remembered it. She heard students practicing as they walked—a waltz on a cello, a lively jig being played by a horn. She kept her eyes running over the doors until, at last, she found the one she was searching for.

"Professor Gustavo Intero." Evalus squinted at the black paint on the door. "Is that your last name? Intero?"

"Regrettably, yes," Vesper muttered, knocking hard.

The sound of someone cursing cut through the wood, followed moments later by the door being yanked open.

"You *imbecile*, you interrupted my—" The words died. The man standing beyond it, tall and pale with thinning black hair and a pencil mustache, stared down at Vesper as though he was seeing a ghost.

Vesper summoned up all her bravado and met his gaze. "Hello, Uncle."

His face transformed into a scowl. "Where in the *Gates* have you been?" He glanced at Evalus, who was looking between them in some confusion. "And who is *that*?"

"This is Evalus," Vesper said. "We need your help."

Her uncle sucked in a breath. "You think, after your little stunt last year, that I would do anything to help you? You humiliated me, Vesper. And you are no longer a student here." He went to close the door, but she caught it.

"I have the last composition of Cristina Agnici," she bit out. "If you agree to help us, I'll give it to you. And afterwards, I'll never darken your doorstep again."

Gustavo's expression flickered. She could see the gears working behind his eyes. Cristina Agnici was one of the most famous Al'notliri composers to ever live. Anyone who presented a new piece of hers would be lauded across the country—across the world, even—for the discovery. And Gustavo was nothing if not conscious of fame.

The door eased open. "Well then," her uncle said, voice turning oily. "Why don't you both come in?"

"Your uncle is a dick," Evalus muttered. They sat together in Gustavo's office, a set of drained coffee cups on a low table before them. Three of the walls of the palatial room were covered in musical notation, while a massive oil painting took up the fourth, depicting Gustavo in a moody pose in front of a piano. Vesper's stomach twisted when she saw it. She remembered when he'd had that painted. She'd been locked in her room for three days so as not to disturb him on such an important occasion.

"Well, he's a good composer."

"There's gotta be a hundred good composers in Notalto. Why him?"

"He's a brilliant music theorist," Vesper said tiredly. "He can take a very simple melody and figure out the rest of the piece just by that. Since we can't wait for Agnici's work to be completed to get the notation, he seemed like the natural choice. Doesn't mean I'm happy about it."

"He said you used to be a student here."

Vesper's shoulders rose to her ears. "I was."

"You never mentioned." Evalus cleared his throat. "What did you—"

"It's a dirge!" Gustavo, who'd been sitting at his desk, shoved away from it with violent glee, a sheaf of pages in his hand.

Evalus looked at him. "Vesper already knew that," he said flatly.

The composer's jaw tightened. "Yes, thank you, I'm glad some of the Conservatory's teachings managed to stay in her head." He set the pages down before them, spreading them out. The dirge was only four pages long—a mournful melody played over a d minor harmony. It would be stunning performed, Vesper thought. "The primary theme is fairly simple, and Agnici is using pieces of an older sea shanty to create the harmonies, so there was a good amount to work with."

Vesper tore her eyes away from the pages. "Can you play it?" she asked.

"Hmm?" He raised his eyebrows. "*Play* it? You only asked me to transcribe it. Playing it wasn't in the deal."

"Someone has to play it," Evalus said. "That's part of the curse."

"Well, my errant niece should have specified that when she reappeared outside my door after nearly a year. Better yet, you could have brought the death mask with you."

Vesper bristled. "We came via Gate."

"Oh, so we're making excuses again?"

"This isn't about me—"

"Isn't it? You turn up out of nowhere with no explanation, bribing me with Cristina Agnici's last piece, and you expect me to believe this isn't some desperate ploy to get back into my good—"

"*That's enough.*" Suddenly, the pages were off the table. Evalus held them in the air with his good hand, feet braced wide. The Navigator had never been anything less than easy-going, even as the curse traveled up his arm. Now, though, his expression was thunderous.

"You're not the only Gates-cursed composer in this city, and we don't need to sit here and listen to you being an ass! Can you play it or not?"

Gustavo's eyes narrowed. "Give me those pages."

"No."

The composer took a step toward Evalus. Vesper was out of her chair before she could think, standing between them.

"Leave him alone."

Her uncle stared down at her contemptuously. "Why did you come back, Vesper?" he asked, voice dangerously low. "Tell me the truth."

Vesper's mouth went dry. She felt like a student again, sitting in his office as he looked over an exam she hadn't done well enough on. Her hands started to shake.

"Uncle, please. We needed a composer—"

He let out a bark of laughter. "You couldn't even transcribe the music yourself? Even though it's for your own Gates-cursed instrument?"

"What are you talking about?" Evalus demanded. "Ves may have been a student here, but she isn't a composer."

"Evalus—" Vesper started, desperate fear churning in her gut as Gustavo cut her off.

"*Not* a composer? My dear boy, what has Vesper been telling you?" He stepped back. "She's my niece. Of course she's a composer. Not only that, but that music," he said, pointing to the pages, "is for the stormorgan, an instrument she was *allegedly* a prodigy on. I can't speak to the truth of it, as I never heard her play. The one time I had the opportunity to do so was a year ago. She disappeared before the performance took place."

"What—what do you mean?" Evalus's voice was uncertain.

Vesper, hating her uncle and hating herself even more, turned to look at the Navigator. His brow was pinched in confusion. The music was still gripped in one hand, but it had gone slack at his side. His eyes turned from her uncle to her.

"You can't play this, right?" he asked. "Ves?"

"I—it has to be perfect—I couldn't risk it—" Panic clogged her throat, cutting off her words. Behind her, she heard her uncle sigh.

"I'm sorry my niece lied to you, dear boy," he said, voice gentle. "She's always been a disappointment. Even to her own family."

The betrayal in Evalus's eyes bore into her, snapping her control like the neck of a violin. Her heartbeat drummed in her ears, tempo ever increasing, while the room around her grew smaller by the second.

Without thinking—without even realizing she was moving—she turned and sprinted from the room.

Vesper ran blindly, feet slapping out a staccato rhythm against the tiled floor. She didn't know where she was going until she reached the grand doors of the concert hall, their handles carved to look like mermaids and open-mouthed fish. Fingers shaking, she pulled them open and stepped inside.

Despite everything, she'd always loved the Conservatory's concert hall. The space had been designed by some Al'notliri architect centuries ago, and he'd crafted the interior to look as though it had been dredged up from the ocean floor. Seats with sea-foam green cushions slanted down toward the huge stage. The proscenium dripped with coral and barnacles, and a few illusory fish flitted among the carvings, bright specks of red and blue. There was a faint hum in here, as through every piece ever played still echoed inside.

At the back of the stage, imposing and strange, was the stormorgan. She thought of it as *her* stormorgan, although all the students could access it. It resembled a pipe organ, but rather than brass pipes, the stormorgan was backed by massive glass cylinders. Within each, a miniature storm swirled, the colors of the clouds shading from pale gray to a dark, sickly green. Vesper remembered the feel of the keys beneath her fingers, the way the cylinders released clouds into the air in huge, gasping breaths. The storm always encompassed her by the end, making her feel as though she was nothing more than wind and lightning and bitter rain.

The door behind her banged open, and she turned to see Evalus. He'd lost his sling somewhere along the way, and he was panting.

"Ves—" he started, stopping when she let out a shuddering sob.

"I'm sorry, Evalus," she whispered. "I should have told you, but I couldn't, I—I didn't want you to hate me. And now you *do*, and I can't even blame you." She dug her teeth into her lower lip, choking back a wave of tears. "I'm sorry."

A calloused hand landed on her shoulder, and she tensed, waiting for the recriminations. But instead, Evalus just squeezed.

"I don't hate you."

"You should."

"Well, I don't. I couldn't even if I wanted to." He gave her a tiny smile, eyes concerned. "Okay? So, just...tell me what happened last year. Please?"

She hiccupped, staring at the stage without really seeing it. "My family—the Interos—are extremely well-known for their musical gifts," she started. "My grandfather was a conductor, my grandmother a dancer. Gustavo is a composer. My mother was an opera singer. I don't know who my father was—she never told anyone. She died when I was very young, and by then, I didn't have any family left except Gustavo. I think he would have disowned me if he hadn't been afraid of the public shaming he'd get for doing so.

"I can't sing," she continued. "Or dance. Or compose, despite what he told you. I can memorize music almost immediately, but I can't make something from nothing, not the way he can. He tried to make me, though. There were tutors—lots of them. Year after year. They were all horrible. The dance teacher would—" She broke off, her throat clotting, and Evalus squeezed her shoulder again. She didn't need to rehash everything that had happened, the scars they had left.

She took a breath. "Eventually, he sent me here just to get me out of his hair. It was a relief to be free of that house. And then I discovered the stormorgan, and I learned how to play it, and…and it felt like I was finally *worth* something. I would play for hours and hours. I used to sneak down here at night just to listen to the storms in the cylinders."

"Then why did you run?" Evalus asked.

"Because I was afraid! I hate playing in front of people, Evalus. It's too much like being in that house, performing for those horrid tutors again and again and again. I was supposed to give a recital. I thought it would be all right and then—"

"And then you learned Gustavo was going to be there," he finished grimly.

She nodded. "I couldn't bear the thought of him watching me perform. So I ran. I ran as fast and far as I could. Gate after Gate. It didn't matter where, just so long as it was far away from here."

"And you ended up at Ingrid's."

"And I ended up at Ingrid's," she agreed.

Evalus shook his head. "Ves, why didn't you tell me?"

"It has to be perfect," she whispered. "I can't—I've never performed perfectly when someone was listening, Evalus. Not once. I couldn't risk your life on me fumbling my way through it. I thought about telling you, but I couldn't. I'm a coward."

"You aren't a coward," he said, voice firm. "Anyone with two eyes and half a brain can see that. You came back to this place and confronted your absolute twat of an uncle to help me, regardless of what he'd done to you. If that's not bravery, I don't know what is."

"I lost us our composer, though."

Evalus chuckled. "Yeah, about that." He released her shoulder and reached into his pocket, removing a set of crumpled pages.

Vesper's eyes widened. "How did you get away with those?"

"I've always had a pretty good right hook," he said sheepishly. "Your uncle may or may not be laid out flat in his office right now. I'd say I'm sorry, but I'm not."

Carefully, she took the composition, smoothing out its wrinkles. The piece danced over the page in her uncle's spidery writing, melody playing louder than ever in her head. They had the music. Now, they just needed—

Evalus gasped and fell to his knee, good hand going to clutch at his chest.

"Shit," he whispered, voice strangled. "I thought we had more time."

Panicked, Vesper sank down and yanked his shirt open. In the time since they'd arrived, the necrotic music had crept over his left pectoral, ripping through his beautiful tattoos to reach black tendrils toward his heart.

"No," she breathed.

"It's okay." Evalus panted. "It's fine. I'll be fine." Even as he spoke the blood drained from his face.

Vesper stuffed the music into the pocket of her trousers and slid an arm around his waist. "Come on," she pleaded. "Stay with me. We just need to get to the stage."

"The—the stage? But why—"

"I need to set up the organ, and I don't know how close you need to be for the music to work." She began moving down the aisle, Evalus leaning on her. The stormorgan crouched on the stage, staring her down. She was still scared, she realized. Petrified. This performance was for much higher stakes than her Gates-cursed recital.

But she couldn't run. This time, she had to play.

A STORMORGAN HAS THREE KEYBOARDS. ONE FOR THE HANDS, ONE FOR the feet, and one for the storm. Musicians always learn the first two long before they are ever entrusted with the third.

Vesper sat on the bench, her uncle's transcription propped on the music desk. Above, the glass chambers loomed. She'd unlocked the third keyboard, listened to the hiss of pressure as the caps on the cylinders loosened. The storm clouds swirled, ready to be unleashed.

Evalus was on the stage, laid out on a couch she'd dragged from the wings. She knew he was trying to be quiet, but she could hear the wheezing of his breath. They didn't have time to find another player. It was now or never.

Sliding forward on the bench, she set her feet against the pedals and hands to the keys. And, trembling, she began to play.

The stormorgan came alive with the first note. Her feet worked the pedals, spinning out deep, sonorous tones that shook the wood beneath her, while her right hand played a mournful series of chords. With her left, she reached up to set free the first set of clouds.

A gust of wind carrying the smell of snow burst from its chamber. A few moments later, the fog of a jungle storm joined it. As she played, bringing in storms and sea mists, F major chords and d minor melodies, she heard something in the music that she didn't think her uncle had spotted. This was a dirge, but it wasn't a song of mourning. It was a song of remembrance. In its tones, she heard Cristina Agnici's longing, her memories of storm-tossed seas and salt-drenched afternoons. She heard a woman singing the tale of her life, hoping that someone might one day hear it and remember her. Cristina Agnici was gone, but she'd left her soul behind in her music—fearless and unbound. The song rattled the very stage with its force, and in the midst of the storm, Vesper forgot to be afraid. She forgot everything except the music under her hands and the man she played for, lying somewhere behind her.

The final melody softened, the storm dying to a fine mist, then subsiding into nothing. Vesper pulled the lever that sucked the storms back into their chambers, watching the lingering clouds dissipate. In the silence that followed, she realized she could no longer hear the Navigator breathing.

"Evalus!" She scrambled off the bench, slipping over the wet stage.

Evalus lay where she'd left him, eyes closed. As she reached him, she ripped his shirt away.

The black rot of the music was gone.

Beneath her hands, Evalus groaned, his eyes flickering open. "Gates, your fingers are cold," he mumbled.

Vesper jerked back. "Oh, I'm s—"

He caught her hand. "That was not a request for you to stop," he said, pressing her hand over his chest again.

"You're all right?" she asked a little breathlessly.

"I'm fine. The curse is gone, thanks to you." He smiled. "You know, you're a liar twice over. You told me you couldn't play perfectly."

Vesper let out a wet laugh, relief coursing through her as she felt his heart beating beneath her palm. It had worked. It had *worked*.

Someone cleared their throat.

She stiffened, looking around. Standing near the stairs to the stage, bruise darkening his chin, was her uncle. His eyes flickered from her to the music still sitting on the stormorgan.

"Well," he said after a moment, stepping up onto the stage. "Congratulations. Your instructors weren't lying when they said you had some talent. Given your return, and your status as an Intero, I could see my way to getting you reinstated at the Conservatory. You would have to repeat some of your classes, of course, but—"

"No." Vesper's voice was as sharp as the lightning she'd just been playing. She darted back to the bench, snatching the pages off the music desk.

Gustavo's jaw tightened. "Vesper, give me those."

"Why in the Gates should she?" Evalus asked with a groan. "She's the one who played them."

"You stay out of this," the composer hissed. "This is a family matter."

"What the fuck do you know about family?" Vesper's hands were shaking. "You never cared about me. You don't even like me. I guess now that you've seen I have 'some talent' you'd be willing to put up with me to get your hands on Agnici's composition." The only copy of which she held in her hands.

No, that wasn't right. The music was in her head, too. She'd been looking at it for weeks, Gate after Gate. And now she'd played it—it *lived* inside her, even more than it did on the page.

"Now Vesper, calm down—"

"Oh, I'm very calm." Vesper set her jaw, staring at her uncle. He'd been bigger in her imagination, a tower of a man. On the stage before her, though, he looked unbearably small. "Do you know how hard I tried to impress you? I wanted you to love me so badly, and you never did. Giving these to you wouldn't change that. It wouldn't fix anything."

"Those pages are *my* property—"

"You're a composer," she replied. "Compose something new." Then, taking the music in both hands, she tore it to pieces, letting them fall to the wet stage.

"No!" Gustavo collapsed to his knees and scrambled forward, grasping at the shreds. They were soaked through, the ink completely obliterated.

She stared down at her uncle once more, etching him into her mind. Unexpectedly, tears pricked the corners of her eyes, and she swiped them away. Then, she turned and crossed to Evalus, who was beginning to sit up. He looked at her with concern.

"Are you all right?" he asked softly.

She smiled tiredly. "I'm fine," she said. "Come on. Let's go."

THE SUN WAS SETTING OVER THE OCEAN WHEN THEY GOT BACK TO Uanoa.

"I'm just saying, if we stole the plans for one, we could probably build a stormorgan for you," Evalus said. His hand, warm and callused, was wrapped around Vesper's own. "It can't be that hard."

"Do you know the amount of time it takes to catch all those storms?" Vesper laughed. "You'd be bored to tears."

"No, I wouldn't!"

"Yes, you would! Besides, I would hope you've learned your lesson about stealing from the Al'notliri."

He groaned. "Gates, you're going to hang that over my head for the rest of my life, aren't you?"

Vesper smiled. They'd taken the long way back from Notalto, enjoying the sights and sounds of myriad different places. She hadn't even minded when Evalus took them back to the volcano for a stint. She felt free for the first time in her life.

"I'll hang it over your head until you get tired of me, how's that?"

Grinning, the Navigator leaned down and kissed her.

"Now that," he said, "is music to my ears."

THE CLOTHIER OF ALENNI

VICTOR MANIBO

There comes a point in each person's life that decisions become harder not because of two equally enticing options but because of stasis. Choices are no longer thrust upon you, the stakes no longer feel as stark: it no longer becomes a question of picking this suitor or that, or entering this trade or that employ. And that kind of decision—the one where you have to decide to decide—is what you have before you.

It is a question you alone must answer, a journey you alone must make. As with the Gate in our town's piazza, you cannot take me with you. Well, not in that way. Besides, you do not need me. As with those Gates too, you do not need anyone's permission, nor need you use any tool or pay any fare. All you need is will.

Have I ever told you the story of the clothier of Alenni? I must have, back in our early days, when we still exchanged tales of where we'd come from and where we'd been. That's right; it is that island of the most splendiferous gems. It is the same place whence came that ruby resting on your finger. Yes, I probably never told you about the town clothier. I suppose I had no reason to until now.

He ran a small shop right outside a piazza, though not one quite like ours. Alenni was a much smaller town, especially in those days before the jewel trade picked up. Why, their piazza was smaller than the abbey's courtyard, and their water well was no more than a rough-hewn hole in the ground.

They too had a Gate, which in their language they called lagusan. The place where things pierce through. Their Gate allowed one to pierce through to a dense valley in the steppes of Koidev, where the land is covered in barley and sunflowers as far as the eye can see. But I am getting ahead of myself.

His name was Euskar and he ran the only clothier in Alenni. He imported his textiles from nearby islands in Al'notlir, and on occasion he'd also been known to tailor. As I said, it was a small town; its inhabitants knew how to sew, at least enough to stitch two sheaths together and cut holes in them. Yet there were weddings and funerals too, ceremonies that lasted for days, both, oddly enough, involving feasts of cured redfish and stone crab, and requiring some finery. The clothier catered to these needs, though he mostly preferred crafting the basics for those who didn't sew themselves: smocks and tunics, house dresses and trousers. Sturdy, practical wear for sturdy, practical people.

His life was forever changed one cloudless night quite like this one. Euskar, still at his draper's table, hadn't noticed the time. He stretched his spindly fingers, and when he arched his back, it gave a satisfying crack. He looked out his workshop window. The square had fallen quiet; its shops had shuttered. Only the lagusan stood silent and solitary. Its arch and entryway, made of polished obsidian mined from the Alenni hills, glistened in reflected moonlight. As he shuttered his own window, for a second he thought his eyes were playing tricks on him. That, or his vision was finally failing him.

The portal's glassy surface began to glimmer.

Travelers never arrived after sundown, the rare ones that come to Alenni, but the clothier readily jumped into action. He wrapped a cloak around himself, and from his shelves he took another, as well as a loose shirt, some drawstring pants, and a pair of sandals, all roomy enough to accommodate whatever figure this traveler cut. Here was another way the clothier made his living. Travelers mostly came for business, and had some means of repaying him for the clothes he sold on credit. Some came bearing urgent news; some came to deliver some offer or acceptance of a deal. The reasons differed, and though they all arrived completely naked, bearing nothing but themselves, they all left town with money.

Euskar stepped out of the shop and strode toward the square, the bundle of clothes cradled in both hands like an offering.

The portal glowed brighter, and soon, a traveler pierced through the gate. He was young, at least a score younger than the clothier, probably more. The waves of his hair were the color of wheat at harvest time, and his face had a striking beauty the kind of which Euskar had only seen once in his life. Once, a long time ago, when he himself was just as young.

It wasn't possible. "He looks just like…" Euskar found himself whispering. A tightness gripped the clothier's chest, and he lost his hold on his goods.

The traveler turned his head to search the square. The clothier, panicked, collected his goods from the cobblestone ground. As he did, he heard the clopping of horse hooves approach. Timo, a miner who lived on the edge of town, got off his mare and greeted the traveler. He handed him a bundle much like the one Euskar had now gathered.

Before he could be spotted, the clothier rushed back into his shop and quietly shut the door behind him.

His fingers trembled, indeed, his entire body shook, as he searched his shop for a sheaf of paper. He rummaged through his desk and its drawers, but not a single, clean sheet was to be found. He rushed to his board and found a scrap of beige fabric, its edges cut in curves. Good enough. He cleared the surface and straightened the piece, then set off to find paint.

Euskar knew the entire place would have none, but still he went through the cabinets, the chests and boxes in his own quarters above the shop. He searched with an urgency he hadn't felt in ages. At last in his desperation, he took a jar of blue dye from the storeroom, undid its lid, and spilled it on his makeshift canvas.

The scrap warped and transformed, soaking up the dye. Euskar held his hands over the spill and closed his eyes. He recalled the cut of the young man's jaw, the curve of his cheekbone, the slope of his brow. Euskar tried, but he could not disbelieve his eyes, nor his perfect memory. He felt the energy pulse through his veins, in his arms and his fingers. He opened his eyes, his downturned palms glowing, and then he began to paint.

The dye reformed and reassembled itself from a large amorphous blot, gathering in the center of the canvas. It took on a dark, almost black hue. Euskar flicked his index finger ever so slightly, forming a line. He felt a ripple of glee. He had not lost his precision, even after all this time. He flicked his other fingers, each its own brush. The dye followed, thinning and massing where he chose, forming strokes and tendrils and curves of blue, spreading and shrinking as he desired. His pleasure grew the more the figure took shape, the strokes and their gradations forming the face of the man in the square.

When he was done, Euskar sat on his stool and wept.

THE NEXT MORNING, HE CAME TO ON HIS WORKBENCH, ROUSED BY A CUP and saucer being set by his side. His apprentice Janessa towered over him with her hands on her hips.

"What happened here, old man?"

"Nothing," he replied, wiping the sleep from his eyes. "Another late night."

"Didn't look like nothing. Looked like a gale blew through here. Why, if I didn't…"

"Thank you, Janessa." Euskar took a sip of his tea. Her brisk disposition could be a bit much, especially in the morning, but her sewing was as expert as her brewing.

"What's this then?" she asked, hunched over the bench.

Euskar hid the painted fabric under other scraps. "Don't…worry about it."

"That was a panel," she answered, miffed. "For the mayor's vest. What did you do with it?"

The apprentice snatched the piece and held it up in front of her. Her expression turned from annoyance, to mild amusement, to awe.

"Master Euskar, this is…this is extraordinary! You did this?"

The clothier nodded, with no hint of shame nor pride. He himself didn't know how to feel about what he'd created; all he felt was longing, and that, he would never let show.

"Who is he?"

"No one."

"These lines, the shading…it looks so real," Janessa continued, her amazement overcoming her need to confront the obvious lie. Her hand ran over the curls on the young man's temples, hesitant at first. "Real, and at the same time, not real. Almost…"

Dreamlike. The portrait was of a man who had long left this world, and whom the clothier only ever saw in dreams anymore. True, there appeared another quite like that man, one who just last night stood in the empty square like a dazzling vision, bearing the same face and the same body as Euskar remembered it. Yet the clothier was convinced, even as he was painting it, that the vision must have been a dream too.

"…And I didn't know you painted," the apprentice said, setting the piece back down on the board.

"I haven't in a long time. Something just came over me last night."

The apprentice picked up the jar of blue dye and inspected it. "You used this?" She searched the room. "What, with a brush?"

Euskar shook his head. "With my hands." He wiggled his fingers before him, the playful gesture undercut by his monotone. He surprised himself, being so uncharacteristically forthcoming, but he didn't have the energy to maintain yet another lie in the same conversation.

"Oh, what a day of revelation this has been! The clothier of Alenni, a master painter. And, I assume a water shaper, too?"

"Not like the others," he clarified. "My abilities in that regard are quite limited. No great waves or instant wellsprings or anything of the sort."

"You sell yourself short! One of your worst habits, and turns out, you do so not only with our goods."

"I keep telling you, raise even a cent and they'll all gladly sail one island over."

"So, who is he?" she asked again, tenderly this time.

"He's a fiction. He doesn't exist."

Euskar lived right above where he worked, his trade and his personal life separated only by a staircase. In the years that she'd been his apprentice, Janessa had seen everyone who walked through the clothier's door. Every client, every supplier, the occasional distant relative. She knew everyone Euskar knew. His world was small, and he liked to keep it that way. It shouldn't be so hard to believe that the man he had painted was no one. Yet at his response, Janessa's lips curled like she was about to launch a wicked barb. She glared at him, hoping to coax the truth, but he stood firm.

"Fine, don't tell me." She rubbed her chin, transfixed at the painting. Then, she began rifling through the pile of cut cloth, picking out the scraps that matched the clothier's makeshift canvas. She arranged them on the surface, piecing them together where they fit.

"What the devil are you doing?" Euskar asked.

"I have an idea."

THEY STARTED SMALL. THE FIRST PAINTED PIECE THEY SOLD WAS A PAIR of ladies' gloves (the town lacked a glover, too). The clothier painted its edges with purple rapunzel blossoms like the ones in bloom under the shop's window. Janessa marveled at how her master manipulated the indigo dye into the tanned leather without the paint bleeding where it shouldn't. The color stayed, not as though stamped or pressed but as though the bellflowers were a seamless part of the hide itself. The townsfolk marveled too, and the pair didn't stay long on the display window, quickly snatched up by an alderman's daughter.

Soon, the clothier received specific requests.

A stag on the breast of this coat, an intricate latticework pattern on the hem of this dress, a lover's face on this handkerchief. The townsfolk asked for painted items even for their most basic pieces. It quickly became commonplace for a housemaid's bonnet to be lined with lilies or spikes of lavender. The baker's apron, made of tough canvas and usually smeared with dried batter, was now completely covered with cherries. The miners' guild had their emblem—a lantern and crossed pickaxes—emblazoned on the back of their overalls. Euskar was not used to so many orders with such specifications, but he was as patient as he was gifted. Janessa, who used to fulfill the occasional requests for embroidery, was only too happy to be rendered obsolete. What her master could do in a day, she would take a week, and without nearly the same beauty nor precision.

Once in a while, a customer would come into the shop and ask if Euskar would do a portrait. A proper one, with oil on stretched canvas, to be placed over a mantel, or a desk. The first time had been the young merchant Morin, who sought to gift his betrothed a small portrait of her late mother. Euskar declined and drove the man out of his shop as though he'd just been asked to commit a crime.

Janessa chalked this up to exhaustion—the clothier had always been so amenable, but he also had not seen business this brisk for as long as she'd been in his tutelage. But when the mayor himself sought to commission a family portrait, and had been likewise driven away by the master, she understood. She made it known to the customers, through hushed whispers, never to ask Euskar for a portrait or a fresco or any sort of art that wasn't on the clothes he made.

Word about this artisan spread beyond Alenni. The larger islands of Al'notlir and the great cities of Griasta had their painters and their water shapers, though they never applied their skills to creating clothes. One water shaper, from the outer reaches of the Alard, had been doing for years what Euskar had only begun to do, but that clothier lacked the vision and talent that Euskar possessed. Soon, ships began to arrive bearing envoys and orders. Travelers came too from the magical Gate, arriving in the nude and later leaving on those same ships, outfitted with Euskar's creations.

Janessa relished the influx of income, and she'd assumed that her master did too. He put on his brightest smile when entertaining the customers, and at midafternoon, when he closed the storefront so that the two of them could focus on actually creating clothes, he seemed energized by the work ahead. Yet as the weeks drew on, the apprentice saw behind the façade. He was swamped, yes, as much as the butcher is during festival, but this was more than that. This was not tiredness of the body; this was an emptiness in his soul.

"All right, spill it. What's wrong?" she finally asked him, once when he had been short with her. "You've been irritable all week, and when you aren't, you mope like a dejected teenager. Don't think I haven't noticed. Aren't you happy with all the business we've gotten?"

"I am. As I'm sure you're happy with your raise."

She smirked. "You know, I could never set up my own shop and leave you now. I don't think I even want to."

"Whatever you choose to do, you will succeed, I know it."

"So, what is it? It can't just be exhaustion." She approached his board warily, the way an animal wrangler approaches a suckling beast. "Is it the painting?"

"I'm happy to paint, the little of it that I get to do."

"The little? Have you not seen our lists? We'll have to turn people away soon or risk having them wait a season."

"And the more orders we get, the more I realize how little it is. This" —He gestured around the shop— "the artistry, the joy we're able to provide—all this feels like a compromise."

"So paint," she told him encouragingly. "Get your canvases and oils and paint what you want, how you want."

"There are only so many mantelpieces in Alenni. Even the entirety of Al'notlir."

"People travel to wear your clothes. They will travel to see your masterpieces, and they will pay handsomely for them. Why, even I've heard of Valennin of Ullande, with his studios and his exhibitions. I'd reckon you're better than he is, what with your talent and your perfect memory."

Euskar smiled bitterly. "How old are you?"

"Eighteen in a month," Janessa replied, brow knitted. "What does that have to do with anything?"

The clothier gestured for her to wait as he headed to his upstairs quarters. From his closet he took the vest, the one with the painted face from four months back. He returned and laid the vest on the workbench with a somber air of ceremony.

"You once asked me who this was."

"And I haven't stopped wondering."

"You're too young to have known, and I suppose no one talks about it anymore." He took a sharp breath. "This man is the clothier of Alenni."

"What do you mean?" she asked, amused. "*You're* the clothier of Alenni."

"Not long before you were born, and well before you stepped foot in this shop, it was he. I was his apprentice, then his lover, then his husband."

Janessa gazed at the canvas. "There's so much love here," she said almost in a whisper. "What happened?"

Euskar gently ran the back of his hand over the face in blue, over the cheek, as though he felt flesh underneath his skin. "His name was Arsem. He died when he was twenty-six."

FEWER THINGS ARE MORE TRAGIC THAN A YOUNG WIDOWER. FEWER things still when said widower was also an orphan, an itinerant who'd never known stability in his life but once. As a lad, Euskar had traveled through countless Gates and ridden countless ships, seamlessly moving from place to place as artists tend to. In search of beauty, meaning, a sense of purpose, or at least a way to fund his next adventure, the young painter quickly took to a portal if the mood struck him. His wanderings led him to the Gate in Alenni, and when the clothier—also orphaned, recently, when the former town clothier and his wife passed from the plague—greeted him in the square with a bundle of clothes in his hands, Euskar finally understood: all this time, he was in fact in search of a home.

The painter stayed in town, taken with the clothier, who was just as smitten. With blistering vividness, Euskar still recalled the first time he'd entered the workshop. The smells of perfumed fabrics and tanned leather, the sharp sound of shears slicing through linen. He'd never been one for the trades, nor did he have any interest in being a cloth merchant or tailor, but he found a new excuse to drop in every day. The more time Euskar spent in the shop, the more he never wanted to leave it. Arsem, likewise drunk in young, reckless love, asked him to stay.

In time Arsem became his partner both in the trade and in life. Arsem still was the clothier of Alenni, a mantle he'd taken from his late father, who inherited it from his mother before him, and so on. For his part, Euskar was pleased to play the apprentice, though barely any younger than his master and nowhere near as skillful. They labored together, every second shared on workbenches next to one another, exchanging smiles and kisses as they stitched.

They lived together too, eventually, above the shop where they blissfully retired at the end of each day. With needle and thread and textiles and trimmings, with daily annoyances at their customers, with the flux of commerce bringing bounty one day and famine the next, with cups of hibiscus tea in the morning and fervent coupling at night, with love unlike either of them had known, Arsem and Euskar built a life. A home.

The young painter, getting less young by the day, became less of a painter too. He was an apprentice, then lover, then husband. He became one of the two that the town called clothier. And he was happy. So happy in fact that he hadn't noticed how he'd abandoned his gifts completely.

"DEAR HEAVENS, YOU TRULY ARE QUITE THE ARTIST," EXCLAIMED THE stately woman before the mirror. The chief of the merchants' guild twirled around, and the painted quetzals' wings fluttered with the flaps of her skirt. "I've never seen anything so lifelike."

Euskar bowed his head. "I'm happy you're happy, Gerodia."

"Tell me, can we add more berries?" She gestured around the bodice where Euskar had painted tropical shrubbery as requested, though evidently not enough of it. "Or maybe more blooms? I don't know, it's missing…something."

"We can add whatever you want."

Presently, the shop's bell rang. Euskar summoned Janessa, but when he heard no reply, he excused himself to attend to the newcomer himself.

On the threshold stood the young man from six months ago, the one from that cloudless night. As when he stepped out of the lagusan, he stood in the buff, looking exactly the way Arsem once did.

"May I help you?" Euskar asked, a tremble in his voice. He never thought he'd see him again, and though he'd often wondered about the traveler who bore a striking resemblance to his beloved, he knew too that further probing would only lead to disappointment.

"Yes, I think you might," the young man answered breathlessly.

The clothier tensed. Not only did this traveler share Arsem's face; he shared his voice too. Sensing apprehension, the traveler continued. "I was told that this was the place to go for…to get clothes on credit?"

"That it is," Euskar answered just as hesitantly. He hurried to the shelf where he stocked the necessaries. He almost asked the man how tall he was, but Euskar knew. He'd seen his body twice now; it was ingrained in his mind like each of his client's, even more so with this one. "Try these on," he told the traveler, handing him a shirt, pants, and a shearling coat. He directed him to a screen behind which to change.

"Master Euskar?" The merchant chief beckoned from the room.

"I'll be right with you," he answered, before once more yelling for Janessa. When the apprentice emerged from the basement, her arms laden with linen, he pointed her to where Gerodia waited and told her to keep the lady company.

"My usual contact never arrived. He brings me clothes," the traveler said, his sheepishness palpable. Soon enough, he stepped out from behind the screen.

"My name's Hedrik, by the way."

Euskar steadied himself on his stool, stunned. He'd seen it, but now it was undeniable. The young man wore the same kind of clothes that Arsem wore, made in the way that Arsem had once taught him to make. He stood in what used to be Arsem's workshop, with the same guileless calm of Euskar's long-dead husband.

"Timo," the clothier said, stammering. "No—no, that is not my name, I meant Timo was supposed to meet you?"

"Yes," Hedrik replied, arms crossed. "How did you know?"

"Someone had mentioned it, I forget who," he answered, waving off the remark. "My name is Euskar."

Hedrik extended his hand. Upon touching it, Euskar felt an exquisite surge of nostalgia, crisp as a prick of a needle. "You've come through once before, yes?"

"I have, a few months ago. I'm a mineralist, which is how I intend to repay you, if Timo ever decides to show up. Your miners discovered a sizable vein of amethyst, as I'm sure you've heard." He paused, proceeding only once Euskar nodded. "I go from town to town teaching guilds how to excavate gems and precious metals."

"And this, our small town, is your first stop?"

"It's a long voyage from Koidev by ship. Alenni's great for starting off on, before I make my way south to the nearby isles. I catch a ride home once I'm done in Pareeni."

Euskar nodded knowingly. "You must enjoy the nomadic life."

"I do," Hedrik replied, cocking his head to one side. "My people don't look highly on it."

"But you impart such knowledge in your journeys. That must count for something."

"That it does. The gems I pick up on the way help too," the young man winked.

"Ah! A jeweler, then!" Gerodia said from behind them. Janessa followed, gathering the train of an unfinished skirt.

"Well, not exactly, my lady," Hedrik began. "See I'm more of a…"

"I told her you'd be done soon," the apprentice told Euskar.

Gerodia shushed her, then turned to the clothier with a sly smile. "Euskar, I think I know exactly what this garment is missing."

Hedrik cocked his head aside, eyes narrowed at Gerodia's hand as she gestured around the bodice. He then grinned and nodded in agreement, understanding what she meant. His smile was more brilliant than any gem Euskar had ever seen. So ensorcelled, the clothier took a while to get the woman's meaning, and when he finally did, he stammered in his response.

"Whatever the lady wants."

<hr>

WHAT IS A PURSUIT? SOME MIGHT SAY SPENDING ONE'S DAYS IN THE company of sheep doesn't count, certainly my parents thought as much, except maybe on occasion when I've literally had to drive away a wolf or search for a missing kid. Yours is what they'd call one of the nobler ones, if not the greatest of the twelve arts. Your parents certainly never ceased reminding me. They might even call tailoring a noble pursuit, at least at the level Euskar had been doing it, with his sorcery and skill.

And what of Hedrik? No doubt teaching counted as a noble pursuit, and he traveled too. Yet in the months that followed, the young mineralist traded those pursuits for another. His journeys to Alenni grew more frequent, and when he visited the clothier, the mineralist claimed that the miners guild kept calling for him, needing help with mineral formations that they didn't know how to extricate.

Eventually, Hedrik began teaching the guildsmen the fine art of cutting and polishing gems. Before long, he let a room above a tavern in the square. It was more convenient, he explained to the clothier; this way, the town's newly minted jewelers could call on him more easily. "And so could you…in case you need another set of hands to work the gems, I mean."

Euskar saw this for what it was, and though his first impulse was to drive his young admirer away, he soon learned how valuable Hedrik could be to the business. Demand grew for painted dresses, overlaid with fine embroidery and embellished with jewels. Hedrik could be called on when the local jewelers couldn't fulfill the shop's orders. He knew which cuts of stone would produce the most brilliance for Euskar's designs. He also knew how to drill a hole in the finest gems better than anyone, and he helped Euskar with his more intricate projects.

"You might as well stay on," the clothier asked Hedrik, in time. He was quite certain the younger man would say yes, but still Euskar sensed that he might be making a mistake. "Janessa and I could really use the help."

Hedrik's face lit up. "Do you mean it?"

Euskar gestured toward the back of the workshop. "That bench is yours if you want it. Your tools have certainly gouged its surface enough."

Hedrik ran his hand over the board, smiling, ruminating. "Maybe for a little while," he finally responded, his eyes downcast. "Until the road calls to me again."

Euskar nodded. Was that disappointment he felt, or relief?

Hedrik's hand inched toward his, grazing the clothier's fingers on the workbench. "There's so much of the world left to see. You yourself must have seen so much of it."

"Not in a long time," Euskar replied. Hedrik leaned in, close enough to feel his breath. "But I've lived a long and happy life."

Hedrik smiled. "You speak as though you are dead."

"I *have* lived a long and happy life *so far*."

"So far indeed."

Hedrik leaned in and kissed him.

That night, after Hedrik had left, Euskar handed Janessa a few coins for some errands. From the woodworker he needed a frame for a canvas, and at the port, he needed whatever pigments had arrived on the day's ships. The apprentice happily obliged, knowing what a change such requests portended.

Every night thereafter, once he and Hedrik exchanged their good-byes, once the town had gone to bed and the only thing standing in the square was the silvery portal and its obsidian enclosure, Euskar retired to his room above the shop and painted. He always painted the same thing and never finished, clearing each night's work with a few waves of the hand, then starting all over again. He wore out the canvas and used up his paints, but he never completed the portrait, fearing what he might do if he kept going.

<hr>

THE MINERALIST WAS NOTHING IF NOT PERSISTENT. DESPITE THE clothier's restraint, Hedrik continued to woo him, and the more time they spent working together, the more Euskar came to see the young man as a beautiful reminder, both of his late husband and his own youth. At length, when his desire could no longer be bottled, Euskar gave in to the young man's entreaties. They spent nights together, sometimes above the shop, sometimes in Hedrik's room in the public house, where they'd go drinking after a long day of filling orders, a new nightly ritual. Each time, Euskar learned more and more of Hedrik's body, and with uncanny precision, the clothier's memories of him overlapped with those of Arsem.

"Come away with me," Hedrik asked him after one of those sweaty nights that left them both spent and invigorated. He nestled against the clothier, lazily drawing circles on his chest.

"No."

"I haven't even said where."

Euskar held the young man's hand and kissed it. "Everything we need is here."

"When was the last time you left Alenni?"

"When was the last time you stayed in one place for longer than a season?" Euskar sat up with a patient grin on his face. "We can't keep having this conversation."

"You're not just one of my stops. And yes, I could stay in one place for longer. I could stay here. It's just that…you never asked."

"I've taken you on as apprentice, haven't I?"

"It's not the same and you know it."

"This is what it is," Euskar answered. He stroked the younger man's flaxen hair, fingers catching on ringlets. "And what it is, is beautiful."

THE THIRTEEN FAMILIES SENT THEIR EMISSARIES, EXTENDING invitations for the clothier of Alenni to grace their courts for a spell. Some offered a price that could make Euskar a rich man many times over, yet he flatly refused every offer. They would have to come to the island, Janessa told these envoys, or risk failing to keep up with the latest trends. She was miffed with her master's intransigence, but it never stopped her from using it to drive up demand, and their prices. She'd also learned to leave the subject be, until the invitation came.

No one rejects Lord Umberthorne of the Council of Diviners, not only on account of his position, but of his stature. The de facto head of the Thirteen Families was the hero of the Thousand-Year Deluge and the chief broker of the Unification. Surely, a tailor from a far-flung island would not spurn one of history's greatest figures, especially not now that Umberthorne was a hundred and twelve and had a permanent, though comfortable, seat by death's door.

Of course, Janessa knew better than to pester Euskar, but this opportunity could not be missed, and so she turned to Hedrik. He himself needed little convincing, and between the two apprentices, he could persuade the master in ways she could not.

"Yes, I've read it," the clothier told Hedrik when they closed up shop that night. "And I've kept the papers and seal in one of our jewel boxes. It's not every day one gets an invitation from a legend."

"Well, what do you think?" Hedrik set down their teas on his desk.

"I think it's very flattering to get an invitation from a legend."

"It's a single long coat. It'll take us two days at most if we work around the clock."

"And leave the shop?"

"Janessa's been running the place well and fine."

"You really will say anything to get me to walk through a portal, won't you?"

"Or ride a horse more than ten miles. Or set foot on a sailing ship. Or ride a great, flying jaguar, or…" Hedrik's laugh lowered. "And I'll be there with you."

"Anywhere but here."

"Here is fine too," he started, sipping on his tea. "As long as we're together. The world can wait."

Euskar reached for Hedrik's hand and kissed it. "Together is what you already have."

Hedrik smiled ruefully. He cleared his throat. "I want to be with you. Not around you or beside you. *With* you."

"I've already said…" Euskar replied, withdrawing. He knew where this would lead. "I could never marry again."

"I'm not asking for marriage. You haven't even told me you love me. How many times must I say the words before you return it?"

"If you have to hear it to know for sure, then maybe that's not love you're feeling."

"Do you? Love me?"

"No."

Hedrik recoiled, fuming. He marched up to Euskar's bedroom in a huff. "He wants you to make him a coat of his greatest victories. Do you know what that means?" the younger man yelled. Euskar followed, scrambling. "Do you understand how that man intends to wear you to his pyre? Umberthorne will put this island on the map."

"Yes, yes, and our rickety port will teem with trade, and our sleepy town will turn into a city, et cetera, et cetera," Euskar answered wearily. "And I will have to keep painting flowers on fancy dresses until the day I die."

"Then don't! Don't do dresses! Do what you fucking want, no one is stopping you!"

"I can't paint, I've told you."

"No, you haven't—" Hedrik snapped. He rummaged through his closet and pulled out a canvas and a box of paints, then dropped them on the bed. "You haven't, and you can."

The painting, forever unfinished, showed Hedrik's profile rendered in striking verisimilitude. Hedrik's eyes welled in hot tears. "How many times have you painted this, huh? I know, Janessa knows. I see your lamp light from across the square. Every night you paint, and only one canvas in this entire place. Now tell me you don't love me."

Euskar blanched. "It's not you. The painting, it's not you. It never has been. This…is Arsem." The older man lowered himself onto the bed, quivering. "This is how he looked when…how I will always remember him."

Hedrik shook his head, wiping his face dry. "Why do you deny yourself so?" He knelt in front of Euskar and clasped Euskar's hand in his. Hedrik pressed it against his own chest. "This is real. I know it is."

Euskar nodded, his tears finally flowing. "It is too real."

"It will always be him, won't it?" Hedrik's voice cracked as he asked, as though fearing an answer he already knew. "*I will always be him.*"

"You are your own person. That to me is clear. But you are also a reminder. A brilliant, beautiful, living reminder."

And what use did the clothier of Alenni, a man of flawless recollection, have of such?

The two men held each other through the night, curled up in that bed, sharing the span with a painting that was done and undone and never done. They wept, knowing where they had arrived. Euskar had made his choice long ago; Hedrik had to make his choice now. Whatever he chose, Euskar knew it would break his heart.

Hedrik gazed at him, his soulful blue eyes made red. "I still remember the first time I saw you."

"A morning I'll never forget."

"No, not that. At the square that night."

"You saw me?"

Hedrik nodded, laugh-sighing. He skimmed his hand across Euskar's face. "You looked like a fox, all crouched in the shadow."

"Hedrik, I…"

"There's no more to say," he answered tenderly. "I will be alright."

"In time." Euskar held him tighter. "You should be out there, seeing the world. Living a life."

"I will. And I will wait for you," Hedrik answered, his tone unwavering and unwilling to receive any reply, as though it was a known truth like the setting of the sun in Fjallanir. Euskar did not protest; indeed, he doubted he wanted to.

Before he left, the young traveler asked of the clothier one last request. A memento.

Euskar hesitated to accede; he had never used his gifts to meld pigment to flesh before. "Are you sure you want to mar your skin?" he asked.

"I am not like you, and I won't want to forget."

The clothier readied the crushed cinnabar, hoping that the process would be no different from what he did with the cowhides. He mixed the pigment with tinctures and oils, grinding and swirling until the sludge became runny and the color lightened. He kissed Hedrik on his forehead, tasting salt. Euskar lingered there, inhaling the younger man's essence, feeling his breath on his neck.

"I will miss you too," Hedrik said.

Euskar gently smeared the pigment on Hedrik's chest, on a spot below his collarbone. Over his heart. He closed his eyes, feeling the threads of magic flow from his fingertips, and when he was ready, he opened them once more, and he painted.

IT MIGHT HAVE ENDED THERE, THE STORY OF THE LONELY CLOTHIER AND the traveling mineralist. With Hedrik never to return, having taught the Alenni guilds all they needed to know, with Euskar never finding cause to leave Alenni, dutifully playing the role he'd grown too comfortable performing for the last twenty years, the resentment only somewhat soothed by success. No adventures, no missed opportunities either, just a long life of stolid contentment. It was more than anyone could ask for; it was more than what most people get.

The clothier still painted over the same canvas each night, although now he was never truly sure: was it Arsem or Hedrik? He too would grow comfortable not knowing.

What would it mean for me to stop here? What would this story tell you, my sweet, steadfast Nella, if this is where I chose to end things? Will it convince you to leave me? Will you finally understand why I am willing to stay behind while you saw the world and lived a life bigger than what you would have with me? Or would you grow more stubborn, scoff at me as though this were a mere display of martyrdom? The clothier of Alenni could have had it all, I can hear you saying. He did not have to set him free.

Yet in truth, he did. And it was for the best.

The tale does not end there, as you might guess. It ends, or begins to end, in a shipwreck.

On that horrid monsoon season when the merchant vessel *Iranun* crashed onto the rocks on the southern end of the island of Alenni, only one surviving boat made it around the cape onto the beach. It carried the first mate, a couple of deckhands, and a mineralist from Koidev. The physicker attended to the rescued in short order, but all were in good health, considering.

Word of the disaster had reached Euskar, though it was not until a week later that the Koidevi, in tattered hand-me-downs, stepped through his shop door, giving the clothier a sublime fright.

Hedrik had grown fuller, taller, his jaw covered by a brambly brown beard, his hair pulled back high in a top knot. He wore a different face, one that barely revealed the features of the visage in Euskar's nightly portrait. This was the face of the Arsem that Euskar had never seen, the

Arsem that he never met and never lost—no, this was the face of the man Hedrik had become.

"I've come for some clothes." He greeted Euskar with an uncertain smile. Even his voice had changed—it still had that deep mellifluousness, but he sounded more assured, anchored. Entire. "I hear people travel far and wide to get theirs from this shop."

"Hello again, Hedrik."

The traveler approached the clothier, pinned to where he stood. "It's been a long time, Euskar. You look well."

"As do you. When I heard a Koidevi had been on that poor ship…"

"Yes, I didn't think I'd return. Not like this, anyhow."

Euskar smiled ruefully. "You could use a new coat, yes? Boots too?"

"Yes, and trousers," Hedrik answered. "You know what? Make it a full set. Head to toe. In that sorcerous waterproof fabric if you have it." He smirked. "In case the return ship hits the rocks again."

Euskar assembled a selection while the transformed Hedrik studied the shop, its bolts of textiles, the thimbles and shears and threads, the stool he used to sit on, still in that same spot before the same workbench with the same gouges on its surface.

"And Janessa?"

"Married the publican if you'll believe it. Two daughters. They live in the cottage next to my own."

"A cottage! Well, who lives upstairs now?"

"No one," the clothier replied. "We needed space for a couple of new apprentices. Cleared out the back too, put in another station."

"And here I was thinking this place looked exactly as it did the day I left it."

The clothier handed a bundle over to Hedrik, who needed no directing toward the changing screen. He soon emerged, his old clothing replaced with new. "What do you think?" he asked, turning to and fro.

Euskar approached to inspect the edges, the way the clothes fell on the body. His eyes fell on Hedrik's collar, on the line of his exposed clavicle. He saw a peek of the fox's ear, the one he had imprinted on the man's chest a decade ago. Euskar averted his gaze, but a moment too late.

"Yes…it's still there." Hedrik buttoned his shirt awkwardly. "I've tried—asked, and well…I—there it is."

Euskar smiled meekly and turned away.

"So, tell me about this cottage," Hedrik said, collecting himself. "On the windward side of the hill, I assume. You always said you liked the view from there."

"I do. It's a good house. I'm happy."

Time stood still. Euskar heard nothing but his own breath and a silence waiting to be filled.

"I'm sailing back to Koidev tonight," Hedrik said.

"The seas should be calm."

Hedrik nodded, expectant. After a while, he leaned over and gave the clothier a tight hug. "I'm glad to see you again, Euskar."

"Me too."

The clothier did not sleep a wink that night. He did not paint either. Till dawn he thought of Hedrik, the old and the new, the young and the old, the Hedrik as he'd always seen, the one he'd never seen before. How many years had Euskar languished, how many years could he have had with someone who was no longer a facsimile? Someone who Euskar understood in his heart had never been a mere reminder?

What a waste.

When the morning light broke, the clothier came down to his desk and wrote a letter.

If it is not too late, meet me a month hence…

Euskar wound up his affairs, handing Janessa the keys to the shop. She'd long proven herself more valuable than an apprentice. She assured Euskar that the place would be waiting for him when he returned, but not too soon, if at all. She offered this in jest, but they both understood.

Euskar had allowed himself to hope, to risk, and there was no certainty of what awaited him once he stepped through the Gate in the square. He would arrive in as new a place as he'd ever seen since his youth, wearing not a single stitch of thread on his person. All he would carry were his memories of Alenni, his life in that small town on that small island, and of Arsem, the man he stayed for. As he stood in front of the Gate, the clothier carried Arsem in his heart, knowing that it had space for more. For a new love, a new home. One worth leaving everything behind for.

And so, hoping Hedrik waited on the other side, Euskar pierced the veil.

In some ways, the story of the clothier of Alenni does end there. You might also say it ends here, at least for now, with my retelling of it. There comes a time in each person's life when the choice is between action and inaction, between a life of comfort and familiarity, or a life of unknown, unspeakable beauty. For the clothier, comfort eventually proved lacking. I've found it so, and despite your qualms, deep inside, you know it too. Love is a stronger reason to stay, but for it to be a hindrance to a fuller life only cheapens that love.

I tell you this story not to drive you away, but to tell you that I will wait. No matter how long it takes, with no expectation of your return. I shall be content to live with a flicker of hope, nourished by the knowledge that you are in pursuit of your dreams. And you will achieve them, my dear Nella. I know it, in the same way I know I will have the strength to wait, the same way my grandfather waited, for the erstwhile clothier of Alenni.

CANDIDATE ELEVEN

KATE ELLIOTT

Frankly, I would have preferred to go on about my usual routine as chief clerk in the Ministry of Civil Appointments and Ceremonial Rites.

While it is true that ignorant people do not comprehend the relationship between efficient bureaucracy and the proper rituals that keep the community in a stable order, I had early on shown a gift for record keeping. Specifically, I mastered the skills needed for precisely cross-checking nominations for academic and work placement, alliances both business and family, and participation in the Circuit of Ambrosial Temples and the annual Paean Festival against the law court proceedings, the lineage registers, and annual donations to the temple.

Thus, I moved up the ranks in the ministry, perfectly content to keep my ledgers in good order. That was really all I asked in the world.

Then, of course, a Gate opened in our proudly Gate-less nation.

What a calamity for our orderly existence!

We Karsofdians are an illustrious people with a dignified history. When our attempts to share our godly worship of the Five Ambrosial Siblings with our neighbors ended in their closing all borders, we did not take it personally, nor did our Ambrosial Family. Ours is an ambrosial land of plenty, as the saying goes. We have remained content to keep ourselves to ourselves and to make sure all the hungry are fed and every person has a place in which they belong, even the persons or places I do not myself particularly approve of. Yet that is the will of the Ambrosial Family: be as you are.

Yet some folk will nevertheless remain discontented. Some would always find a path out along the monster-haunted slopes of the Skar Mountains or beyond the smoking shallows of the Tar Sea. Most of these malcontents did not return, whether dead or imprisoned or satisfied in their chosen exile, I cannot know. Unfortunately, a few did return over time, bringing with them, like rose-drop candies, tales of other lands, other gods or lack thereof, and of the mysterious Gates by which people in far places could travel as they wished in the blink of an eye, although with the unexpected side effect of having to arrive at their destination naked.

Blasphemy! We pray in the private confines of the Inner Womb of the Ambrosial Temple in the sanctified blessing of nudity, as the gods brought us forth in our first moments before our elders swaddled us in the fabric of profane life. How can the Gates be a godly venture if they thus strip us of the very garments that conceal our sacred and most blessed nature? If passage through the Gates leaves us bare for all to see!

For this reason, I never thought we of the righteous law, lineage, and temple would ever have to trouble ourselves with Gates.

I was wrong.

For it did so happen that on a drowsy summer's day in the season of the Soft Brother, one of these mysterious Gates appeared, unbidden and unexpected, on an island in a lake outside the capital city.

Something had to be done.

That was how I found myself drafted by the Five-Headed Secretariat to sit as clerk in Fragrant Purity Hall when proceedings were opened to determine which Karsofdian would be an appropriate first envoy to the wide world beyond. I have long used a complex system within my ledgers that allows me to spy lines of connection that others might miss. Many a poor appointment choice has been avoided for that reason, many a misalliance prevented. So, when the Secretariat decided that any adult person could present themselves at the hall as a candidate, naturally I was drafted to make sure no unsuitable individual slipped through during the selection proceedings.

I am not one who desires to sit at the front of the room, cynosure of all eyes. A plain desk was placed to the right of the selection bench where the notables sat, raised above the floor so they could better cast their gazes across the multitude. I paid no attention to the crowd, most of whom were merely there to gawk and comment, as is the Karsofdian way. Far more wanted to watch than to present themselves as candidates. The capacity of Fragrant Purity Hall, standing room only, amounts to exactly one thousand and twenty according to the Methodical Inventory of Ceremony. One thousand for the audience, fifteen officials to maintain order and record the proceedings of the day, and the five members of the Secretariat to preside.

At exactly the noon-day bell, a list was presented to me with the names of those who had recorded their intent to be considered for the position of envoy. There were only eleven, a curious number, you will admit, for those of us who bear five fingers per hand and five toes per foot.

The hall herald rapped her gavel on the lectern and, with a piercing warble, sang the assembly into silence. Once the hall lay quiet, she called out in a stentorian voice, "Candidate One."

Only I had been handed the list of names, as it is considered ill luck to vie for an appointment by revealing one's name and associations, lest there be accusations of favoritism. As a path through the crowd opened, and the first candidate emerged, I immediately set to work with my ledgers to see what I could discover about them.

Candidate One was an elegant woman of middle years, brisk and knowing. She climbed the three steps to stand on the dais. First, she pressed her clasped hands to her chest as a show of piety toward the statue of the Five Ambrosial Siblings at the back of the hall. Then, she turned to display her face and hands to the crowd. Finally, she addressed the presiding bench where the five members of the Five-Headed Secretariat sat.

"I present myself and my qualifications," she proclaimed. "I am a scholar of history. We know little of the world beyond our borders, since it has been over one hundred years since our last diplomatic embassy. I have read everything there is to read about those days. Thus, I can best negotiate with foreigners without offending them."

The Secretariat questioned her closely. After they were done, the usual questions were shouted from the audience, some ignored and some hailed and answered. My cross-checking complete, I wrote beside her name that she had two weak disqualifying connections against her, not enough to condemn her outright, but enough to make her a losing candidate against one with no disqualifying marks.

Candidate Two was a sly, wiry soul who had spent many years as an actor on the summer stages in a troupe that toured the towns and villages of Karsofdia. His qualification was the ability to speak smoothly and rapidly. He boasted as well of having the knack of turning a skeptical audience to his favor, something that might prove quite useful for an envoy headed into unknown territory. Fortunately, he had a clear disqualifying connection. I made the note and waited for Candidate Three.

This lithe warrior sprang onto the dais with a graceful bound, all wag and verve, audacity and bounce. Indeed, the crowd cheered upon seeing them, because Candidate Three was well-known in the arena for feats of strength and agility, and had on five famous occasions adventured into the Skar Mountains and, every time, brought back the head of a monster, each more gruesome than the last.

"Who better," the warrior cried, "to venture into unknown spaces? Should it come to that, I can fight off any hostile who might attack, for I need no weapons but my sinews and my mighty kick!"

Some in the audience launched into a popular arena song colloquially known as "Whack Whack Whack." It was with difficulty that the herald warbled and whooped them back down into silence. Even then, scattered voices called out an acclamation. Heroic monster-killers have a long tradition of being elected later in life as town mayors and provincial governors, able to confront any sort of intractable public nuisance. But although an argument could be made that the position of envoy was a political position similar in function to mayor or governor, it would be carried out beneath the sovereignty of the Ambrosial Siblings, so therefore it also would count as a temple office. As law and custom decree, contact with monsters, even the most heroic of deeds, of itself means a person is disqualified from serving a term as a Blood in the temple. Thus, I could immediately disqualify Candidate Three.

Candidates Four, Five, and Six all had tedious bureaucratic backgrounds, colorless folk with no blemish but no bloom either. Forgettable. And all with minor disqualifications, should such be needed.

Candidate Seven trod up the steps weighed down with several thick volumes. These he set on the lectern and opened. He proceeded to read out excerpts that spoke of Karsofdian history, the founding of our ambrosial land in an isolated region by a community of believers never tolerated in close-minded climes. For a long while we had prospered, and of course we prospered still. No one went hungry. Every person had a place.

"But," he thundered, everyone in the hall startling as if a clap and a rumble had broken over us all, "we are fewer than we were, generation by generation. If we do not increase our numbers, then shall we slowly fade and the worship of our Ambrosial Family will fade as well. What then!"

No one had any answer. Dread cracked the air, choking every voice.

"For you see," he went on, compellingly, "this Gate is a gift from our Five Ambrosial Siblings. By its opening, so shall we live, for now people who wish for a better life can come to us, to live among us. Should they wish to do so. But the envoy needs to be a person who understands what is at stake. And that person is *me*."

The uproar after this lengthy diatribe went on for quite a while, after which the Secretariat broke for luncheon. I alone did not leave my seat.

The assembly resumed one bell later, by which time I had found an obscure disqualification for Candidate Seven. Not that I am biased, you understand. But I had to do what I had to do.

A good meal and a mug of ale had invigorated everyone, although whispers still raced around the assembly as folk discussed Candidate Seven's dire tidings. It wasn't that people didn't know that our numbers were decreasing, that certain small signs might offer an uneasy look into a future where we might dwindle into oblivion. It was that life went on in its usual orderly routine. It is more painless to not see what might jar one's cozy day-to-day with a glimpse of unpleasant storm clouds, when those clouds may not pummel one with rain for another few generations.

But what if Candidate Seven was wrong? People are wrong all the time. What if he saw what he wanted to see? How could he possibly know the heart and intention of the Five Ambrosial Siblings?

The herald called the assembly to order.

Candidate Eight was an experienced merchant, one of the rare individuals who had departed our gracious land as a feckless youth and returned some years later, although she had brought no rose-drop candies but rather three children she had birthed to three different sires, whose names and backgrounds she had dutifully given to the ministry so her children might be recognized as people rather than animals. She had fallen without ripple back into the smooth pool of Karsofdian life. Besides authoring two pamphlets describing unusual geological landmarks in the world beyond, she had never again brought up what she had seen or done in her time away. Her children had grown up and married young, to suitable partners. There was even a first grandchild. Now she spoke without grandiosity or braggadocio to point out that her experience gave her knowledge that would be precious to an envoy's duty.

"It is true we have space and need for people who might wish to settle here, if they can be persuaded to accept our way of life, which may seem strange to outsiders. But that is the very question, is it not? How do we persuade people?"

She spoke somewhat longer on this refrain, making a good deal of sense.

I searched and searched, but I could find nothing disqualifying. Even her departure and return could not ban her from the job. She wasn't wrong: her experience of the world beyond the Skar Mountains and the Tar Sea gave her insight that others might lack.

By the time she finished answering questions, it was getting rather late in the afternoon, and there were still three candidates to go, as I knew quite well from the list of names I had tucked beneath the ledgers opened on my desk.

Candidate Nine was currently serving as a Blood in the Ambrosial Temple of the Five Ambrosial Siblings, one who could act on the

Siblings' behalf in the community and also clean and sanctify the Inner Womb and answer arcane questions of theology and practice. As with every person serving as a Blood, ze wore loose garments and a hairstyle that eschewed the usual gender markings people delight in.

First, ze raised arms skyward and groundward, then forward and backward, then outward and heart-ward. Intoning, ze sang the offering prayer:

"Let us walk above and beneath,

Let us walk in front and behind,

Let us walk in the world and in our own deep heart.

Let the Soft Brother lay a gentle and reassuring hand on our shoulder.

Let the Lost Sister's invisible tread guide our righteous footsteps.

Let the Angry Fire light our darkened path.

Let Spoonless grant us the strength we need when we grow most weary.

Let I-Will-Hold-All-Your-Hands-As-I-Have-Enough-To-Go-Around bring us all together hand-in-hand to the ambrosial land where we shall prosper.

So shall it be, by the will and the mercy of the Ambrosial Family."

After everyone spoke the proper response, ze turned to the Secretariat. "I am adept in all the prayers. I have served many years in the temples. I am righteous. I am clean."

You are disqualified, I thought as I noted one major and three minor disqualifications. But I said nothing. It was not yet time. I am not a chief clerk for nothing.

My name came last, Candidate Eleven. My speech would be simple: *I alone have no disqualifications. Thus, I must be chosen.* And I would sacrifice my sanctified blessing of nudity, of remaining clothed in the sight of all except the Inner Womb of the Ambrosial Temple. I would pass through the Gate. Once in the unknown land beyond, I would make such a hostile hash of the initial meeting that my behavior would cause the Gate to be blocked from the other side forever. I did not relish this task, and I already mourned the loss of my beloved routine. But someone had to do it, lest we be overrun by people who cared nothing for our Ambrosial Family, our modest but fair-minded way of life, our lightly-inhabited valleys that could so easily be overwhelmed by a great influx of unknown and uncooperative unbelievers. That is what the others did not understand.

So I allowed Candidate Nine to go on about why ze would be the best envoy because the foreigners would respect a person of dignity who had lived a life utterly beyond reproach. A persuasive speech, in its way. I might even have been convinced. But I was determined on my path to save Karsofdia. No one else could.

When ze finished and stepped aside, the hall herald rapped her gavel on the lectern. "Candidate Ten!"

The gathered people looked about themselves, seeking that stir amid the bodies that meant a person was making their way forward. Yet at first, nothing happened. No ripples blasphemed the pool's smooth surface.

"Candidate Ten!" the herald repeated.

For a moment, I thought Candidate Ten had decided against appearing, which of course would have to be noted in the ledger against future appointments. Those who commit must either make the try or say they have chosen against the try, rather than just not show up and leave people in the lurch!

For a moment, I thought that was what had happened.

Then, as a whisper of wind blows light kisses on a pond's glassy surface, the people in the hall began to shift, making a path. A sleek, dark head zigged and zagged, deftly winding a way forward until, as on the exhalation on a long-held breath, a man emerged out of the assembly. Gravely, he ascended the three steps and halted on the dais.

He was a handsome, youthful person, dressed in a loose, orange robe. He acknowledged the Ambrosial Family with clasped hands pressed to his chest, then the Five-Headed Secretariat likewise, then the people in the hall as well, as if all had a godly seeming in his eyes. He even nodded at me, not that I blushed to see a knowing twinkle in his brilliant gaze. I never blush. Never.

He shifted, standing tall, chin lifted the better to display his bold chin and noble profile, his luxuriant black hair and his shapely lips. I thought he was about to begin his speech.

Instead, he unpinned the shoulders of the robe. With a rustle and rush of cloth, the garment dropped to the ground to leave him stark naked in front of us all. In front of us all! His body had grace and proportion, muscular legs and lean waist and broad shoulders, every part a pleasure to look upon. Not ogle, not that. What the gods have made cannot be vulgar or profane.

Even so, the shock of seeing a person nude in the midst of a public meeting was so mighty that one might have heard a pin drop, and indeed he dropped the pins as a final gesture. *Tink tunk.*

No one said a word. No one laughed, nor cried out a scolding reprimand. No one bolted for the doors to the outside. No one could look away. No one covered their eyes. Not even me.

In all his face and form, he was very beautiful.

At last he spoke aloud, perhaps to the gods, perhaps to the Secretariat, perhaps to the rest of us. Perhaps to all of creation.

"I am a divine weapon," he said in a resonant voice as lovely as his figure. "This you can yourselves see. The gods have made me as I am, for this day. Send me through the Gate as envoy, and those who look upon me shall stop in their tracks, at least for one moment. They shall say, 'This is Karsofdia?' and thus they will remember the name of our humble and resolute land, this I shall promise you, in the Names of the Five Ambrosial Siblings."

It was true. No one who saw him could forget him.

No one had yet spoken, too slack-jawed to manage a single word.

He picked up the pins, pulled up the cloth of the robe, and fastened it back into place, covering himself but not the memory of what we had all seen. There came a shuffling and a general sigh from the assembly. The Five-Headed Secretariat shifted on their chairs. He waited in modest patience. At length they found their voices.

The Secretariat asked, "What of those beyond the Gate who might wish us harm?"

"If their hearts are turned away from wishing harm upon us, then we will suffer no ill from meeting them."

"What of those who might wish to trade with us?" the Secretariat asked. "Can anything good come of that?"

"If we negotiate well, and gain what we wish, then we shall prosper."

"What of those who chose to avoid us in the days long ago? Who closed their borders with us back in those dark days?"

"Should they choose to open them again, now that we have a Gate, then we will no longer be shut off from the rest of the world."

"And what if these open borders should come to pass?" demanded the Secretariat. "What if people choose to come here, where we have lived for so long, alone and in peace? What shall happen to our ambrosial land then?"

"Then those who come in good faith and with open hearts shall join their lives with ours."

"Do you mean to say that such people will pledge to join us in the worship of the Ambrosial Family?"

"If that is their wish, then, yes, they will."

They had no more questions. Everyone was still too stunned and no doubt lost in recollection of what we could no longer see but could not forget. Candidate Ten stepped to one side, into line with the previous nine candidates, whose resigned features suggested they had accepted they would not be chosen.

The herald rapped her gavel upon the lectern.

"Candidate Eleven."

I did not stand. Most likely, my trembling legs would not have held my frame upright. After the herald called for Candidate Eleven three times, that candidate was announced as disqualified.

The gods make us as we are. It is our task in life to find a path that suits us, if we can. Those who are fortunate find their feet fitted to a way that opens. And sometimes, the gods make a road for us to walk on before we know we are destined for it.

You may ask yourself if Candidate Ten had a disqualifying mark. But I could not tell you, for I had entirely neglected to cross-check my ledgers. No matter what I might have discovered, the matter was already settled.

SILVER AND GOLD

ROWENNA MILLER

Abelin Rosemani Holyoke hauled a cart half-filled with century pine branches and half-filled with her giggling four-year-old. The burn pile was just far enough from the stretch of ground cleared by the centennial failure of the pines to be a nuisance, and Lanashonin wasn't old enough to be particularly helpful. Hanti was, but he was inside, ostensibly studying his math but probably making watercolors of a new-bloomed water iris.

She shoveled a few more bent branches into the cart, ignoring the visitor who waited in the gravel drive of the farm with deliberate intensity. She didn't sell directly to gardeners, and she made herself hard enough to find that the only people who showed up unannounced were bulb dealers, competition in the rare plant trade, and treasure hunters. She detested all three. The bulb dealers arrived with the irritating frequency of hay fever, but she could usually shake them off with a peek at her exclusive contracts with Dryam's Exports; the competition was obnoxious but fumbling and quickly outed themselves. But the treasure hunters.

The treasure hunters were the worst, and the thick glasses and thicker book accessorizing the man in the driveway identified him as, most likely, some mawkish treasure hunter.

Abelin dragged the cart down the hill, the wheels rattling and the four-year-old giggling. They sought her out once, twice a year at most, but getting them to leave was a hassle disproportionate to their infrequency. They heard that Abelin Rosemani Holyoke could scent an Emperor jonquil with one sniff, that Abelin Rosemani Holyoke could spot the tendrils of the first spores of Esseni Valley moss at a hundred yards, that Abelin Rosemani Holyoke could extract the glass-fragile bulbs of the Undine tulip from the rock-hard clay they overwintered in.

They weren't wrong. But she wasn't interested in hunting horticultural treasures. Not anymore. She had her growing stock and her suppliers and her dealers, and she had a plot of land in the temperate rain forest valley just close enough to the city that it wasn't hard to procure books and tea, and she had two children who didn't need their mother getting arrested for trespassing in the National Botanical Gardens. Not again.

The man was still there when she crested the hill on the return trip. She shooed Lana inside despite protests that she was owed at least one more ride up the hill in the cart. She wheeled the cart behind the shed. She sighed.

"Well?"

Ilber Framer had done his research. Not just the research that brought him here, of course, but his research on Abelin Rosemani Holyoke. He knew she was prickly as the hothouse cacti she grew on the glassed alcove on the south-facing corner of her house, and that she was uninterested in solicitors of all kinds. He knew she was widowed with two children. For some reason, the combination of facts had produced a picture of a woman much older and frowsier and far less imposing than the real life person standing in front of him.

"Hello, I'm—" He coughed. "I'm Ilber Framer. I have it on good authority you're the woman I want to talk to about a most interesting opportunity."

"Your sources are as underdeveloped and unimpressive as your manners."

Prickly, indeed. He strode toward her house and noticed a patch of green shoots. "These are lovely," he offered.

"They're garlic. Plain old garlic. For eating. Now either spit out what you want so I can refuse quickly or save us the trouble and get out now."

"I don't think you'll—" His voice waned as her frigid stare intensified. "I need a partner, that's the long and short of it. Someone who knows plants."

"Someone who knows plants."

"I should back up a bit."

"Perhaps you should back right out of my driveway."

He wasn't sure if he was supposed to laugh or simply leave, so Ilber did what he usually did when he was nervous. He forged ahead, talking at double speed. "You know that the ancient ruins of the castle of the Gann family have never been found. They would house a treasure trove of valuable antiquities, of course, but also the foundational documents of the Al'notliri proto-republic."

"One of *those*, then." Abelin stripped her gloves with a disgusted sigh. The republic-seekers, the antiquarians who idealized the past and turned it into some kind of blueprint for the future. Framer was either a centralist, then, or working for one—deluded sops who wanted to strengthen the Concert part of the Concert of States and undercut the power of individual princes. Not that she cared. "You may kindly leave."

"The ruins would—"

"Kindly leave."

"An absolute fortune, not to mention recognition in—"

"Kindly. Leave."

If a large centennial pine branch hadn't fallen at that precise moment, Abelin would have successfully chased Ilber from the premises and the gambit would have been defunct. But as it happened, a large russet-needled branch plummeted to the grassy hillock, bringing with it a very large and positively thrumming blue hornet nest. Abelin considered only momentarily before giving her revised orders to Ilber Framer, in clipped, hushed tones.

"Back away very slowly until you reach that gilded birch on the other side of the drive. If they're not on you by then, run for the door."

It was a good thing that Ilber was fairly decent under pressure, as the blue-black insects swarmed out of the paper shreds of their former home with the vindictiveness of tiny wet cats and boasting inch-long stingers to reinforce their displeasure with anyone and anything they judged potentially responsible for the demise of their nest—namely, anything moving within a visible radius. Ilber edged backwards slowly and deliberately, his boots gently scraping the gravel. Abelin seemed to make no sound at all, yet reached the opposite side of the drive before him and bolted toward the door. The buzzing intensified as Ilber followed suit, boots kicking a cloud of dust that drew the attention of the hornets.

He was surprised Abelin held the door for him, even as a single intrepid hornet found its mark. He smothered an obscenity as the stinger sunk through his jacket and into his biceps, and another as Abelin swept it from his arm and onto the floor with an unnecessarily large book, and then swiftly dispatched it with her shoe.

"Thanks," he managed through clenched teeth.

"Get your shirt off," she replied. "You'll want something to draw the worst of it out."

It was already beginning to swell and hurt like— "Fucking death!" he exclaimed, then looked up at a pair of eyes staring at him from the courtyard just past the entryway. "I'm sorry," he added.

"They've heard worse from me," Abelin replied, returning with a ratty towel and a jar sloshing with milky liquid. "Shirt off," she repeated, and he complied, though dragging even the fine cotton over the apple-sized welt drew a few more choice words this time suppressed under his breath.

Abelin washed some tonic into the towel and pressed it onto the impressive welt. "You must be extra and specially allergic," she muttered with an unsympathetic smirk. "You should see what they do to Hanti." She nodded toward her eldest, a boy swiftly cresting the first waves of adolescence. "I can't let him out if there's a swarm."

"I looked like I'd been punched," Hanti offered helpfully.

Lana grinned. "He swelled up like a balloon!"

"Here, hold that," Abelin said, shoving the towel into Ilber's hand. He had to admit that the tonic was helping. Already the worst of the throbbing had dissipated, and the redness was cooling. "What is this stuff?"

"Emerald shadeweed." She replaced the cork of the jar and stashed it back on a shelf. "It grows everywhere on most of the islands. Nothing to interest a treasure hunter, I'm sure."

"It's got my interest now," he replied. "The thing is—thank you," he added, accepting a finely glazed earthenware cup of water from Hanti. "The thing is, there's no one else who could make the sorts of identifications that you could. I've found a source that no one—"

"I'm not sure how many ways I can tell you that I'm not interested," Abelin said. Attack by a blue hornet hadn't softened her any. "I could not be more uninterested, in fact. I have garlic to harvest, and several grafts to attend to, and—"

"I found the plans of the royal gardens and orangerie of Gann."

"Those were lost! They're not in existence, that's impossible—" Abelin stopped herself, painfully aware that she had cleanly contradicted a half an hour of very well-feigned disinterest. "I don't care."

"Oh, but you do." Ilber smiled. "It would be awfully hard, wouldn't it, to avoid caring about such a horticultural treasure? Even if you were not a botanist."

"It's impossible." Abelin conceded the point of interest and retreated to the safer position. It was almost certainly impossible that those documents had been found. The royal gardens and orangerie of Gann were famed, the stuff of fairy tales and legends—and no documentation had survived after the catastrophic destruction of their city and port when a longstanding disagreement with the Lappinale family erupted into war, a decimating fire, and a land so scarred and cursed no one even considered the profit of grave robbing and treasure hunting until too much time had passed and the thick rainforest had enclosed the whole of the island in a blessed screen of vegetation.

"I am a librarian. At the Kal Mat'in University." He paused, letting Abelin react to the name of the most prestigious seat of learning, with the largest collection of books in the archipelago. "The university has accessioned so many collections from so many dead patrons that there are many priceless treasures sitting in boxes. When I found the plans, I knew what I had."

"Then why isn't the university botany department here, or the history department, or—or whoever is handling this expedition?"

"I'm no fool. I copied the documents and promptly tendered my resignation."

"No. No, no, no, you're not roping me in on whatever half-legal caper you're planning, stealing priceless antique documents and—"

"Madam! Everything is purely legal! It's a public library; the entire point is for people to use the materials." She eyed him suspiciously. "I may have made some errors in accessioning the documents so that it will be years, decades probably, before anyone else finds them. But I did not *steal* anything."

He waited. She didn't speak. The children hovered in the arch that led into the courtyard, both unwilling to step away and miss anything about this most unusual exchange. The visits from the bulb dealers were never this exciting.

"Don't you at least want to know what was in them?"

A slow smile spread over Abelin's face.

THE TRUTH WAS, AS SOON AS ILBER HAD PULLED OUT THE COPIES OF THE hand-drawn sketches, the centuries-old bulb inventories, the diagrams, and even a notebook of a long-dead gardener's schedule and watering notes, she was hooked. She had arranged for the children to stay with her sister, packed her sturdiest boots and wool walking skirt, and booked passage for two on the next ship to Gann. She pored over the minute details of each sketch on the journey, noting the exact location of each exotic fruit tree and clapping with delight when she discovered that the greenhouses had included an orchid hothouse.

"Though that will be useless now," she conceded, as the schooner Bluenose dipped and swayed in a gentle rainstorm. "The orchids can't have survived without proper ministrations. However." She pointed to the banks of snowbells, lady's drops, and gilded jonquils. "Those will have naturalized and spread."

"And you're sure—even after the fire and the encroachment of the forest—"

"They're known for being hardy little plants. They'll survive almost anything, and fire only helps them naturalize—clears the way for the next bloom cycle."

The map of the gardens had also revealed confirmation of a long-standing myth: the presence of a Gate in the castle of Gann. Rumored but never confirmed, it had been under the control of the Gann family, Abelin realized, quite literally—the labyrinth of the water gardens had been built around the Gate. Outgoing only, surely, or someone would have discovered the ruins long ago.

"Once we find the flowers, we're close to the gardens. And when we find the gardens—"

"We've found the ruins."

"Did you have a plan to bring in additional hires for excavating what is sure to be several acres on your own, or are you completely delusional?" They'd agreed from the beginning—they would split the profits of whatever they found equally, regardless of what each put into the operation. The trouble was, after the initial recovery, laws relegating the continuation of the excavation to whichever university won the bid went into effect. Only the first find was protected.

"It won't be necessary. The most valuable find is the documents, and I intend to find them myself. They were supposed to have been sealed in the lower courts of the judicial halls, 'beneath the eye of the storm.' That is almost certainly a reference to the Gann family crest bearing the Storm Father, their ancestral deity. Now, if they are beneath the eye, then that should narrow the search quite a bit as I expect the figure to be looking at the spot the documents are hidden."

"What if the Storm Father is on the floor?" Abelin asked, deadpan. "What if it's a mosaic? What if the documents are actually under the Storm Father's real, actual eye?"

"Then I suppose I'd have to excavate—"

"But you'd destroy a priceless, ancient work of art, a pristine Gann mosaic in the process." Abelin feigned horror. "What would you do?"

Ilber finally realized she'd been harassing him. "There are methods of careful removal of mosaics. I'd have to accept giving up a quick recovery of the documents, but I don't mind."

"Quick may be necessary," Abelin cautioned him. "There's always the possibility of others following our trail."

Ilber stopped folding his map. "Others?"

Abelin smirked. "You didn't think that the treasure hunting industry was entirely honorable, did you?" Abelin chose not to disclose that, on occasion, she had been privy to such mercenary expeditions. "There are a decent number of them who let other people do the hard work of research and tracking through mud or desert or thorny jungle and then…"

"But that's illegal!"

"You think they care?" She handed Ilber the stack of books he'd left piled in front of her. "Barimen, now, he tends to operate out of these islands, and he was the worst I—" She stopped before she said *worked for*. Hadrian Barimen terminated their partnership, to put it politely, only after she'd misled him on the real value of some tulip bulbs, even though he'd made a tidy profit on the scheme. "He was the worst one operating, last I knew. Scouts in the usual port towns and way stations, and they report to him, and he's just smart enough to weed out the real possibilities from the wild goose chases."

"I highly doubt anyone would take our foray seriously—the ruins of Gann have been the subject of more abandoned quests than I can count. As long as you're sure you can let the trail of plants lead you, we'll both retire early."

"And do what?" Abelin asked. She'd never dreamed of a life of leisure—though most people didn't believe it, she liked work, liked the feel of dirt under her nails and the smell of growing things. Any gains she'd made treasure-hunting—and there had been a few lucrative ones —she had set aside for her children. And built that greenhouse on the south-facing side of her house.

"Read, I suppose. Write the treatise on comparative ancient forms of governance I've been planning."

"So you'd work."

"Yes, but I'd work at what I *want* to do. Very different from keeping to the library's schedule and answering to the head archivist and kicking youths out of the physics annex."

"Why do you kick kids out of the physics annex?"

"Oh," he replied, startled, "they only go there to have sex. Forgot no one else would know that."

Abelin burst out laughing. "So there they are, mid-coitus, and then you—"

"Yes, and it's terribly uncomfortable! And no one uses the annex for anything else, so you know that if a couple of students go that way, pretty soon the head archivist is going to make me go and kick them out."

"Then why bother at all?"

"Because it's—why, it's not—" He stopped. "I have no idea. We should just turn the whole annex into a brothel."

"Well, a little luck and you won't have to play hall monitor anymore."

"I won't, regardless of our luck," Ilber said, confident for perhaps the first time in his life. "I'll find something else even if our expedition comes to naught. I suppose hauling crates would leave me more time to write than working for the library, come right down to it."

Abelin considered his reedy arms and almost delicate shoulders. "Yes, that would be a viable career alternative for you."

Ilber, immune to sarcasm, cheerfully continued plotting their search of the island.

After a dull voyage and a night in a port town as seedy as it was crumbling, Abelin and Ilber set out with a rented donkey laden with supplies. It was at this point that Abelin began to question her sanity at joining this hunt, not only because she did not like working with donkeys, but because the thick forests of Gann were thick with flies. Large flies, small flies, brightly colored flies, drab black flies—and all of them seemed to prefer her blood to any other food source.

"What did they eat before I got here?" she lamented as they stopped for the first night, camping by a spring that had apparently birthed a million jade-colored blood-suckers.

"What's that?" Ilber, unbothered, turned to see Abelin covered in angry red bumps. "How awful—you're covered in bites! You take the tent—I know we said it was my turn first, but that's—that's really awful."

Abelin knew that the sporting thing to do would be to argue, but she was beyond caring about the niceties of pretending she was interested in fairness while besieged by bloodletters. She didn't even protest when Ilber helped set up the tent he wouldn't even be using. Ensconced inside, however, Abelin felt the uncomfortable pang of an unfamiliar feeling—something very close to loneliness. She was hardly ever alone; parenting two children had that effect, to the degree that on rare occasions when both were sleeping or distracted, she relished the silence. But now Lanashonin and Hanti were far away, safe from wild jungles and vicious flies, and she felt the thickening darkness of the untamed night pressing close.

"Ilber?" she said, more urgently than she intended.

"Here," he replied, with dutiful cheer as though answering morning roll call. "What is it?"

What was it, indeed? She hadn't considered what she actually wanted to say once she had Ilber's attention; she had been more concerned with the reassurance of another human voice. Now she flushed and floundered for something innocuous to take up a few words between them.

"Do you think," she began, "that we're camped a little close to the road?"

"Why should that matter?" Ilber replied. He scooted closer to the tent, his bedroll dragging behind him.

"It's only…don't you worry about hitchhikers?"

"Well, I don't see why they'd bother with us, and at night, and we've only got the donkey, anyway—we can't give anyone a ride—"

"No," Abelin said, seeing the opportunity and setting the trap. "*Hitchhikers.* They appear out of nowhere, like mist. Only on roads, though. But if you see one, up close, you notice that they're not—not really there."

"Whatever does that mean?" Ilber's irritated retort told Abelin she'd had the desired effect.

"There's the form of a person, but there's no face. They're covered in strange symbols, some say it's a map of places they've been that humans could never rightfully go. No one knows for sure, because if you look too long, the symbols start to twist and bend and you feel right sick, like being on shipboard in a storm." She paused, letting the silence bleed into the space between them. "And if you so much as touch one, they crumple on themselves like leftover ash. But what's left—it seems like a boon, at first, but it's a curse."

"Stuff and nonsense."

Abelin fished in her pocket and closed her fingers around what she found there. "It's true! The little gift inside is no gift—it might be a coin, or a silk handkerchief, or a gossamer glove, or even a jewel, but if you make the mistake to pick it up—oh, the road looks dark, Ilber. And so close."

"What happens if you pick it up?" Ilber was closer now, just outside the flap of the tent.

"You're driven to find more of them. Find more hitchhikers, find more treasures. Travel down roads ever darker and more fearsome, do things ever darker and more loathsome—all to find more hidden bits and bobs in the carcasses of the wraiths."

"I don't believe a word of it," Ilber said in a voice that suggested he did in fact believe at least a little.

"I should know," Abelin said in a flat, bleak tone. "How else would I have found this?" With a deft flick, she tossed the string of spare buttons she kept in her pocket out of the tent and toward Ilber.

He sprang back with a yelp and scrambled from the harmless buttons, while Abelin doubled over with laughter.

"I hardly think that funny!" Ilber said, though he was clearly laughing, too.

"I'm sorry," Abelin said, gasping for air. "I just—it was too perfect, the story and—"

A slap from outside the tent interrupted her. "Damned flies," Ilber said by way of explanation.

Perhaps it was guilt over frightening Ilber, or sympathy for the incessant irritation of the flies, or a growing appreciation for having another human being nearby in the encroaching night. Whatever it was, Abelin spoke before she could think too hard about it. "I know we said we'd trade off on the tent, Ilber, but there's really nothing untoward about sharing it. If we're head to toe and back to back, we can pretend the other isn't even there."

Whether it was the flies, the lonely darkness, or the lingering effects of Abelin's story, Ilber conceded immediately to the suggestion. He wouldn't have admitted it, but the rising mist on the road unnerved him even more than the flies.

The morning dawned dolorous and damp through the jungle mists. It seemed a waste to Abelin not to make use of the netting barring the tent from flies, so she arranged it like a veil over her head instead of packing it on the donkey, not caring that she looked like a demented ghost.

"Are you going to be able to see the trail?" Ilber said, doubtful.

"I can see just fine. And the kinds of plants we're looking for—they're obvious in this terrain."

If Ilber looked incredulous, it was with good reason. The trail of garden plants overgrowing the bounds of the former royal gardens was likely to be obvious only to an expert like Abelin, and when she gasped with delight and took off down a narrow ravine, Ilber had no idea what she had seen.

"Snowbells!" she shouted back to him as he tugged the donkey along. "It's not indigenous to this region at all. It shouldn't be here."

The green plants Abelin pointed to were not in bloom and so looked nothing like either snow or bells, but like every other plant in the vicinity to a layman like Ilber. But not to Abelin, who saw each notch and curve of each leaf like a signature. Before long, she had discovered another patch of something that meant something—gilded jonquil, she said. It was not gilded. It was green. Like everything in the forest save the flies, which, denied Abelin, circled Ilber.

Abelin followed patch after thickening patch of what she called naturalized bulbs, finally discovering a plant even Ilber recognized as domesticated rather than wild—a dainty spray of seafoam roses.

"That's—it's real, then," he breathed. "The rest of the ruins, they must be close, they must—"

"Look up." Abelin said.

As Ilber did, he saw Abelin. She was grinning like a fool.

Behind her was the remnant of a low, moss-covered wall: crumbling into the ground around it, half-buried in new growth and old fall branches, but most assuredly human handiwork.

Ilber slowly strolled into the courtyard of the ruined castle of Gann.

ABELIN LET ILBER WORK. HE HAD HIS CHARTS AND MAPS OUT BEFORE she could blink, and had marked off several possible entry points to judicial halls, which he was sure held the ancient scrolls.

He didn't need or want her help. She had served her part in the expedition. Now he had his. Instead, she explored the ruined gardens. They were half-overrun with the plants that were of the ordinary sort in Gann, but here and there the original layout of the garden came through. The water gardens, the labyrinth—Abelin found these easily. With passing interest, she noted the archways of carved stone crafting a decorative pavilion around the Gate nestled in the water gardens. At any other time, to any other person, the lost Gate of Gann would have been deserving of a full dose of wonder and accompanying curiosity, but not for Abelin. Not when she saw what else lay hidden in the garden.

Blooming in majestic fronds of purple and blue, spilling their clean water scent into the air, stood a sea of celestial irises.

They're extinct, Abelin thought, denying the flowers bobbing directly in front of her. *Gone! No more!*

But here they were—alive, growing, in full corporeal bloom. She looked around. They weren't the only ones. Most of the flowers were fairly commonplace, sparrowsbreath and daintyfoot, gilded jonquils. But in patches and stands, among the loose bouquet of flowers scattered over the forest floor, were varietals thought lost. Silverleaf jonquils. Ashburn's waylily. Scarlet crocus. All of them brilliant, beautiful, priceless.

Priceless.

She dropped to her knees and began excavating. The root structure of even the most prized, the rarest of bulbs was the same as any common crocus. They could be transferred, moved, replanted—now, after they had bloomed, was a good time to do so, but it wouldn't hurt them anytime.

Abelin lifted the first celestial iris bulb carefully from the ground, loosening the soil and letting it cling to the delicate tendrils of the roots. She took several more, and a collection of silverleafs and waylilies.

They looked altogether ordinary, not terribly unlike ginger or garlic bought at the market, dirty and undistinguished.

At some point the stalks and their flowers must be trimmed, but not yet. She laid the bulbs on the ground, letting the flowers bob on the stems, just for the joy of looking at them. She had begun unearthing a scarlet crocus when Ilber ran into the garden, panic and dismay vying for control of his startled face.

"They're here! It's—followed us—they—"

"Who, Ilber??

"Hunters." He panted. "*Professional* hunters. Not like me. Not academics. Professional," he stressed.

"You mean armed," Abelin answered slowly, rising from the ground. "Uninterested in the legalities of first rights. *That* kind of professional." .

"That kind," he confirmed.

Abelin knew that kind. It didn't pay to try to argue or negotiate, not unless you had something really useful to negotiate with. Like throwing knives, or the knowledge you'd poisoned their water and had the only antidote, or a hostage taken in advance. They did not have anything so very useful.

"They must have followed us. I didn't like the look of that innkeeper. Well, no use trying to figure the whole thing out now," she said, deliberately gathering her things with the perfunctory motions of packing up after a picnic. "Let me see who we're working with."

She crept back up the path, silencing her footfalls on thick moss and keeping behind the crumbling stone walls. Peering around a column long since covered in vines, she spotted a quartet of thick-armed men bristling with thick-bladed knives. And there, with the same unruly beard and well-worn leather boots was Hadrian Barimen. She bit her lip to quiet the torrent of curses that welled in her throat. Damned Barimen, probably still mad about the damned tulips.

Even if they had any leverage to negotiate, Abelin was not going to risk meeting Hadrian Barimen anywhere he could easily dispatch her and hide the evidence. She hurried back to Ilber.

"Ilber, we need to go." Abelin kept her voice low and calm, trained by years of practice soothing tears and tantrums in much lower-stakes disasters with Hanti and Lana. "That is not a man we want to meddle with. Nothing else is important right now—just getting out of his way."

"They're blocking the trail. We can't go the way we came, not without...." His voice pinched off before he could finish.

"Well." Abelin sighed. "The donkey?"

A loud bray answered that question, followed by the rustle and crash of four hooves tearing through the underbrush. "I guess he'll find his own way home," Abelin said. "All the better we don't have to fight with that lazy idiot. Only one option, really." She nodded toward the stone pavilion, its intricate symbols filtered over with lichen and the Gate within, half obscured by trumpet vine. "The Gate."

Abelin hadn't traveled frequently by Gate, and she doubted Ilber had, either. They didn't know where it went, but it went somewhere, and at the moment, that was the priority—being anywhere but the ruins of the castle of Gann facing down Hadrian Barimen and his goons.

"The Gate?"

"Of course, you dolt—if they've got the trail blocked, how do you think we're getting out of here? I don't relish breaking trail through the jungle in the wrong direction, do you?"

"No, but—but all of our things. And—and all of the things *here*." He caught her arm, pleading with her as though there was anything that could be done. "The scrolls."

There it was. Failure, defeat, staring them in the face. They had laid out a nominal amount into the equipment and the rented donkey, but it didn't begin to compete with the greater loss of leaving behind the newly discovered site. Leaving the treasures of Gann behind meant, for Abelin, leaving behind her payout—and for Ilber, even more. The money, yes, but he had almost had the scrolls. Almost touched the first documents of the proto-republic, almost held history in his hands.

From across the overgrown courtyard, the noise of the scavenging treasure hunters paused, then increased. They didn't have long if they wanted to avoid a confrontation.

Abelin's eyes landed on the bulbs. The flowers drooped on the ground. "Not everything. Take as many as you can hold." She gathered bulbs in her hands, piling them a dozen deep in the crook of her arm, piling more on top of that, nestling her chin on the top of the pile. "Hurry!"

She ran for the Gate, the path half-obstructed by a twining silver clematis. It was beautiful, blooming in the shimmer of sunlight that filtered through the forest canopy. Ilber followed, balancing an armload of bulbs. The racket in the castle ruins echoed as the armed men now clearly looking for them clambered over the fallen walls and overgrown courtyards. They would find the equipment, the notes, the maps Ilber had drawn—but they wouldn't find Abelin or Ilber.

The Gate was right there and ready to deliver them to safety. She had no idea where this Gate led to—nowhere special, likely, but it didn't matter, because Abelin knew something that most treasure hunters didn't.

The bulbs were alive. Dug from the ground living, the hairs on their roots still seeking water, their stems still stretching to meet the sun. Blooming, growing, inarguably and conclusively alive—and each of the bulbs they carried was worth its weight in gold.

Ilber stumbled after her, meeting her eyes, trusting her. She gave him a small but very real smile.

"Now," she ordered, and they stepped through the gate.

MARIT THE RESOLUTE

LINDSEY CARMICHAEL

Marit gripped the railing and glared up at the warped metal of her harness swinging from the rigging. Moments ago she'd been supported in her own invention, mobile and free with the sea breeze in her face, ready to help or move as needed. She'd been a head above everyone else, for a change. Now she lay at their feet, propped against a shipping crate, her hip aching almost as much as her pride. She was more furious that the harness had failed to carry her through the rite of passage than she was at the fresh injury.

Captain Ingvar, his crew, and every other 18-year-old from the whole island of Brödel gaped at her more than they usually did. Families who had gathered proudly along the pier to celebrate now shifted uneasily.

Marit's foster-parent Loke radiated anxiety from where they waited among the spectators with Marit's rolling chair. Even their pet otter Fysker had caught the tension, hovering at the dock as if ready to jump in and come rescue her.

She weathered the looks. If there was one thing she knew how to endure, it was people staring. She locked eyes with the captain and held her chin high.

"I see what went wrong. I just need my toolkit, and I could try again. With your leave, sir, Aleksander could get it."

Murmurs simmered through the crowd as her childhood friend Aleksander stepped forward, smiling. It had been years since she'd given up pining for him, but her heart still lifted at his willingness to stand by her side. He wore the traditional Brödelian red shirt and trousers, symbolic of the sunrise and all the lands to the east. It made him look ready for anything in a way her own ancient hand-mended reds did not. Of course, he had a mother to tailor and press his clothes for such an important day. Marit had Loke. They had brought a long list of precious skills from Fjallanir a generation ago, just before the Gate closed on their isolated island. Sewing was not on the list, so Marit made do. She was already rigging equipment for herself. Why not hem pants, too?

The rite tested a person's seafaring abilities. According to tradition, each young person brought themselves and nothing else aboard. Marit had argued that her experimental harness was a safe and useful addition to the ship itself, but she was aware the captain had considered it an "act of kindness" to "bend the rules" for her.

"I give you all my sympathies, but we do not have the time, child. The tide is calling."

Marit gritted her teeth and tried to smile with confidence. The whole point of today was that none of them were children anymore.

"I can fix it. Please, half an hour more. Let me prove it to you. Loke—"

Loke took a step toward the ship, but the captain shook his head. "Beg pardon, Loke Leifki, but that won't be necessary. You run your smithy your way, and I run my ship mine."

She had to find a way through this mess. She tried one more time. "I can be of use to you and the crew!"

As if he hadn't heard her, he barked, "Aleksander Jenavar, bring down the harness."

Her friend hesitated, and Marit felt a last flare of hope. But the moment stretched, and a sick feeling rose in her stomach when Aleksander wouldn't meet her eye. He ducked his head, then turned and fled up the rigging.

The captain's voice washed over her like waves on tired, eroded stones. "Marit, you've already proven you've a clever mind, and clever hands. You know I'll buy as many of those new crab traps as you can make. They work like a charm, really."

Marit bit her tongue and aimed her fury out to the sea, out to the eastern horizon. Looking away to the nearest place that was not here. Around her, rigging was readied, knots were lashed tight, instructions were given. None of it included her.

Aleksander appeared, handing her the broken harness like a bandage for a wound. "I'm sorry," he said. "At least this happened before we sailed?"

She stared at the warped buckle, the tear in the leather, all of it blurring with livid, unshed tears.

The captain put his hand on her shoulder. "I'm sorry, too, girl. We all are. But that's just the way things are." Somewhere in her gut, an anchor dropped straight to the harbor sea floor. She wanted to swat him away but refrained, to remain in his good graces.

His hand retreated and some time later Loke's heavy boots appeared in her line of sight. When she turned to face them, their eyes were unbearable, so she focused instead on the fact they were holding both of her beloved wooden canes in a single huge hand.

"Do you need me to carry…?"

Marit scowled at them, which was unfair, but so were the tears rising like the damn tide in the back of her throat. "Last. Resort. Only." She slipped her own small, twisted hands onto the familiar curve of the canes and lifted herself and her body full of pain.

As she made her way across the deck and the gangway, she kept her focus divided equally between the placement of her feet, the tips of her crutches, and the feel of Loke's hand on her shoulder. It was a relief after the unwelcome touch of the captain. Loke was steadying. Understanding. Forgiving.

Though she knew it would cost her, Marit remained standing until the ship pulled away. None of the family here were sitting, except a pair of toddlers, and she could not bear to set herself apart even more. Now that the unpleasantness of Merit's injury and request had passed, the crowd of parents, aunties, uncles, and grandparents put extra effort into cheering and waving goodbye, as if volume could erase awkwardness. None looked at her.

Fysker stood anxiously on the cushion of her chair, his little paws scrabbling on the backrest as he butted his head against her arm. She reached out a hand for him to nuzzle.

"We could try again," Loke said, their voice hoarse and straining to be heard above the noise. "I'll harvest reeds. We can make more crab baskets to keep him happy. He'll take you out for your rite eventually if we just keep trying."

Marit smiled softly at Loke's use of "we."

She watched the ship as it rose and fell on the waves. They passed under the cliffs where the old hospital, once the pride of the island, stood abandoned. It was surrounded by fields of bushy green shrubs, row after ragged row of Golden Mugwort, all escaped from their carefully tended boundaries to seed themselves wild. Useful, potent medicine when fresh and full of island magic. Useless when dry. And impossible to export.

A fortune waved in the wind, unharvested.

Near the hospital stood a ring of stones in a perfect upright circle, hollow and empty as a shell. The elders who had survived the famine ruled that the broken Gate should stand as a memorial. A constant reminder that the world could change at any moment, and all you could trust were your own two hands to see you through it.

Her eyes traveled to the south end of the field. The sight of the familiar cottage and smithy gave her a pang of yearning. She wished she could teleport there, instead of pushing her chair up the long path that crisscrossed the town. Loke and Marit's home lay in liminal space, at the point where the hospital grounds ended, at the very outskirts of the town, on their island at the edge of the world.

She still wondered how Loke could bear to make their home in full view of the Gate. But she knew what it meant for necessity to outweigh comfort.

She entertained Fysker with a gentle paw massage, partly to distract herself from the throbbing in her hip. Eventually he scampered down off her chair to dive into the harbor.

Slowly, the ship full of her year-mates tacked beyond the safety of the cove.

The crowd drained away like water from a sieve, back to work.

Always to work. Sailors on small merchant vessels moved about their day, one crew from Al-Notlir breaking into a lighthearted shanty. As if she hadn't just been denied the right to become an adult in the eyes of her people. As if nothing at all had happened. And really, nothing of consequence *had* happened on Brödel, not for fifty years. What had this place been like when Loke first arrived?

Marit secured her canes to the back of her chair with shaking hands, then sank into the cushion with a groan of deep relief. She tossed the harness onto the pier with a clank. Fysker scrambled out of the water to investigate, chirping when he realized it wasn't edible.

"Maybe I don't want to keep trying." She fetched a small waxed packet of pain salve from her pocket. With a quick glance around, she untucked her shirt and slid her hand into her trousers to tend to the injury on her hip. Loke moved close to shield her from view of the town. Fysker splashed down into the water to float on his back, where he began to rub his whiskers in small circles.

Marit used the tail end of her shirt to clean the oily medicine from her hand, no longer caring that her reds looked untidy. Scandalous. She fixed Loke with a tired look.

"I would rather crawl through a damn Gate on my hands and knees than beg the Captain to treat me like an adult."

Loke wheezed a laugh, gravelly and bitter, at the memory. "It wasn't so bad. I got through it."

Marit raised an eyebrow, and then they were both smiling together. "You're changing the story again? The Gate Guardian whisked you through with a velvet robe this time, did he? Gave you a chariot to crawl into?"

Loke laughed until they coughed. Then they coughed until they doubled over, hands on their knees and face darkening. Marit put her hand on their back, frowning as she felt the guttural, grinding vibration inside. Loke pulled a flask of mugwort brew from their cloak pocket and took a face-pinching sip.

Marit waited, offering the kind of patience no healthy person had ever shown her. Only when the spasm passed did she pull her hand away.

Loke lifted the harness off the pier and stood up again with a sigh that hissed like a leaky bellows. They looked closely at where the fatigued metal had given way. Marit's hands itched to take it up and repair it.

"None of 'em are ever gonna make it easy for us," Loke said finally.

Hands on her wheel rims, Marit turned her chair to face the town and rolled over the bumpy boards. "It doesn't matter how old I am, how skilled, or how many times I redesign a workable system for me to be mobile while not in the way on his ship. He'll never see me as a worthy crew member. All I want at this point is someone to take me out of this place."

Loke snorted, keeping pace at her side. "You and me both, Sprocket. I wish I could uproot you, me, Fysker, and a whole row of mugwort. Pack up your notes, prototypes, all my tools, and sail to my family in Fjallanir."

"The plants would wither as soon as we left the cove."

Loke ignored this. "My cousins would show you their foundry. It's larger than a whole city block! My brother would feed you the best fire-fish soup in Ullande. His wife has almost no sight and trained a guide wyvern named Snarglefoomf, who helps light all the fires. To hear my brother tell it in his letters, Foomf is almost as cute as Fysker."

"Doubtful!" But Marit couldn't help wondering what she might train a guide wyvern to do. The incendiary possibilities alone were tempting.

"It's summer, so we'd travel upriver beyond the marshes for a soak in the hot springs. I'd teach you how to harvest the sweetest cloudber-ries, each one bright red-orange like a little sunset, and we'd eat them with honey and cream." They beamed at her and held out the harness. "Oh, Marit, you've no idea just how you would thrive there."

"It sounds delicious," she said. "Like a dream." She took the evidence of her failure back from her foster-parent. They passed the Al'notliri ship and watched the sailors dance a jig to another shanty.

"And then! I would drop you at the doorstep of the University of the Resolute, where they'd take one look at you and your creations and fling you right into class, I'm sure of it."

"They wouldn't!" Marit shook her head. "Loke, what is the point of me? I'm only good for tricking crustaceans into wicker boxes. I can't even fathom what I'd have to do to prove myself of value to a formal school. Let alone a Fjallaniri university." She set her jaw and flung the harness into the harbor with a plunk so loud Fysker gave a chirping yelp.

"Hey! I had a use for those buckles." They both watched as Fysker corkscrewed under the surface and disappeared. She mumbled an apology.

"Sprocket, your skills are good. Drawing, figuring sums, solving puzzles when we have to make do. But your ideas! Those are proof enough. What about your chair-cannon design?"

Marit laughed for the first time in a week, her voice reaching far enough to startle one of the sailors. His heavily tattooed arms, clapping to the song a moment before, went still as he caught sight of her. It was a potent stare, and she met his gaze with a level one of her own, confident that she'd never have to interact with him again once their ship sailed. What would it be like to have a whole city of people whose stares wouldn't matter, because she didn't have to know or rely on them?

"What's funny? We could have you there and settled before classes begin in the fall." Loke pointed toward the sailors. "It's only six days to Remor. You could use the Gate there."

"You want me to use a Gate?" Marit stared.

"Why not?"

Incredulous, she gestured to her elaborate rolling chair and the gear shift lever extensions she'd designed and built herself to navigate the steep village paths. She twisted to reach one of her canes, running her fingers over the perfect angle of the handle grip, remembering the painstaking hours of carving, shaping, redesigning. The many discarded prototypes were now used to prop up vegetables in Loke's garden. She savored the way it cradled her hand, comforted, strengthened.

It would fit no other hand. It would serve no other person in the world, except her.

And she couldn't take any of it with her, not through a Gate. Only by sea.

For the 55 days needed to sail to Loke's home country of Fjallanir, she'd be little more than glorified cargo. Even Captain Ingvar, who had known her all her life, considered her a burden.

Fysker popped up again like a cork. She clicked her tongue to call him out of the water, then maneuvered her chair onto the smoother paving stones of the street by the docks.

Would she be willing to spend so long at sea, if it meant a chance at a new life? She'd arrive too late to even try applying for a school.

"If I had the money to sail all the way there, maybe I could get work with my foster-cousins at the foundry," she said slowly. "Make something more than crab baskets."

"Take the Gate," Loke said. "Make something of *yourself*."

Marit shook her head. "It's too great a risk. And either way, I'd have to leave you behind. Don't be silly."

"Marit, I'm serious. I know you think you're safer here, but that's only because it's all you've ever known." Loke nodded up the road lined with shops and shade trees. "This is only a *tiny corner* of the world and not worthy of your talents."

Marit frowned. Together they passed under the ancient, craggy linden tree at the edge of the town square, its branches full with blossoms and the buzz of summertime. Loke was in the habit of collecting the flowers for their flavor and soothing medicine.

"This isn't all I've ever known, though," she said. "I have eyes to read. Ears to hear the stories of everyone who comes ashore." Seeing Loke reach high overhead to pluck from the branches made her feel small, so she watched Fysker instead. She pulled out one of her canes to nudge him away from a honey-drunk bumblebee. "And you. You told me plenty. Gates are no place for the likes of us."

"Well, maybe I shouldn't have told you that story," Loke snapped. "It was a bad day for everyone. Bad days happen." They waved a flower toward the tiny ship on the horizon for emphasis, before stuffing it into their belt pouch.

"Right." Marit snorted. "I'm sure that Gate Guardian lost a lot of sleep over what amounted to the most shameful moment of your life."

Loke closed their eyes, and Marit closed her mouth.

They left behind the tree and its bees, moving in a pocket of quiet broken only by her wheels creaking on the uneven paving stones. The ship shrank ever smaller in the distance.

Marit angled her chair off the main road and up the path to the smithy.

"Wait!" called a tenor voice.

Marit jolted, turning to find the tattooed sailor from before approaching at a jog. He came to a breathless stop before them, blocking their way.

Fysker squeaked, then gave a single huffing growl. "Excuse me," Marit said. "Were you following us?" She felt Loke's hand on her shoulder and was grateful to not be alone.

The sailor crouched down to her eye level, a gesture that annoyed her until he gave her a nod of respect as he might any other adult. He held out his forearms to show her the tattoos, black lines of maps skating across his light brown skin.

Marit gasped.

"You're a Navigator," Loke whispered.

"And an eavesdropper." He looked a little sheepish. "My apologies. But you were staring at us from the pier, and I became curious…" He trailed off, noticing Loke's height and forearms twice the size of his own. "I heard talk of the Gate at Remor."

Marit and Loke stared with awe at the Navigator, then both spoke at once.

"What path through the Gates—?" Loke broke off, waving at her to speak.

"It's true I couldn't take my canes with me through the Gate, isn't it? They might as well be part of my body. But it's not the same as a pegleg."

"Prosthetic, they call it, in the cities," the Navigator remarked. He admired her canes. "But you're right. They *might as well* be part of you. But each time you set them aside, they become not-you again. The Gate would claim them for the void if you tried."

"How do people like me travel through Gates?"

"Hmm." He said nothing for a long moment, scanning the town as if committing it to memory. "They mostly don't."

Marit huffed in disgust. "I wonder why."

"Could someone carry her?" asked Loke.

Marit flinched away from their question. Old unease welled up from her hips like water from a poisoned spring. She willed her tightening throat to soften, to open, to just breathe.

"Sorry," Loke said softly. "I had to ask." She nodded, petting Fysker as if he required her complete attention.

The Navigator ran his hands through his dark hair. "I've never tried it. Some Gates might let you. Some might not. Perhaps someone could hold your hand and pull you through." He shrugged. "An animal, now. If you can get it to approach the Gate, an animal will be able to bear you through."

"Oh, certainly, I'll just mount my trusty stallion—"

Loke cleared their throat with a sound like scrap iron sliding down a mountain. "Show some respect," they said, before a deep cough took them.

Marit held her tongue and waited, noting the Navigator's discomfort. He offered his hand to Fysker, who sniffed it and apparently decided no more growls were needed.

When Loke found words again, they kept it short. "Please. The path? To Ullande?"

The Navigator unfolded slowly to his full height, unlacing his vest and shirt until he was able to pull the fabric down over his shoulder. If he was aware of how inappropriate this was for their literal straight-laced town, he didn't care. He jerked his chin toward the tattoos along the back of his shoulder.

"Remor to the Hawk Markets of the Indeya Delta. To the south and the west of Al'nar. It's warm there, sunny enough to scorch skin pale as yours, but they'll give you linen robes as a token of the Merchant Guild's hospitality. If you have a chance to try the gazelle pepper steaks, it will be an experience you won't soon forget. The stew is cheaper, though, and almost as good."

"And from the Hawk Markets?" Loke prompted, as impatient with this description as if they hadn't just been waxing eloquent about cloud-berries.

"The Gate to Ullande is but a stone's throw from the northern side of the market." The Navigator said it with a carefree smile, as if it would of course be nothing for her to cross a bustling market in a strange city, alone, without her canes.

Loke's hand tightened gently on her shoulder. "I still have contacts at the university who'd give you a chance. People like us, who'd love your designs, who'd understand the value in your skills."

"Like us?" she said sharply, turning to look up at them. "You didn't say that, before."

"Like us. People who will get it."

A wave of tears rose in the back of her throat, just as they had on the ship. This tide felt different. Hopeful.

"Marit. A week at sea, two Gates, and you'd be free."

She put her hand over Loke's, realizing how she'd taken her foster-parent's presence for granted. The thought of being instantly so far from them left her cold. And thrilled.

Now that the Navigator was standing, he spoke over her head, directly to Loke. "I know it has been a generation since the tragedy of this place, but if any among you keep the needle and the ink, I can tattoo her with your mark of credit." He gestured to Loke's wrist, where their faded tattoo had once provided a link to their family and personal bank accounts. A lifetime ago.

"This crew will depart for the mainland in three days and leave me on Remor in nine. I can take her in my charge if you like." He righted and laced up his shirt, gave Loke a friendly nod, and left.

Marit felt too unmoored to scowl at the man's back.

"You're not a child," Loke said.

"Thank you," she said, her voice almost as hoarse as theirs. "I shouldn't have said what I said about the day at the Gate. I'm sorry he heard it."

Loke nodded, their face and their grip on her shoulder both softening. "You're not a child. And everyone knows you're brave. One thing that I don't know how to teach you is that sometimes..." Their voice became strangled. "Sometimes shame is a thing we all endure. Just like pain."

Marit made a fist, clinging tightly to Loke's fingers.

She let the tears flow.

Loke knelt beside her and took her hands in their own huge grip, with charcoal-ringed nails and skin that smelled of linden flowers. "I for one would like to find out where you and your clever mind and clever hands actually belong. Do you really believe it's here in my garden shed, weaving crab baskets until the day you die? For the likes of Ingvar?"

"You can't come with me or visit," Marit said, gulping in air. Fysker put his paws on her knees and chirped softly. She stroked his head and cried harder. "Promise you won't try. Six days to Remor? Your lungs…"

"I stay where my medicine grows. I promise. There's no fault, nor shame, in having a body. And all bodies have their own needs. Right, Sprocket?"

She nodded, taking deep breaths, but it left space for a new wave of old pain to bubble up. "I want to be among people who get it, Loke. People like us. I know it's wrong of me, but sometimes I wish the hospital were full of sick people again. I know… I know the tragedy… when the Gate broke, and there wasn't enough food to go around… their sacrifice was…" She couldn't get the words past her tears.

"Marit." Loke's voice had the quality of molten lead. They nudged Fysker to one side, took her shoulders in their hands, and looked intently into her eyes. "I was there. It was not 'a sacrifice.' It was sacrilege. It was wrong. One Griastan took a walk in the sea, according to the ways of her people. Her journey to Brödel had taken too long, she was too sick, too hungry, and the dark mind won. It was her right. But that didn't make it right for some of the people of this place to call for other patients to join her."

Loke's face broke then, and their eyes shone. Marit covered her mouth with grief and wondered if she had ever seen them cry.

"If my own life weren't tied to the mugwort, I'd have left on the very first ship off the island. You have value. I have value. And every one of those people had value even when they were too sick to 'contribute.'" They spat the word. "Even when your hands hurt too much to weave or whittle or tinker with gears, I still love you. Not because you're clever. But because I love *you*, Marit, my foster-daughter. My friend. And it's why I will get you off this island if I have to row you to the mainland myself."

Marit hugged them tightly. She made a decision.

Slowly, giving each other the gift of patience, the two humans and their otter made their way to the first home Marit had ever known and the last one Loke would ever know.

MARIT'S FIRST INSTINCT WAS TO LAUGH. ALEKSANDER LOOKED uncertainly between her and Loke and then back at the donkey he'd led from his family's croft. The beast was named Muckgabber, according to his love of complaints, but Aleksander had saddled him with soft blankets and tack clearly stolen from the family's pony. "Mucker is as softhearted as he is stubborn, and has been a steadfast friend to my family for decades."

Aleksander tried to meet her eye, but lifting her own gaze to his would be too like forgiveness. He'd proven the quality of his friendship when he caved to Captain Ingvar. He went through the rite without her, avoided her on his return, and here he was, days later, with a donkey instead of an apology.

"Well, it's technically still a step above crawling," Marit said to Loke with a tight smile. The irony did not escape her that a donkey might prove more helpful than Ingvar.

Loke peeled off their work gloves and tugged the soaked bandana from their face, leaving behind smudges of soot. "Thank you, lad. She can keep the saddle and kit on till the last minute." They passed him a small purse, but he refused. A little dance of pride ensued.

Marit rolled closer to the donkey. He lowered his head to sniff her chair with big gusty snorts. Aleksander's mother Jena was generous to give up an important farm animal right before harvest. Marit tried to feel grateful.

"I can barely ride with a saddle to hold onto," she said. "Isn't bareback risky? Especially since I can't grip with my legs?"

Aleksander gave a small, awkward cough. "Tug on his mane all you like. He might complain—loudly—but he'll stand solid." From the corner of her eye, she watched him offer a grin that would have left her swooning as a girl.

She knew it might be her last chance. Marit craned her head back and finally met his gaze. Taking in this strong, healthy person, this yearmate of hers who had strolled onto the ship and claimed the birthright of his future, she attempted a smile.

"You can handle Mucker," he said. "As long as you keep that famous temper in check."

Her smile hardened until she could crush oyster shells in her teeth. Mucker took a step toward her chair and nudged her in the stomach with his nose. Acknowledging her anger.

She softened immediately. Definitely an improvement over Captain Ingvar.

It took seven days to sail to Remor. Marit had never been so bored or so lonely while surrounded by so many people. She'd brought two old castoff canes from Loke's garden patch and wore the cheapest dress she owned. She brought nothing else.

The Al'notliri were polite but distant, so Marit kept to herself. Forced by rain to remain below decks and in her cabin, she spent the time asking the Navigator questions and pretending Mucker was actually a large, curious otter. She didn't have much success in either pursuit.

"Why can prosthetics go through Gates? Don't they cease to become part of the body every night when they come off for sleep?"

The Navigator frowned. "People take them off?"

Marit stared at him in the watery blue light from the porthole. She reminded herself that there would be people like her on the other end of all this. Loke had promised. Somewhere out there, someone would understand.

"Unless you can afford magic buffers to protect the skin, then yes, prosthetics come off to sleep. When I was young, I explored the empty hospital and found a silver gripping arm. The magic had faded, but I was able to fix the rest with Loke's help. My first big repair."

"What happened to them? Your foster-parent."

Marit was impressed it had taken him this long to ask. "People get sick. Nothing has to *happen* for a person to get sick."

She waited for him to dig for her own worn-out story. Instead, the Navigator shook his head. "With Loke and the Gate Guardian, I mean. What happened on the 'most shameful day of their life?'"

Marit toyed with the grip of one weathered cane.

"Not sure which Gate it was. Somewhere on the old path to Brödel. The Gate Guardian didn't think much of invalids, I suppose. Loke asked for help. Guardian said they looked fine. But they coughed too hard and collapsed." Marit's throat was so tight she had to whisper to finish the story. "They had to crawl through like an infant. Everyone just stared." She shuddered.

They held the story in silence together a while. Muffled music rang through the ship's hull, punctuated by braying from a tired donkey.

Eventually, he asked about the Gate.

"It died within the year. People used to coming and going for medicine were trapped, and there wasn't enough food for winter. Not many ships, too few sailors. That's why everyone learns to sail now. Only the 'useful' can earn their place on Brödel."

"Thank you," he said.

"For the story?"

"For trusting me."

She nodded. She let go of the cane as the ship lifted on a swell. For a moment, it appeared to balance on its own.

Remor proved to be a rock covered in mossy tundra with a single, lonely Gate.

In the end, she did manage to handle Mucker. She rode him up the island path using a death-grip on the saddle, but this lasted only until he caught sight of the Gate through the downpour. After that he would not budge.

Adani, the single Al'notliri who came with them up the rock, nodded as if he had expected this. "The animals, they sense the space between."

The Navigator looked from Adani, to Mucker, to her. She had abandoned her canes on the ship that waited far below, telling herself a sailor might be grateful for them someday. Now she wished she had planned better. How would she get through the city without a ride? How could she face any of these unknowns without her chair? She felt more nude without it than she would actually disrobing to go through the Gate.

"Do you want to go back?" the Navigator asked. "Or do you want me to carry you?"

Every single tiny bone in her hands ached with the cold, but at his words, frustration boiled hot in her stomach. Frustration, and fear.

Mucker brayed loudly, startling her. She ran a hand over his coat. It was sodden and coarse, nothing like an otter. "Sorry, my friend. We all have limits."

She had risked her health, her future, on the gamble she could find a way through. To a new home and family. To a university.

To people like her.

She looked at the Al'notliri and the Navigator and summoned a shaky smile.

"I need help to dismount. Then if you're able, I would ask you both to walk on either side of me. At least to the Gate. I need you to be my canes."

It was a long, soggy, embarrassing process. The arms of both men felt twig-like, compared to the oak tree strength of Loke.

Adani offered his arm for balance as she and the Navigator hastily peeled off their sodden clothes. "We really are on the edge of the world!" he said, averting his eyes. "I wish I could offer you better hospitality." He accepted her dress and gave her a sip from his canteen, a fruity liquor that burned warm in her throat. "You come to my home sometime, they'll give you hot tea and places to rest."

Marit actually whimpered at the thought. She was inches from the blurry otherworld of the Gate, but all she could think about was her desire to sit down. She wanted her chair so badly that it eclipsed even the rawness of baring her twisted body to these strange men. Swaying from foot to foot on moss and clinging to the rain-slick stone of the Gate wall, she felt her legs give a warning tremble.

"Navigator? I need to do this now, before I fall through."

He passed his own clothes to the sailor and held his bare arm to her. It was covered in tattoos, but also raindrops and bumps like her own.

He took her hand and made it disappear into the Gate, where the numbing blur enveloped her arm with strange familiarity.

All her life she'd dulled her own pain by diving into details of everything around her. Stories from sailors. Crabs on the seashore. A silver prosthetic. The Gate was the same: full of everything, and nothing.

In the end, her fury and determination propelled her forward.

She fell anyway.

Marit emerged on her hands and knees into blessedly clear air. Sun-baked tile steps warmed her aching palms. Stairs? Of course there were stairs. Completely unnecessary stairs. A giggle bubbled up through her outrage.

"Welcome to the Hawk Market," said a bored voice with an unknown accent, somewhere above her. "Name, please? Origin? Destination?"

She hadn't even found her feet again, she thought with a laugh. Not that she'd be able to walk again anytime soon. She was crawling down stairs!

She couldn't wait to write to Loke about this.

She pushed her strangely dry hair from her face and looked up to find the Gate Guardian—or whatever passed for one here—watching her with mild interest.

The Navigator was nowhere to be seen.

Marit sprawled on the ground, laughing harder.

"Sprocket," she said, a wave of giddy freedom running through her. She should be terrified. Who could she trust? What could she do?

Maybe nothing.

Or maybe, almost anything.

She thought she should feel ashamed, with her warped, messy body taking up space here in public on the other side of the world. But the stares of other travelers slid off her like water from Fysker's back. She could find no fault, nor shame, in having a body.

The only shame was this place and its pointless stairs, this whole process, indifferent to the point of hostility to people like her, navigated by healthy travelers who never stopped to ask why people like her never used the Gates.

"My name is Sprocket Lokevar." She leveraged herself somehow to a sitting position, not bothering to cover her nudity. She grinned defiantly at the Guardian. "I'm from the edge of the world. I'm going to find my people in Ullande. I'm going to enroll in classes at the University of the Resolute."

She held up her wrist with the still-healing mark of credit. "I need to borrow or buy two canes, please."

The Navigator appeared, still nude with a robe thrown casually over one shoulder, pushing a wheelbarrow through the crowd. He grinned when he saw her. "What do you want first, a robe, a pepper steak, or to see the world?"

"Never mind on the canes," she said to the Gate Guardian, who hadn't moved an inch. "I found another way through."

LUMI & THE NAVIGATOR

NATANIA BARRON

Lumi was, admittedly, napping, when the Navigator fell through the Gate. Well, she assumed he fell, because when she finally reached him—after being rudely awakened by a clatter down the hall—he was sprawled out on the smooth, slate flagstones in the inner chamber, unconscious.

There was a not insignificant amount of drool pooling out of his mouth, staining the slate a darker shade of gray. Peaceful as his face was, he had a youthful look about him in slumber, sooty lashes drawn delicately down over his freckled cheeks as he breathed evenly. She marked the map tattoos over every inch of his back, arms, and…

By the bells, she had to get him covered.

Hardly anyone came through the Gate this far downstream. Lumi wasn't even supposed to be here tonight, taking the watch over from Rurik who was still too drunk to take his shift after celebrating Beda's pregnancy. They had been hoping for a babe by the summer, and—

She really, really had to get this man covered.

Lumi wrestled one of the heavy woolen robes off the rack, hitting it a few times to remove the layer of dust, and then, at a distance, almost averting her eyes, she threw it over him and winced, waiting for him to wake up.

He didn't. He stirred slightly but was otherwise unresponsive. No. How could this have happened? Why her? Why now?

There was no point in wallowing in fear and panic. This was her responsibility, and she had been trusted on this watch, just as she had countless other shifts. She'd been trained. Even if scarcely anyone among them had to use that training, she was not helpless.

Lumi leaned on one foot, taking the pressure off her shorter limb, then the other, hands on hips, as she tried to contemplate her options. The labyrinthine Gate building was not easy to traverse, and if she left him alone while she went in search of other clothing or implements of awakening—pots and pans and the like—she ran the risk of him waking up and being disoriented. He could hurt himself. He would feel abandoned.

He was a Navigator.

Just like her brother Kalle wanted to be. Before he died of the crawling fever. The fever that had taken his life and left her in need of a magical device to use her leg. That she had lived—always the smaller, weaker twin—and he had not, seemed a great injustice to the world.

Yet even in death, Kalle's bravery sang to her sometimes.

If Kalle were here, he would have demanded Lumi do everything in her power to save this man, this noble Navigator.

But Lumi was frightened.

So, she did what any other sensible person would do: she poked the Navigator with the long staff she carried until he woke up. Her brother never would have approved of such cowardly behavior, but he wasn't here to judge her. Even if she felt like his shadow lingered just out of sight. Sometimes, late at night when fatigue threatened to undo her, she thought she could see the spectre of him, watching and musing. Lumi wanted to know what it was like to be dead—they had shared everything else in life until he'd gone. Surely death shouldn't have kept him.

It was as if the entire world stopped when her brother Kalle died. She stopped growing. Stopped caring. Stopped seeing. All her dreams had been extinguished as surely as incense smothered in the dark.

The moment the Navigator's eyes flew open, she scurried back into the darkness, holding out her staff defensively. Her whole body snapped awake in that moment, shimmering energy crackling through her veins.

It was the same way she felt when she finally spotted a deer in the woods while hunting. Fear tinged with excitement.

"Don't move!" Lumi shouted loud enough for the chamber to echo, making her sound far more ominous than she was.

"Hunnnnhhh," the Navigator moaned, his eyes scrunching closed as he turned over, planting his large hands down to steady himself.

"I mean it!" Did she?

Time stretched and thinned as Lumi watched the Navigator shake his head like an irritated pony and finally manage to get on his knees. The robe slipped off, pooling on the ground around him, and Lumi averted her eyes. And then she didn't because the man started laughing.

His raspy, percussive laugh was so unexpected, Lumi started looking around the chamber for some sign of humor she had missed. Was this one of Rurik's pranks? It wasn't a very good one, if that was the case. And she'd have to have Beda chastise him for it. This is why she preferred animals to people. They weren't half so tricksy.

The Navigator laughed so long and so hard tears began streaming from his eyes, pattering down his chest.

Lumi remained frozen, watching him, her cheeks burning with a mix of shame and another emotion best left unexplained.

When he started coughing, Lumi sprang to action—suddenly remembering her duty and her basic manners—and clumsily scooped a ladle full of water into one of the old wooden bowls they kept for just such an occasion.

The Navigator took it, and after a few sips seemed to soothe the worst of his coughing, he could actually hold a conversation.

"You must think I am mad," he said, blessedly wrapping himself in the gown. He was much too tall for it, but at least it covered the majority of his most vulnerable parts. "My sincerest apologies." He looked to the right and the left, wiping his mouth with the back of his hand.

"It's been a long time since someone came through here."

"Fjallanir, yes?"

Lumi nodded. "Far upriver, though. Most of the Gates are in Ullande, and there's so many connections there, so folk mostly avoid us here."

A Navigator. If Kalle could see him! His eyes would light up, and he'd barely be able to contain his joy. He could never suppress his emotions, much to the chagrin of their father who believed his son ought to be far more stoic in life. Lumi was the one who never could let out her feelings, even though she felt them all sharp as knives inside.

The Navigator stretched out his arm, studying the tattoos there. They were too dark for Lumi to make specific sense of.

"So, we're in Harlek."

He had no doubt in his voice. Utterly confident. What it must be like to live one's life with such certainty! She would love even a sip of that sensation.

"Yes," Lumi said. "I'm Lumi Harkis, a Gate docent."

The barest suggestion of a smile crossed the Navigator's lips. "My name is Eldin. I'm a Navigator. Or I was."

Lumi did not understand how one could *have been* a Navigator, but she nodded anyway. It was customary to tell the date to travelers through the Gates, so she did.

At her statement, Eldin fell back on his hands again, closing his eyes. "Six years," he said with a weary sigh. "It's been six years."

THE LITTLE WEASEL BEAR COULD STILL SMELL ANOTHER TREE. NO, OTHER trees. A whole forest. It had plagued her for two cycles of the moons, and this night she vowed to find the source. Deep inside her mind she knew, resolutely, that it was the answer to her pain. Another forest. Other trees. Beckoning her to them without ceasing.

Two days before, her kits were taken from her. They were still so small, so vulnerable. She thought the den was safe. She had lined their chamber well with mouse skins, the downy fur a perfect patchwork of comfort. When she'd looked upon her work, she had been so proud.

Not her first litter, not her first kits, and not even the first she'd lost. But their violent end, the memory of the smell of their blood and the way the earth itself had been torn open, had twisted something inside of her that did not go back the way it should. Every breath smelled like owls. Like foxes. Like death.

She had dreamed of them grown, running beside her, climbing up the trees. They might begin smaller than mice, but at maturity her kits could squish a mouse with their paws, bat it away, inconsequential. How their pelts would glisten, their tails fluff out behind them. She would revel in their beauty, their claws, their individual markings and scents.

That hope had been extinguished. Her world altered. Stopped.

Until she'd found that other tree smell.

Since then, she could think of nothing but the other tree smell. Cold and bright, but not the same as her trees. Far away, colder, harder to reach. She had a feeling if she were to run day and night for a month she would not be able to reach it, and yet she could smell it.

Maddening.

Every time she thought she was nearing the place, it moved again. Flickered. That feeling, that connection, vanished, leaving her teeth aching and her claws tight. Whatever trees called her, they were toying with her. Testing her. She knew this to be true.

She devoured mice and voles, even rabbits when she could get them young enough. Nothing filled the void inside of her, even though she knew she was pregnant again, because that was her lot in life.

She dared not hope. She dared not think of her kits full grown.

If there was any chance she could dream again, to see her future with her kits, it could not be here, in this bloody place. This haunted place. This terrible place.

The weasel bear decided she needed to find those trees, no matter what. It was her quest; her duty. For herself, for the kits she now held inside her body. A new start.

RURIK KEPT STARING ACROSS THE KITCHEN TABLE TO ELDIN THE Navigator, while Lumi explained what had happened again. In the cover of the first morning light, just as the next docent came to relieve her, Lumi had decided to take Eldin to Rurik and Beda's, because the longer she spoke with the Navigator the clearer it became that something was terribly off.

Eldin ate as if he hadn't eaten in years, and perhaps he hadn't if what he said was true. He also marveled at the humble magical items in the house: the self-snuffing candles, the ever-warming pot, the supportive brace Lumi wore on her left leg, which adapted to her body's curvature.

"We don't have smiths of such remarkable affinity where I came from," said Eldin after Beda snuffed out the cooking fire with a crank of the stove. "I had heard you all were industrious, but I'd only ever seen your big magical machines. How many little ways you've wrought magic."

"And where do you come from, Navigator?" Beda asked, always the most forward among them.

"Eldin is fine," said the Navigator. "And I'm from Mirraden. Originally. Made my first mark at fifteen and have rarely been back since."

"Mirraden!" Beda breathed in wonder. "Is it true what they say? You collect spider silk from the highest canopies, harvesters living above for weeks at a time?"

Eldin nodded. In the bright light of morning, Lumi noticed how the lines of his tattoos drew her eyes again and again, stark against the man's pale skin. He wore Rurik's clothes well, though they were a bit small on his hefty frame. Had he visited all the places depicted there? Was there a ritual involved before he could mark them? Did he have to learn all the customs before traveling? Did it hurt to make the tattoos? Did he make them himself? She needed to know, a longing deep inside of her threatening to crack her open.

She startled when Rurik snapped his fingers before her face.

"Lumi?" Beda asked, tilting her head so her long beaded braids clinked against one another. "I think you need some rest."

Lumi most certainly did not. Not when there was this much adventure to be had. "I just got lost in thought," she said, taking another bite of morning porridge. Beda had even added some dried citrus to it to make a good impression.

"I was talking about Kalle," Rurik said. "How he wanted to be a Navigator."

Swallowing was much harder than it had been a moment ago. Lumi took another bite and then a long sip of warm lemon balm tisane. "He did," she finally said. "But that was a long time ago."

Eldin looked from Rurik back to Lumi. "You speak with the weight of the dead," he said.

"Kalle left us some years ago," Rurik said.

"Two thousand and nine hundred and six days," Lumi said. "We haven't had a Navigator in the village since Great-Great-Grand Uncle Olet."

"Olet of Nines?" asked Eldin.

"We just knew him as Olet," Lumi said. Other than Kalle, no one in her family had ever spoken of Navigators, not with any real conviction. Knowing she'd had one in her ancestry made her nose tingle, and a warm, welcoming feeling spread through her chest. For all of Kalle's dreams, for all of their shared hopes—hadn't she wanted it a little, too?

Eldin's expression went a little distant, as if he was thinking so deeply, he could not focus on the matters at hand. Lumi understood that sensation quite well. She often felt as if she were on the outskirts of the present, ever skating about the edges like frost at the joining of the windowpane.

"Well, you might have guessed by now that I did not intend to come here, exactly," Eldin said a moment later, after everyone had fallen into the easy silence of eating. "And I cannot stay too much longer. But I first have some business to attend to, if Lumi could assist me."

"Me?" Lumi asked.

"Is there another person in the room named Lumi?" Rurik scolded. "Honestly! What an opportunity."

Lumi remembered the Navigator said he'd been gone perhaps years, but she had not shared that with her friends. It was not her place to do so. Eldin, as a Navigator, reserved the respect of being able to tell his own story without her weighing in on what she had learned.

Still, he wanted her help.

"You're welcome as our guest, however long or short it might be," said Beda, her cheeks dimpling with a kind smile. "And whether or not you'd like to address the village is entirely up to you, of course. Lumi will help you in whatever ways you need."

Eldin nodded, returning a somewhat strained smile. "For now, I'd be glad to help with whatever needs doing about the house. It's the least I can do. And I'm afraid I'm a bit out of practice with household chores. Then, once I've rested, I'll go about my task and take my leave."

———

TOGETHER, LUMI AND ELDIN HELPED CORRAL THE SHEEP, REORDERED the herbs in the storehouse, and put out the linens to dry. This gave Beda and Rurik some much needed time together, which would be nonexistent soon enough with the babe on the way. And if Beda was like her sister Gutnel, she might even have twins!

Lumi couldn't imagine a life with twins at the breast. Unlike her peers, she had never dreamed of having children of her own. She was much more comfortable with sheep and goats and chickens, and that's where she found herself on days she wasn't tending the Gate. Being a Gatekeeper was simply part of her heritage, as her family had always done so. Though she was not often asked, given everything that had happened with Kalle. Lumi often got the feeling they pitied her for losing her brother, knowing how much she had changed after his death, and wanted only to extend kindness rather than responsibility. Except she was tired of pity. She was tired of kindness.

"How old are you, Lumi, if you don't mind the question?" Eldin asked. They had just finished pinning the last of Beda's beautifully embroidered linens between the house and the thick oak tree where she often found Visska, the cat, lying in wait for her next prey.

Lumi chewed on her lips a moment before answering. "Twenty-three. But people think I'm younger. They seem to forget."

"Why do you think that is?" Eldin asked, though it was not asked in an unkind way as some folks often did.

"Because Kalle died when he was only fifteen, and he was my twin, and they say sometimes a twin left behind freezes in time," Lumi said. She sighed. "That, and I never had the gift of getting along with people like Kalle did. I like animals better."

"I noticed that," Eldin said. "The sheep listen to you before you even speak. It's a rare gift, that."

Lumi swatted the air in modesty. "Anyone can teach a sheep to obey. They've got fewer brains than an acorn."

"But you don't treat them like it," Eldin said. "And besides, inside an acorn is the entire pattern for how to grow a tree. It is ancient, deep knowledge, greater than any other, to understand how a tiny seed can become a tree."

She liked the way Eldin spoke. It was not often, but almost always with care and with intention. Speaking was exhausting around most people, and she always felt she shared too much or too little. With Eldin, she didn't feel that way.

It was a shame he would leave soon.

THE WEASEL BEAR COULD NOT REMEMBER EVER BEING SO COLD. PERHAPS it was because the growing kits inside her demanded more and more of her energy, or because the winter was unrelenting. Still, she would not give up in her quest.

"What are you?"

"I am none of your business," the weasel bear said, shivering.

The source of the voice was a horned and hoofed creature, coat as white as her own, with gray eyes like the last light of dusk. They had found her, despite her tidy spot in the snow. Their snout was annoyingly close to her.

"Everything in this wood is my business," said the creature, without the haughtiness such a statement might imply. "I am the wood. But you are not of this wood."

"No, I am not. I am on a quest to seek the other trees," said the weasel bear.

"A weasel on a quest? Quite a strange circumstance. And one with kits upon the way, too," said the horned beast, pounding the ground with a pristine hoof.

"I am no weasel," she replied. "You are some kind of deer."

"Perhaps. But I am more than any deer, and then, I am all of them. You may call me Reini, king of this wood."

She thought it prudent to bow, but she was too cold. So, instead, she just inclined her head. "They call me a weasel bear, for my kind are neither bears nor weasels, as you have observed."

"A weasel bear," Reini mused. "Indeed, you have great teeth and sharp claws, and a coat that changes hue. Do you live in the trees?"

"When we can. We are lithe and graceful, fierce in battle, with great teeth and vicious jaws. Now, though, I am cold, and I do not know where to go."

"Well, first, I will give you a name, brave weasel bear. I will call you Eska."

Eska had never had a name before, not one she could share with others outside the family she once had.

"What does it mean?" she asked Reini.

Reini tossed his head, the little hairs under his chin swaying with the motion. "It means you."

That made her feel better, warmer. If she had a name, it meant she could be remembered.

"Do you know where the other trees are? I can smell them, but I cannot find them, and my young will be born soon...or else I will die first."

"Do you believe the trees are calling you?" Reini asked.

Eska thought that was a very strange question. "I hope they are."

Reini went very still, then lowered his head a little more. "Then that is enough. Climb upon my horns and I will take you there, Eska. But you will have to go the last part on your own, and it will be perilous."

"It will be worth it," Eska said, summoning the remainder of her strength to climb up into the bramble of Reini's horns. They were so vast she thought, for a moment, she was back at home in her own tree, before it had burned, before the blood, before she had lost herself. She did not have time to be afraid, though, for she fell asleep almost right away.

Lumi couldn't quite understand what she was looking for. Eldin said he had a friend follow him through the Gate, and it would be waiting for him—and stated it was an animal that defied description.

When she pressed, he said it was better if she didn't know. Well, that was quite an assumption for the Navigator to make. He barely knew her. But it was rude to contradict a Navigator, and the fact he'd given her any kind of quest or duty was enough of a compliment that she couldn't refuse. Kalle would never forgive her, even from the grave, if she were to insult Eldin.

So, that was how she ended up high in the barn rafters, holding out a wedge of cheese, calling out to a shadowy shape. It smelled like roasted bread, which was strange, and slightly musky. But no matter how she had moved her head, she could not quite make out the form of the animal. It was larger than a cat, smaller than a dog; at first, she counted five legs, then realized one was a tail. A long tail, thick and the same length as its body.

Perhaps Eldin was right, and it was beyond description.

She didn't use her people voice when it came to animals. Few seemed to appreciate the noises humans made, and instead preferred clicks or whistles or, sometimes, even low growls.

When Lumi went *pzzt pzzt* like she would at a cat, the creature hissed. But when she said *nuu nuu* like she did to the horses, it stopped, listening. Lumi felt the tension between them unravel as surely as a snapped thread in the loom.

Just enough light came through the thatch to illuminate the creature's amber eyes, a contrast against the slate gray fur of its muzzle. Indeed, were it not for its graceful gait, Lumi would have thought it a small bear. Its ears were rounded, the snout a bit shorter than a fox's but still blocked like a bear. The creature's claws were impressive, sharp and curved, grasping the wooden beams with expert care.

"Well, there she is," came Eldin's voice from below.

The creature sniffed the air, then shuffled its rear as if preparing to spray. Lumi hoped it would not.

"She's mad at me," said Eldin, by way of explanation. "As she should be. Come now, Wen. Now that Lumi's brought you out, there's no more hiding."

Wen, presumably, gave Lumi a dolorous look as if to say, "See what I must endure?" before skittering down the main beam of the barn as if born to such movement.

"What is she?" Lumi asked.

Eldin laughed as Wen sprung upon him, climbing up his body like a tree and then curling around his shoulders. She looked like a great, burly cloak, her tail draped down his front and ending somewhere near his knees. "She's a nuisance, that's what she is."

"I mean, what do you call her, besides Wen."

"She's what we call an *eskin*. Some call them weasel bears. She wasn't supposed to follow me through the Gate, and I suppose that's one of the reasons I was so delayed. The Gates have their own sense of humor."

"When did she come through?" Lumi felt her face flush with shame. She'd missed an entire creature arriving through the Gate. Some Gatekeeper she was.

"Hard to say," Eldin said. "Sometimes I think they have smaller Gates of their own. Or, she came through after me and skulked around until she found me."

"And you were both really gone years?" Lumi asked, jumping down into the soft straw. Her brace rattled, but the magic stabilized her quickly. She beat at her skirts to free herself of sticks and hay.

"I suppose we were. Six winters ago, I went to Mirraden. Now and again, I do that, to see where I came from once again. I had to leave Wen when I became a Navigator, and she did not take it well. So upon my arrival, I think she believed I was staying. I tried to give her the slip at noontide, when they're most likely to sleep, but she clearly followed."

"You think she was lost with you for six years, then," Lumi mused, amazed at such a loyal, strange creature.

"I know it. These creatures are long-lived and slow to age. Their behavior is strange, often flitting between lesser known Gates. She must have been terribly upset when I didn't show up," Eldin said. "They say each chooses a person for life, and that their oldest ancestors came from smaller creatures which originated here. No one is sure how they ended up all the way up in Mirraden, though, as there are no others like them anywhere in between."

"Some ancient *eskin* must have made quite a journey," Lumi said. Wen chirruped and then licked her paw, sharp claws gleaming. She truly was magnificent.

"Indeed. And we are grateful for her, for the *eskin* help us in many ways."

"Poor thing," Lumi said with a sigh. "That Gate had a mind of its own, separating you both."

Eldin scratched the *eskin* under the chin, the lines at his eyes deepening with genuine affection. "I suppose it does. Perhaps it was just waiting for you."

"Me?" Lumi asked.

REINI'S VOICE CAME FROM EVERYWHERE AND NOWHERE AS THE SCENT OF new trees and new horizons filled Eska's nose. "There is always a price for escape, Eska. What will you give?"

Eska leapt from antler to antler atop Reini's head, but she never could get to the end of it. "I will give some of my teeth," she said, knowing she had plenty to spare.

With a pop of pressure, she felt her teeth—the very last ones toward the back—disappear, leaving strange, empty sockets before they filled back in with flesh. And just as she gave them away, she could see the archway in the distance now, snow falling all about her and melting on her nose.

"What else will you give?"

Eska squeezed through a small gap, her spine twisting as she did so. "I give my love of the sun," she said. "I will not need its light when I find the promise of this new land."

Just as she spoke, her eyes flashed, suddenly sensitive to the light. But in the absence of her vision, she could smell even more clearly now. She would only have to leap, just to make the jump, and certainly, that was her greatest strength...

"I require one more sacrifice, Eska."

Shivering with anticipation, Eska knew what she had to do. "I give you my fleet feet, my nimble limbs. I give you my fearless jumping."

Too late, she felt her body shift: it became thicker, stronger, the muscles in her legs shortening and losing their limberness.

"Now you must leap," Reini said.

Eska gasped. She had just given away her ability to jump! How could she close the last distance between the great archway and her safe home?

"But I cannot; I have given it away."

"There is always hope in believing, and power in pushing beyond what we have lost."

"I have only ever wanted a happy ending," Eska said, readying herself for the last leap—for herself, for her kits, for the future.

Reini laughed, the sound following her into her next life: "There are no happy endings, little one. Only temporary soft landings."

LUMI LOOKED BACK AT THE VILLAGE AS SHE FOLLOWED THE NAVIGATOR toward the Gate complex.

He hadn't asked her, not directly, but she knew he expected her to follow him. Like the animals she knew and loved, she could sense things about Eldin before he even said them. Being with him, she felt *more*. More than she saw herself, and more than anyone in the village ever had.

"Part of me doesn't want to go," Lumi said as they reached the first doors of the Gate complex. She took out her great key and turned the mechanism, the gears moving easily beneath her ministrations.

"I know," said the Navigator, adjusting his gait so Wen sat more squarely on his shoulders. She was sleeping, snoring even, the smell of baked bread wafting about her. "Lucky is the person who leaves part of their heart behind."

"Kalle was the one who should have been the Navigator," Lumi said, thinking about losing part of her heart. She could not stay here, mourning him forever. "It was his dream."

"I find that hard to believe. You may not have begun that dream, Lumi, but you can carry it forward. For your family, for your legacy. If you are happy here, then I will not press any further. But if there is even a chance, even a spark of hope inside of you, I think it is worth it."

They stood by the second set of doors now, their voices barely audible in the tiny, stone room.

"I have never imagined I'd have such a destiny," Lumi whispered, tears burning her eyes.

"No one is destined one way or another. They are simply waiting at the right time—there is always chaos, no matter our plans. But know this: Wen and her kind only speak to a select few folk, and she brought me here, to you. You will help me return her to her home, and then, if you choose, you can take the leap."

Side by side, Lumi and the Navigator entered the innermost Gate chamber. She ought to have felt embarrassed to strip down naked, but she did not. She ought to have been shaking, second-guessing, thinking about Beda and the baby, about Rurik and the next harvest.

But she was not.

"What if we get lost for another six years?" Lumi asked, hesitating just as her toes reached the last tiles leading up to the Gate.

"Then we will meet again at the beginning of the next adventure," Eldin said, holding out his hand.

She put a hand on her brace, the metal wrapping her leg so well. "My brace. I'll come out the other side without it." The magic device had given her freedom back, but the sudden idea of jumping into the Gate fully vulnerable made her lose her breath.

"We will find you another," Eldin said, as if reading her thoughts. "There are many smiths about—and in the meantime, you will have us both to help."

Lumi felt the soft pressure of Wen's tail against her leg and looked down to see the creature's amber eyes flashing, almost in a mischievous challenge.

She took a deep breath and undid the fastenings at her hip. To keep her balance, she grabbed the Navigator's hand. He did not balk and did not change his mind.

And so, together, they leapt forward, into the future.

COURIER'S HONOR

VALERIE VALDES

The bells of the Clockspire rang out to signal the imminent turning of the massive, interlocked gears of Girruna, the cliffside city some ancient, whimsical genius had decided to construct as a mechanical marvel for reasons many speculated about but no one truly knew. Some of the gears were as large as a village, others as small as a house, and people lived happily within the hollow centers of their towering granite walls.

Nevane waited with the crowds in Cobblestone Commons to enter the Gategear when it became accessible, the air warm and thick from the press of people and the slanting sunlight of afternoon. She loved the precision of Girruna's motion, the regularity of it, the blessed routine. She loved the bridges that arched between certain gears, the lifts that let people reach the tops of the walls and wander among the vast, winding paths that shifted with every turning.

Most of all, Nevane loved being the best courier in the Black Dragonfly clan, racing around the city delivering messages and packages. Like any good courier, she knew the layout of the gears, the locations of all the doorways cut into their teeth and walls, and what times they were open or inaccessible. She knew which gears had lifts and which had ladders, which had handholds spackled onto the stone and which had nothing but a test of one's patience. She'd never failed in her duty, never let one of her clan's enemies steal from her, never compromised her integrity for her own gain.

Because of that, her clan's leader, Ifreda, had tasked Nevane with an especially important delivery. Rumari, one of the clan's lieutenants, brought Nevane to Ifreda's office personally, then waited outside as Ifreda explained the assignment: go to the Gategear, find a specific locker, retrieve its contents. Tell no one, stop for nothing, return promptly. Do not fail.

On her honor as a courier, Nevane would put the package into Ifreda's hands herself.

The bells ceased chiming, and with eerie magical smoothness, the ground beneath her feet turned clockwise. The gear's massive teeth shifted so a previously obstructed doorway overlapped with its counterpart, forming a tunnel through which people began to rush in both directions. It would only be open for another half hour, at which point the gears would turn again, and the doorway would vanish.

Nevane let the crowd carry her into the gear that held Girruna's only Gate, the magical portal shimmering in the air at the far end of the circular space. Many had already disrobed in Cobblestone Commons, and those who hadn't did so now. Privacy screens stood to the left, for those who didn't wish to strip in front of their neighbors, but the necessary nudity for the quick journey to Stahlven, in Fjallanir, bothered few travelers. Shirts and trousers, skirts and dresses, linen and silk and leather all quickly gave way to bare flesh, and few gazes wandered because everyone was in a great hurry to be about their business.

While some people handed their discarded clothing and personal items to friends or loved ones, others made use of a local amenity. Along the curved walls, some enterprising official a century past had erected lockers in which travelers could stash their clothing and any items they didn't want magically lost in transit. Each locker opened with whatever code the user selected, a series of simple shapes that could have endless combinations.

Nevane consulted the locker number she'd been given by the clan leader, scanning rows and columns of identical metal doors until she found it near the ground a dozen steps from the Gate. The code worked; the door opened, and she peered into the narrow box with mild interest.

A nondescript leather scroll case rested inside. Nevane pulled it out and slipped it into her stingbag, which promptly sealed itself shut. It was spelled to her and had no visible seams or openings unless she opened it. Even better, anyone else who touched it would feel a painful stinging all over their skin that intensified the longer they held on.

People rarely tried to hold on.

In her time as a courier, Nevane had learned that she needed the best tools available to ensure she made her deliveries. Clans engaged in struggles for power often targeted couriers in the hopes of obtaining useful secrets or obstructing business. She had her stingbag, she had hard-earned fighting skills from running the gears, and she had lungs and legs that wouldn't quit.

If all went smoothly, she'd reach Longbridge within two turns and be in Deepwall before dinner was served. And tonight was curried goat night. Her favorite.

Nevane joined the dwindling line of stragglers returning to Cobblestone Commons, only to find a trio of goons looming in front of her, wearing the plated headbands that marked them as Iron Scorpion clan members. Two had muscles on their muscles and spikes on their knuckles, while the third carried a baton that would sting like Nevane's backpack.

"Hello, little runner," Baton said with a sneer. "We've come to relieve you of your package."

"Is that an innuendo?" Nevane asked, subtly stretching her calves. "Because you're not my type."

"It's a chance to keep your teeth in your mouth." Baton held out a hand. "Let's have it, and you can go on your way, none the wiser."

"Certainly nothing could make you three wiser. I'm taking this to its intended recipient and no one else. Courier's honor."

Muscles One and Two advanced as Nevane backed toward the rapidly nudifying crowd behind her, offering Baton a cocky grin.

"Come on, then," she said. "I haven't all turn."

Muscle One rushed her. Nevane sidestepped, and he slammed into a half-naked woman, who screamed and slapped him repeatedly with the metal buckle of her belt. Muscle Two moved more deliberately, spike-knuckled hands curled into fists, watching Nevane's eyes and feet. She glanced left and feinted, then ducked right. Her steps took her past a portly man with a glimmering tattoo on his back, then between a merchant and his wife arguing about something she'd found in his pockets.

Baton tried to pin her against the wall. As he swung his weapon, she kicked up and off the stone blocks, leaping over him. Muscle Two managed to touch her bag, but the magical sting made him flinch away. She sprinted for the doorway.

A fourth Iron Scorpion manifested in front of her, arms outstretched, legs wide to brace for impact. Nevane slid along the ground underneath him as his hands closed on empty air, then sprang up to continue her dash into the next gear.

Cobblestone Commons bustled with merchants attempting to take advantage of those leaving through or arriving from the Gate, and customers looking to be taken advantage of as they rattled off credit codes to pay for their purchases. The sounds of good-natured haggling over snacks, toiletries and other essentials blended with the scents of fresh cheese bread, spiced meat, and mushroom skewers. No time to eat with people chasing her, though. And curried goat awaited her.

Thankfully, it was easier to lose pursuers in the Commons than Gategear, and soon Nevane had put enough booths, carts, and warm bodies between her and the Iron Scorpions that she could slow to a jog. Her thoughts, however, sped up.

Strange that someone had been waiting for her at the lockers. They hadn't said they knew what was in the package, only that they were there to take it. Who had sent them and why? Or had they simply spotted her and decided to seize an opportunity?

She considered the path she needed to take to reach the Black Dragonfly stronghold at Deepwall. Far, certainly, but not onerous as long as she wasn't waylaid further. A few minutes later, she passed through the door to Gristmill, whistling a jaunty tune under her breath and looking forward to another job well done.

WHY HAD SHE THOUGHT THE REST OF HER RUN WOULD GO SMOOTHLY?

In Kilnside, smoke rose from the kilns and ovens that gave the gear its name. Artisans blew glass and baked clay and handed off their finished products to customers or merchants bound for farther gears. Nevane eyed the Scarlet Beetle clan members closing in on her, their red scarves tucked into black vests. She recognized one of them: Charys, who combined her weighted scarf with poisoned needles. They'd had drinks together a few times, sloppy kisses once.

"Give us the map, Nev," Charys said.

"What map?" Nevane asked.

"The one you're delivering," Charys replied, unwinding the scarf from her neck as she spoke. "Every clan between here and Deepwall is going to be after it soon."

How had that happened? She'd picked it up less than a turn ago. There were various mundane and magical methods to communicate quickly between individuals in the city, but the only way to spread word that widely at such speed was through the notice boards posted in various gears. They were connected to each other by magic, but only a Blazoner should be able to scribe on them…

"That's a lot of clans," Nevane said. "You think they'll just let you keep it if you manage to take it from me?"

"Not your problem. Come on, Nev, I don't want to hurt you."

Nevane tugged at her silver neckcloth, embroidered with thin black dragonflies. "You know I take my job seriously, Char. I'm loyal. My clan leader wants this, so she's getting it."

"Stop talking," another Beetle said. "We copy the map, we turn her in for the bounty."

Bounty? Nevane's blood iced. Who'd put a bounty on her head? And why? For the package, or something else?

"Fine," Charys said. "Can't say I didn't try." She held her scarf with both hands and spun one end, face calm as if she were preparing to order a glass vase rather than commit violence.

Nevane barely dodged as the length of cloth whipped straight at her. Her next moments were spent ducking, jumping, and skipping backward as Charys flicked and swirled her weapon in a flurry of deadly fabric. Arms wrapped around Nevane from behind, pinning her briefly, but her assailant shrieked and dropped her as the stingbag did its work.

There were too many Beetles and only one of her. She had to get away before they wore her down or called for—

More Scarlet Beetles appeared as if summoned by magic.

—reinforcements. Grind her to dust.

Nevane darted into a glassworks, the white heat of the fires warming her right side. Glassblowers embroiled in their labor ignored her as they spun and shaped their molten crafts; some barked a warning or stared curiously at her through protective goggles. She grabbed two handfuls of sand from a bin in passing, and immediately tossed one at two pursuing Beetles. One enemy took it in the eyes, then stumbled into hot glass backside-first and screamed. The other sprang to the right, straight into a podium displaying a star-patterned bowl that wobbled precariously.

Glass shattered behind Nevane as she dashed out of that workshop, followed by an angry shout. She entered a pottery maker's studio next, snatching a glob of wet clay from an unattended wheel with her free hand. A rough grip seized her arm, and she turned and smeared the clay into her attacker's face. They released her, swiping at the sticky mess while Nevane continued running toward the doorway to the next gear.

Charys's scarf whipped past her cheek, so close she felt the wind of its motion. Reflexively, she flinched backward, but Charys had swung the weapon around. The hard weight struck her shoulder, along with the poisoned needles, sending a wave of frigid pain down her arm.

"The map, Nev," Charys snapped.

"I deliver," Nevane said between gritted teeth. "Courier's honor."

"Suit yourself." The end of the scarf flew again, toward Nevane's chest.

Nevane leaned back, then tossed the remaining handful of sand into Charys's eyes. The woman roared and shook her head like an enraged animal.

Nevane bolted through the doorway, her left arm hanging uselessly at her side.

Now that she knew she was being hunted, Nevane decided Longbridge or the tops of the walls would leave her too exposed. The winding way she took instead led through gears both familiar and rarely crossed. Curious greetings met her in the second-hand markets of Cheapmeet; the few scholars in the Orrery ignored her, intent on their studies; the ice peddlers in Chillturn had long since finished their deliveries and gone home for the day. The sun sank lower and lower in the purpling sky until finally it took itself off to bed as well, leaving a sliver of moon and a dazzling spray of stars to observe her progress.

Nevane reached the Nightbloom Gardens earlier than most lovers of nocturnal flora or romance, so she had the glowing bluestone paths and luminescent plants to herself. Massive white flowers perfumed the air with intoxicating scents. Clusters of stepped mushrooms and swathes of soft moss gleamed in faint yellows, oranges, and pinks among the trunks of tall trees, whose leaves cast dappled shadows. The doorway to Fruitfall waited on the opposite side of the gear, a single blazing lamp set high in the wall as a beacon, and it had just opened if she'd gauged the tolling of the Clockspire correctly.

The air seemed to thicken as she walked, no doubt due to the burbling streams winding between clusters of plants and beneath elegantly carved bridges. The pain in her arm gave way to numbness and fatigue. Nevane had spent enough time running the length and breadth of the city for her body to be accustomed to the effort, but today was different. She'd never had a bounty on her head, never had multiple clans chasing her, trying to keep her from making her delivery.

Questions shadowed her steps. Who'd ordered the bounty? Did they want her, or the so-called map? Not knowing what it might even be a map of, she could barely speculate. She also rarely delved into clan politics, except to track the shifting alliances that would make certain gears hospitable or hazardous. If this package was valuable to her clan, one of their enemies in Copper Mantis or Silver Butterfly might want it on principle.

And yet, how had someone outside her clan learned of it in the first place?

One thing was certain: whoever was behind this had access to a Blazoner, and that narrowed the possibilities to public officials, people with enough power and coin to pay bribes without fear of consequences, and, of course, clan leaders and their representatives.

A ghostly murmur interrupted her reverie. She froze, knees bent, prepared to sprint down the path. When nothing more happened, she continued, heart pounding, the metallic taste of fear slicking across her tongue.

Another susurrus of whispers rose, accompanied by a shimmering figure dancing in the corner of her vision. Nevane bolted, legs pumping like pistons. More visions flanked her, hazy and indistinct. Voices muttered, incomprehensible, as if heard through a wall. Her limbs felt heavier with every step. Where was the doorway? The beacon? She slowed and turned in a circle, finally finding it. Leaves rustled nearby, but no wind kissed her skin.

"Lie down and rest," a voice said softly, seductively.

Yes. Rest.

"You've run so far, so long. You deserve sleep."

Sleep would be—no, she had to deliver the scroll case.

"See that comfortable bed? You'd love to find out how soft it is, wouldn't you?"

A bed appeared in front of Nevane. She skidded to a halt before she ran into it, and her thoughts did the same. What was a bed doing in the middle of the Nightbloom Gardens?

This made no sense. And the flowers' scent had changed to something spicy and strange, like cardamom with a hint of camphor. Oh no.

Nevane pulled her neck cloth up to cover her mouth and nose. One clan favored this type of hypnotic, soporific magic: the Steel Spiders. The Gardens weren't part of their territory, but they'd been known to ambush people here when it suited them. She'd wandered right into their web, and now she had to find a way out.

The mental haze lifted slightly now that she wasn't breathing in the harmful fumes, but she didn't have to fake the unsteadiness of her gait as she avoided the nonexistent bed. She would soon be out of time to reach the doorway, but if she tried to race for it when she was still so far away, her invisible foes would close their trap. She had to be crafty.

"I suppose you want the map, too?" Nevane asked.

A mocking laugh answered, echoing as if it surrounded her like the spelled mist. "The mythical map? Supposedly leading to a secret Gate filled with expensive treasures? Nonsense."

Is that what she was delivering? Nevane hadn't been told, and she hadn't asked. It was none of her business; she was only the courier.

"Who knows whether that rumor is even true," the hidden Spider continued. "Such a Gate could be anywhere. It could open to some isolated place from which treasure would be difficult to extract. Not as if items could be brought through it. No, we have no interest in such a thing. It's far easier to drag you in for the bounty."

Sadly sensible, but not to her advantage. "Does the bounty specify whether I'm to be taken alive?"

"It does not."

Ouch. "Whose bounty is it, anyway?"

Another laugh, deep-throated and cruel. "You don't know? Your own clan is looking for you. Hauling you to them means we benefit from improved relations between our clans. And, of course, they remove a traitor from their ranks."

Traitor? What?

"I'm not a traitor," Nevane spat. "What do I stand accused of?"

"Stealing the map. You must admit, you're a long way from Deepwall, little bug."

Only because she was taking a roundabout route there, trading speed for security. Curse it. And yet, something about this felt wrong. If only the Spider magic wasn't scattering her thoughts like birds, she might figure it out.

"They'll know I'm not a traitor when I finish my delivery," Nevane said. She had to believe that. Ifreda had trusted her, and that trust wouldn't change to doubt in a few turns of the gears. Would it?

Silence replied. Were they closing in? The faint glow from the plants and flashes of moonlight hid more than they revealed. If she wanted to get away, she needed to bring the Spiders closer, to use a special trick she had up her sleeve for situations like this.

Nevane wandered toward a deeper patch of shadows near the path, keeping the beacon of the doorway in sight. She would only get one chance.

"Why are there so many feathers?" Nevane groaned, flapping her functional hand as if warding off hallucinations. A few still hovered here and there, but she was able to blink them away more easily now. And the arm Charys had poisoned was slowly recovering; she could wiggle her fingers, even if they still felt like they belonged to someone else.

"Lie still," the Spider coaxed. "Let your end be soft and sweet."

She could reach the beacon if she ran. This was her chance.

"Yes, time to sleep," Nevane said, slurring her words. She collapsed past a tree covered in pink lichen, the scent of cool earth a welcome change from the cloying spell. Sliding her numb arm above her head, she gripped the bracelet on that wrist with her other hand and waited.

Quiet. Peace. Then, the scuffling of footsteps in soil. How many Spiders were there? Through slitted eyes she saw one, two, three shadows pass in front of the glowing tree trunk. They'd be on her in a moment.

"Don't touch the bag," the Spider warned. "It stings."

Someone crouched next to her.

Nevane squeezed her eyes closed and twisted her bracelet. A burst of blinding light flashed from it, bright white even with her face averted. The nearest Spider shouted, and without further ado, she rolled to her feet and ran for the doorway. Her boots pounded against the ground, breath coming in labored gasps through her neck cloth. She would make it. She had to.

The bells of Clockspire began to toll. No! She was still too far away. A rock tripped her and she stumbled, barely catching herself with her numb arm, pushing back up and throwing all her remaining energy into her every loping stride. The beacon above the gear's tooth beckoned. Closer… closer…

The chiming stopped, and the gears turned. Nevane slid straight into a solid wall and bounced off, pounding it with her fist in frustration.

She had to get out. The Steel Spiders wouldn't be blinded for long. They would know she was heading for the doorway.

The lift was on the opposite side of the gear, and no wily resident had dropped a ladder here. Nevane would have to do this the hard way.

Clockwise from the doorway, she found a tree whose branches reached the top of the wall. She shook out her poisoned hand, which tingled as if it were being stabbed by tiny needles, then started to climb the tree. Clearly someone had at least done this much before, because grooves had been carved in the trunk, up to where the lowest branch grew. Progress was slow and awkward, but the prospect of death at her back lent her strength and stamina.

"Where is she?" a distant voice called.

Nevane sped up. She could see the lip of the wall now, limned in starlight.

"There! On that tree!"

Curses. She wrapped her good arm around a limb and pulled herself higher. The thwack of a projectile hit the trunk near her. She didn't stop to see what it was.

Someone started climbing up after her. Nevane couldn't rush, though, or she'd risk falling.

Abruptly, the next branch put her above the top of the gear. The city spread out in front of her, its hundreds of gears, large and small, lit from within by torches and candles and enchanted lamps. Beacons illuminated the walls themselves at regular intervals, tended by the sect of wall walkers who considered it a holy task to wander the concentric paths formed by the ancient stones. Sometimes people left them food, or spare shoes to replace ones worn by near-constant constant motion; it was considered a way of earning future luck.

Nevane needed that luck now. She crept across the branch, which swayed perilously beneath her weight. Another projectile sang past her head. Abandoning caution, she moved more quickly, then jumped across the small gap to the wall.

Her feet touched stone and she rolled onto her injured shoulder. Sucking her teeth from the pain, Nevane scrambled to her feet and ran.

THE SHAMBLING FORMS OF WALL WALKERS AND OTHER PERAMBULATORS occasionally passed in front of the lights above and below, casting eerie shadows across the tops of the gears and down inside them. Only the flimsy cover of night hid Nevane from the enemies stalking her across the city. Pulling up the collar of her jacket, she slowed her pace, impersonating a walker, and hoped for a brief respite.

A yellow flare landed at her feet. She skittered away from it, throwing an arm over her face protectively, but it was too late.

"There she is!" someone shouted. A whine was followed by the clang of metal hitting rock. She'd heard the sound often enough to recognize it: a Granite Strider's hooked rope catching on the lip of the gear's wall.

Nevane had to get down into a gear, but which one? And how? She wracked her brain for options nearby, but she couldn't—wait. Printer's Nook. Not a gear, but a long, narrow space between Graverside, Inkwell and Waxworks. Wooden walls protected those inside from falling into the dangerous gaps between teeth, whose pits were deep enough to break legs if one was lucky or kill outright if not. None of their door-ways would be usable at this hour, but the lift ran more or less day and night since the press never slept, and ladders and poles had been rigged up for people to climb or slide down if they were in a hurry.

Footsteps told her the Striders hadn't lost her, and no doubt they were far less exhausted. She needed to stay sharp, but between Charys's fading poison, the clinging cobwebs of visions from the Steel Spider's hypnotic spell, and the sheer amount of running she'd done, Nevane feared she was reaching her limit.

One thing at a time. Get to Printer's Nook, then Graverside, then… Turnbridge would do nicely. At this hour, the bridge would be facing North Turnbridge, which would put her only two gears from Deepwall. She was so close, she could almost taste the curried goat.

The wall curved left, and she followed it, then jumped to another gear and kept going. On and on, pursuit behind her, beside her, before her.

Finally, mingled scents on the breeze—hot metal and paper, ink and acid, molten wax—announced her imminent arrival at her destination. She'd almost reached the lift when a Strider appeared in front of her, twirling his hooked rope. Nevane slid to a stop, kicking up dust, then changed direction to move straight for the Nook. Surely there would be a ladder, a rope, something she could use—there!

Nevane leaped onto a pole holding up a tarp and slid down, her arms and thighs warming from the friction. When she got close to the ground, she jumped the rest of the way and took off like a thrown rock.

Printing presses large and small rose and fell as people slid papers in and out of the frames or spread a fresh coat of ink on metal plates. Two women argued about a headline while a third watched; a man crumpled up a caricature and threw it at his hapless associate; a gaggle of writers traded quips and gossip while drawing mugs of mead from a tapped keg.

One of them noticed the courier dashing headlong between the ramshackle buildings, because she heard a shouted question: "Ey, is that the Black Dragonfly with the bounty?"

"Get a quote, fool!" someone else shouted.

"No comment!" Nevane called over her shoulder.

Grinding teeth, did everyone know about the cursed price on her head?

A table ahead held scroll cases, into which a bored-looking girl was stuffing rolled sheaves of paper. An idea flashed into Nevane's mind, and with a rushed apology, she grabbed an empty case as she hurtled past. Either the girl didn't care, or she hadn't noticed, because no cries demanded that the thief be stopped. Nevane made a mental note to return later to pay for it.

Nevane finally reached the end of the Nook. She fumbled the pilfered scroll case into her stingbag, clambered up the wooden interior wall, then crossed a rickety plank bridging the gap to the gear wall. It swayed alarmingly beneath her boots, but held long enough for her to reach solid stone. Away she went, toward Turnbridge, ignoring the stitch in her side and the fiery tingling in her poisoned arm as best she could.

The Granite Striders hadn't given up, unfortunately. A half dozen of them trailed behind her like the tail of an unruly kite. If they caught her…no, they wouldn't. She was the best courier in her clan.

The huge arch of the bridge that gave Turnbridge its name rose above the wall, still connected to its counterpart in Northbridge. She had only a few minutes to reach it before the Clockspire chimed the next turn. The steps leading down into the gear were guarded by two Striders. Despite her fatigue, Nevane moved like air around them, ducking thick-gloved hands and vaulting over an attempted leg sweep. Down the steps she went, as fast as she dared so she wouldn't fall or twist an ankle, not now when she was so close.

Tired and focused as she was on the bridge, Nevane didn't register the danger on the ground until it was too late. She made it halfway across the open space when it suddenly…wasn't.

She was entirely surrounded. Clan members from Iron Scorpion, Scarlet Beetle, Steel Spider, Copper Mantis, Silver Butterfly, Granite Strider and more circled her, eying each other warily. Worse, along the wall, Black Dragonfly allies waited, but they seemed disinclined to help her, either because they were outnumbered or because they thought she was a traitor.

Then again, unless she was mistaken, most of them reported to the same lieutenant…

A slow clap broke the eerie silence. Bylon Keth stepped forward, muscled arms bare, bald, tattooed head gleaming in the moonlight. Bully boy for the Copper Mantis clan, he absolutely hated Nevane for her refusal to let her limbs be broken the last time they tangled. Instead, she'd left him with a torn shirt and a boot print to the ass, in full view of enough people to dent his reputation.

"Look what the teeth spit out," Keth said. "Having a bad day, runner?"

"Keth," Nevane said coolly. "You think you're going to be the lucky one who takes the map from me, instead of anyone else here?" She waved her good arm at the assembled crowd.

Keth's sneer dismissed the other clan members as insignificant. "I'll take my chances. Our numbers are good, and you've hit a wall, haven't you? A stiff wind would knock you down." He stamped a foot and blew at her sharply. She refused to flinch.

"We had her first," shouted an Iron Scorpion.

Charys muscled her way forward, scarf flung around her neck. "I tagged her arm. She's mine."

A dark-garbed figure with a gray mask gave Nevane a sarcastic bow. "We snared her in Nightbloom. We don't want the map, only the courier."

"Cut her up and share her!" a Strider shouted. Laughter and hooting answered.

Nevane sucked in a breath and reached for her pack. "How about this." She pulled out the scroll case she'd filched from Printer's Nook and raised it above her head. "I trade the map for my life."

"How about I get both?" Keth snapped. Protests replied, and the mood of the crowd degenerated from amused to angry. Nevane waited a few more heartbeats, letting the tension grow. As the circle of bodies tightened around her, she waved the case like a flag.

"How about…you get neither?" Nevane threw the leather tube into the air. Everyone's gaze tracked it as it tumbled end over end. She bolted for the bridge.

The crowd exploded into motion as people tried to catch the scroll case, then fought over it. Hands reached for her, but she danced out of the way, letting her stingbag protect her when it could. Someone tugged at the knot of her neck cloth, cutting off her air, but she grabbed their wrist and rammed their thumb into the back of her neck, eliciting a yelp of pain. They released her and she pressed onward, rubbing her aching throat.

The fighting intensified, thuds of fists and elbows meeting flesh, bones cracking, shouts of pain, tingles of magic suffusing the air like an oncoming thunderstorm. The Steel Spiders must have set off a spell, because that spicy cardamom-camphor scent buried the aromas of sweat and foul breath, and some clan members staggered or flailed at nothing.

Nevane's focus narrowed, her every action like a second ticked on a clock. Duck a punch. Sidestep a kick. Push someone into the person behind them. An Iron Scorpion doubled over from a blow to the gut, and Nevane vaulted over their back. The bridge was a dozen steps away when Keth landed a slap to the side of her head that sent her reeling.

"No, you don't, Dragonfly," Keth said. He exploded into a flurry of punches and kicks she was hard pressed to avoid or redirect. A feint, and he caught her full in the breastbone, knocking her onto her back. The breath whooshed out of her, pain clamping down on her chest like a vise. She managed to get her legs up in time to catch him in the gut as he charged her, sending him sailing over her head and into the roiling mass of other fighters.

The bells of the Clockspire chimed. Get up, each peal seemed to say. Get up. Get up. Nevane struggled to her feet and limped to the bridge, picking up speed as she climbed it. Halfway to the seam at the middle, a cry behind her announced her escape had been noticed. A stone sailed past her head, then a dart. The bell's final peal rang out.

Beneath her boots, the bridge moved. Nevane sprinted the last few steps and jumped off the edge, flying toward the also-moving portion on the North Turnbridge gear. She barely caught the edge of it, clinging for her life as her legs dangled over empty air.

Finally the gear stopped, and she hauled herself up, flopping onto her back and gasping like a fish on land. Alive. Still alive. And with her package intact.

Nevane gave herself a thirty-count before getting up. Any longer and she'd stay there for the rest of the night. Possibly the rest of her life, if some rioters disengaged and came after her.

Down the bridge she went, her boots like lead weights, her entire body tender and aching as if bruised all over. She'd examine her injuries later. Now, she had a delivery to make.

———

NEVANE'S HEART LIGHTENED AS THE SILVER AND BLACK PENNANTS flying at the four corners of the clan's stronghold came into view. Deepwall filled most of a medium-small gear that had changed hands a few times since it was occupied centuries earlier. The Black Dragonfly clan had held it since the current clan leader's great-great-grandparents' time, and it had survived any number of raids and sieges, though none since Nevane took her oaths.

The gear-tooth door was closed, so she had to climb in from Stillhaven, which was blessedly quiet since all but a handful of the distillers had gone to their beds. She saluted the guards at their post as she passed the first row of thick perimeter walls, then the second. At the third, a separate pair of guards arrived to escort her inside, neither of whom mentioned any bounty when she said she'd come to deliver a package to the clan leader.

Within minutes, Nevane sat on a padded bench in a cozy antechamber, cooling her aching heels. A stack of pillows invited her to recline, but she didn't want to fall asleep despite her various pains. After she completed her delivery, she intended to find some food, then collapse into bed in her tiny room on the second floor near the garderobe. What could she scrounge up in the kitchens at this hour? Dared she hope there was leftover curried goat? Mushroom pies? Thin-crusted, buttered bread and milky coffee, at least?

The door opened and Nevane stood at attention, expecting the clan leader. It wasn't.

"You made it," said Rumari as he closed the door behind him. His hair was slicked back as if he'd recently bathed, his orange blossom scent supporting that assumption. Nevane found him greasy nonetheless, as he seemed to have risen through the ranks by quietly ensuring others above him fell.

He'd also been the clan lieutenant who brought her to Ifreda earlier, and the one whose subordinates had watched her from the walls at Turnbridge. Thoughts slid into place in Nevane's mind like a gear's teeth.

Nevane saluted, fist to shoulder. "A tough run, but I deliver."

"Well done." Rumari smiled, more teeth than humor. "Let's have it, then, and you can go rest until your next assignment."

The splinter of suspicion lodged at the base of her skull now bled. "With respect, I'm meant to give the package to the clan leader."

Rumari's smile remained fixed. "Ifreda is occupied, hence my presence instead."

"I don't mind waiting for her summons. The bench is comfortable enough."

"Very well." Rumari returned to the door, but instead of leaving, he locked it and turned around, his smile gone. "You're going to be difficult, I see. After the mess you made of things today, I'm not sure why I'm surprised."

"You put the bounty on my head," Nevane said, keeping her tone even. "Why?"

"For the map, you little fool." He stalked toward her, a knife appearing in his hand as if by magic. "The Iron Scorpions were supposed to take it from you quietly, and I'd split the proceeds with them. But once they informed me they'd failed, I had to change tactics."

"So you set everyone against me. Why not just let me get here and then take it?"

"Too risky. I might have been seen. Better that you have no safe gear to hide in, and everyone working to flush you out."

Nevane watched the knife. "But somehow word of the map spread, and half the people after me wanted the supposed treasure, too."

Rumari scowled. "Iron Scorpions have loose lips, it seems. And now I'm forced to deal with you here in our very own walls, instead of far away, where my hands could stay clean until I had the treasure safely stolen."

"You'll never be safe again," Nevane warned.

"I'll be gone before anyone figures out what happened. I'd hoped to remain here and steal the treasure in a more leisurely fashion, but needs must."

He slashed at her throat. Nevane leaped back, grabbing a pillow to use as a shield. She knocked away his hand once, twice. The blade tore through the linen fabric, sending a burst of downy feathers into the air. Rumari growled, swinging and stabbing with practiced skill, but he'd always been more for talk and scheming than bloodying his hands. Nevane had trained on the streets since she was old enough to run. Her foe fought for treasure; she fought for her life.

And yet, she was exhausted, and he was fresh as cool mint tea. The knife's point drew a line of bright pain across her chest. Blood beaded on her skin and seeped into her shirt. Another pillow was sacrificed to the cause, feathers drifting to the floor. She lured him into a thrust that went straight through the cloth, fabric circling his wrist. Twisting it, she yanked his hand into the wall and he dropped the knife. Before he could free himself, she kicked the weapon under the bench and kneed him in the kidney. His back arched as he grunted in pain, then threw her off.

"Why won't you die, curse you!" Rumari bellowed.

"Can't die," Nevane replied between ragged breaths. "Have to… deliver package. Courier's honor."

Rumari's hands curled into claws as he advanced on her again, eyes murderous. Nevane flipped her stingbag around so it hung in front of her chest like armor.

"Finish it, then, traitor," she taunted.

Rumari tackled her to the floor in a cloud of feathers. As soon as he touched the stingbag, the pain hit him. He tried to get up, get away, but she locked her arms around his neck, legs around his waist, pressing the bag against him. He headbutted her and stars filled her vision, but still she clung. His screams increased in pitch as the bag's magic intensified the hurt past bearing, and his efforts to free himself weakened.

Finally, an eternity later, he passed out, his chin digging into her collarbone. The scent of orange blossoms flooded her mouth; she hoped never to see the fruit again.

With a groan, Nevane rolled the unconscious lump off her, more feathers flying upward. She fought for air, sternly telling herself to get up. The longer she lay there, the harder it would be to rise. And if he awoke before she was gone… That did it.

Brushing feathers off her clothes and out of her hair, Nevane unlocked the door and checked for guards. No one. Apparently Rumari hadn't shared his little plan with more than a few of his loyal minions, if anyone. Or he didn't want to risk any witnesses, loyal or otherwise.

Nevane closed the door behind her and limped toward the clan leader's wing, head aching, chest burning from her wound, hoping against hope that no more surprises were about to pop out from behind a dark corner.

———

While Ifreda, the Black Dragonfly clan leader, had an impressively decorated receiving room where she heard formal petitions, she also had a suite of more modest offices in her private wing. At this hour, she'd likely be in bed, unless she was dealing with lingering concerns—or, for some odd reason, waiting for her missing courier to finally show up.

A pair of guards stopped Nevane, and an aide was dispatched to see whether Ifreda was receiving. The walls seemed to be trying to tilt sideways, or perhaps it was the floor. Blood loss? An aftereffect of the Steel Spider's spell? Or did she have a concussion from Rumari's hard head?

"She'll see you now," the aide said, and Nevane snapped to attention, eyes wide open through sheer willpower.

Ifreda sat behind a desk covered in enough paperwork to be a fire hazard. She was twice Nevane's age, with gray-streaked black hair and skin the color of teak. A dragonfly carved from a single enormous block of obsidian hung on the wall behind her, its wings reflecting the light of the beeswax candles flickering around the room. A thick rug muffled the shuffling of Nevane's boots as she presented herself for inspection between two overstuffed chairs, saluting and then clasping her hands behind her back.

"I believe you have a package for me, Nevane," Ifreda said. Sharp black eyes behind wireframe glasses pinned Nevane like a bug.

Wordlessly, Nevane produced the scroll case from her stingbag and set it on the center of the desk, then stepped away and resumed her stiff posture.

Ifreda regarded the case with a fond smile, twisting it open and removing the contents. "Here you are at last, my beauty," she said softly.

Nevane kept her gaze fixed on the dragonfly since she hadn't been dismissed or asked to sit.

"You took longer to deliver this than expected," Ifreda said. "Report."

How best to explain? Perhaps the clan leader wouldn't believe a mere courier over a lieutenant? So be it; she had no cause to hide the truth. "Rumari sent Iron Scorpions after me to steal the map, then when they failed, he put a bounty on my head, branding me a traitor. I was chased here by near every clan in the city."

"Who told you it was a map?" Ifreda asked, her tone mild enough to pluck a note of fear from Nevane's already taut nerves.

"Charys, of the Scarlet Beetle clan. Everyone else who accosted me after that seemed to know."

"A map to what, did they say?"

Nevane cleared her throat. "A secret Gate, filled with treasure."

Ifreda cracked a laugh like a whip. "I knew that wretched man was listening when I told my son about the map. What a worm. Where did you leave him?"

"An antechamber near the front gate. He may have woken up by now."

Ifreda tapped the scroll case on the edge of the desk. "I wonder if he'll make a run for it or try to cover his ass with lies." She gestured at the aide waiting by the door, whispering something into his ear when he approached. He raced off to do her bidding. Rumari, if he was caught, would no doubt have a worse day than Nevane.

"Do you want to know what this is?" Ifreda asked, lifting the curled paper so Nevane could see the back. It looked like old parchment, yellowed and delicate, and the candlelight rendered it translucent enough to show lines of ink on the other side.

"I'm just a courier," Nevane said. "My task is done. It's none of my business what that is."

"So modest. 'Just a courier' indeed, when you're the best we've got. It's why I sent you on this errand." Ifreda rose and slowly paced toward Nevane. "This is an item passed down in my family, but it was lost in my great-grandfather's time. The daft man used it as a bookmark, then lent the book to someone, and one thing led to another. People died before a new map could be crafted, the knowledge of how to reach the Gate wasn't passed on, and here we are. The book recently ended up in the possession of someone who realized what they had, and they offered to sell the map back to me."

"What if they lied?" Nevane asked. "You already paid them, I presume."

"I had reason to believe their story was true," Ifreda said. "Then, too, sometimes we must extend trust in the hopes of being rewarded accordingly. Honor is one of the few things any of us have that can't be taken from us unless we allow it."

After spending the day guarding her own honor, Nevane wanted to protest that it wasn't so simple, but she'd already let her tongue run away from her once. She held it now.

"The map does lead to a treasure," Ifreda said, leaning against the front of her desk. "Alas, as treasures go, it isn't what Rumari and the other clans might have hoped. The Gate is in a particular cave below Girruna, along the sea cliffs, accessible only at low tide. On the other side is a lush ocean retreat."

"A retreat?"

Ifreda chuckled. "A vacation home for my family. Always warm, and much enjoyed when the weather here turns cold. Good fishing, gentle surf, delicious fruits… I've never been there myself, but now I'll have the chance to go, and I can pass it on to others in the clan so it won't be lost forever."

The notion that she'd almost died over a map to a beach house did not endear Nevane to her clan leader, if she was being honest with herself. Better that she'd left the office thinking she had done some great service for her clan. Still, it wasn't Ifreda's fault that Rumari had schemed and made trouble. And she was sworn to deliver no matter the package. Her honor remained intact; that was its own treasure.

"My thanks again, Nevane," Ifreda said. "I don't suppose you might enjoy a little vacation at my retreat yourself?"

"You honor me, clan leader, but no," Nevane said. "I'll take the doorways of Girruna over a naked Gate trip any day."

"Reliable as the Clockspire, you are," Ifreda muttered, waving the scroll case dismissively. "Go on, then. See the medic before you hole up in your room for an age."

"By your will," Nevane replied, saluting. Her hand was on the door's handle when Ifreda called her name again.

"Have you ever considered becoming a clan lieutenant?" Ifreda asked. "I seem to find myself with an opening. More responsibility, less hurry-scurry all over the city?"

Nevane shook her head. "I'm honored, but I'll stop running when the gears of Girruna do."

That assertion elicited another chuckle from Ifreda, although Nevane had to admit, her own words reeked of bluster. Especially after the medic dosed her with a potion that tasted of burnt eels, then sent her to bed bandaged and poulticed up to her eyeballs. When she reached her room, she found a bowl full of steaming hot curried goat and rice awaiting her, which she consumed with great delight before the bells of the Clockspire sang her to sleep.

CHASING THE SUN

MARSHALL RYAN MARESCA

Zun had been told the rules of caretaking the Midpoint Lodge for the season. Several times. He swore sacred oaths that he understood those rules and would follow them without fail.

He completely failed.

Midpoint Lodge was a simple cabin built on Ogakiir Mountain, at about as high a point where one could possibly build such a thing. Just getting there from Zun's village, deep in the valley, took three days, and that was with the elaborate system of ropes, pulleys, and rising platforms that had been built a generation ago. Not that anyone else from the village would come up. He would be alone for the season, as was the custom. Someone had to be here to mind the lodge.

Midpoint Lodge was notable, and needed minding, for only two reasons.

One was the view, especially at sunrise, which was beyond spectacular. One could see across the range of the Mestikari Mountains, tinted rose as the sun came up, and beyond that the Obanidol Forest, and on clearest days the Esceri Ocean fading into the horizon. Even as Zun was toiling away, cursing the circumstances that brought him here, he was up with the sun every morning to see that view.

The other reason was, of course, why it was called "Midpoint."

Every morning, Zun trudged a mile up the slope to the receiving point: a simple platform with a net and cabinets. First, he made sure the net was clear, that no branches or animals or anything else had fallen into it, and confirmed it was correctly positioned. It was, of course, directly below the shimmering Gate that hung thirty feet in the air. If anyone came through, they needed a safe place to land. Next, the cabinets. He made sure they were properly latched, that no animals had gotten in, and that they were properly stocked with furs and boots. Six sets.

Then down the slope, past the lodge, and down another mile to the ledge. Check that the sled run was clear, that the sled and track hadn't been damaged in any way. That the ropes and knots were secure. Check the cabinets: empty each morning, just as the ones up top were stocked.

Then back to the lodge, where he tended to the fire, made sure there was enough wood to keep it going. Made sure that there was hot food at the ready, that the rooms were tidy, the beds were fresh. He aired out linens every day, swept every mote of dust, and made sure the lodge was ready to receive the Travelers.

Day after day, he kept to his tasks.

Sunrise. Slope. Net. Cabinets. Ledge. Run. Fire. Wood. Food. Beds. Sweep. Prepare.

Nothing else happened for eighty-seven days.

The eighty-eighth day started like the rest. Sunrise. Slope. Net. Cabinets. Ledge. Run. Fire. Wood. Food. Beds. Sweep.

And then the door flew open.

"Thank fuck and brightness!" someone shouted as bodies piled in. "You didn't tell me this place was colder than the tip of a Fjallaniri's cock!"

Five fur-clad people stomped in, tracking snow and dirt onto the freshly swept floor.

"I told you mountaintop in winter," another said. "What were you expecting?"

"I expect you to close the door and leave the cold out there."

The door slammed shut, and the five people tromped over to the fire and started stripping off the furs, leaving them on the floor as they did.

In the time it had taken Zun to react to that, they had made a wet mess of the floor, strewn their fur coats and boots about, and stripped completely naked to bask in front of the fire. Five of them: two men, two women, and one that, even naked, Zun wasn't entirely sure about. Every one of them, their skin—all different shades, like none Zun had ever seen in the village—was intricately tattooed along their arms, chests and backs.

He had been briefed on this, of course. The people who would come, they could be people of any shade he could imagine. They would not care one whit about being naked. They would be heavily tattooed. And they would treat the lodge with casual disregard, as if they owned it. Because, in a way, they did.

He had expected all of that, even though he hadn't been truly prepared to face the reality of these people arriving.

But what he really hadn't expected was there would be five of them.

"It'll be a pack of six," Zun had been told. "When anyone comes, if they come, they'll come in a group of six. That's how it always works."

But there were five.

"Is…is everything all right?" Zun managed to stammer out.

"Oh, the minder," one of the women—skin and eyes as dark as night —said. "Don't be gawking, man, bring us some food."

"I, it is, I just…"

"Are you dense, just…Charestiz, are the translation charms working?"

"They are, you're just rude," Charestiz said. That was the one where neither 'man' nor 'woman' seemed accurate or appropriate. "Sorry, sir, you'll have to forgive her."

"It's not his place to forgive us," one of the men said.

"He is a person who lives here, and we just stormed in." Charestiz got to their feet and wrapped one of the undercloths around their waist. Not that it made much difference in terms of modesty—already their incredibly long, golden hair covered a good portion of their body. "Hello, thank you for hosting us."

"It's our lodge," the first man—rich brown skin and blue eyes—said.

"It's the Travelers' lodge," the tawny-skinned woman said.

"And that's us."

"And this man does us the courtesy of making sure it's well kept for us," Charestiz said. "So the least we can do is treat… I'm sorry, what's your name?"

Zun realized they were addressing him. "Oh, it's Zun."

"Is that short for something?" the dark-skinned woman asked.

"Really, Amarel, do you do none of the reading about the places we're going?" the ruddy-skinned man asked.

"Of course I read them," she said. "Enough to not make the sort of social error that would get you killed or arrested. But this is our sanctuary."

Charestiz responded. "Tended by the Nedikari people, who traditionally use short names until they claim more syllables in their names, after going through milestone sacraments such as marriage or vestment or parenthood. Zun is a young man who has not yet claimed any, and you essentially belittled him."

"Oh, no, gentles, no offense was taken," Zun said. "I did not expect any of you fine people to know our ways."

"Are you thinking we're ignorant?" the brown-skinned man asked.

"Nothing of the sort," Zun said. "I simply would not have thought worldly people as yourself would even care about the ways of our village."

The ruddy-skinned man had stood up and clapped Zun on the shoulder. "Friend, it is because we are worldly that we care about all the ways of all sorts of villages. I am being rude. I'm Ghenii es Qarant, you know Charestiz and Amarel O'nge, and our friends there are Simon Marsh and Koshka Galazzo," indicating the other man and woman. "Thank you so much for your care and hospitality of this lodge. It is an important place for us, if you didn't know."

"I didn't," Zun said. "Or, I mean, of course it is, but I don't know why, or rather—"

"Breathe, Zun," Charestiz said. "Everything is fine."

"But do fetch us meals and robes, already," Amarel said. After a withering glare from Ghenii she added, "Please."

"Of course," Zun said. "And it is for five, yes? Or is there a sixth still out in the snow, perhaps? I was told it would be six."

"It's just five," Simon said, his tone saying volumes about how he felt about that. Zun had no desire to further interrogate that point, and went off to fetch what they needed.

He brought them everything they needed—that was his job—and after they ate he did everything he could to fulfill their further requests. As the evening drew on, Simon and Koshka went to the beds. Ghenii had Zun draw him a bath, and Amarel dozed off in a chair in front of the fire. Charestiz stayed in the main room of the lodge, examining every little detail of the furniture, decorations on the walls, before finally finding the leather-bound guest book and sitting in one of the divans to peruse it.

Zun had looked through the guest book—there was little else to do —but the entries were in languages he didn't understand or recognize. He had to presume they were even languages and not merely nonsense.

While they all slept or relaxed, he got to work cleaning up their mess and making the place presentable for the morning. "They'll probably only stay one night, if they come," he was told. The point, he understood, was to see the sunrise here and then move along. No one wanted to stay here.

"You know," Charestiz said as he was sweeping the floor in the common room. "You forgot something rather crucial."

"Did I?" he asked. He thought through all his duties and expectations. He had set everything as it should be. They were fed and cared for. What had he forgotten?

A light smile crossed Charestiz's lips. "The passcode for the lodge."

The passcode. He was supposed to confirm their identities as Travelers before letting them into the lodge. They had come in so quickly, with so much certainty, he hadn't even thought to question them.

"Right," he said. "Can you confirm?"

Charestiz rolled up the sleeve of their robe, showing the tattoo on their wrist of a compass over a sunset horizon. They were a Traveler, all right.

"The code for this lodge is… *nerifalio.*"

"That's correct," Zun said. "Can I ask you how long you've been, you know—"

"A Traveler?" Charestiz asked. "I'll be honest, I've lost track. I never quite figured out their calendar. Maybe five years?"

"Their calendar?"

"The Traveler calendar is universal for time and season regardless of methods used in other parts of the world." Firelight gleamed in their golden eyes as they leaned closer. "Have you ever been in any other part of the world?"

"Just the village in the valley, and then up here this season."

Charestiz's brow furrowed in thought, and then they hopped to their feet. "I think it's high time for some sleep. Want to see the sunrise in the morning. That's the whole point, yes? Thank you for your exemplary work, Zun. It is very appreciated."

***

Zun awoke when he always did, before the sun rose, as his guests crashed and stumbled through the lodge. They were also arguing —quite loudly—though he couldn't make any sense of it. He could hear them perfectly well, but none of them were speaking a language he understood. Nor did any of them seem to even be speaking the same language; each one sounded radically different.

As he emerged from his bunk to find them in the sitting room, that changed, the cacophony of their voices melting into intelligible speech.

"—we can't keep standing around, timing is everything."

"Exactly, so it's decided. Ah, morning Mister Zun." This was Ghenii, smiling broadly as Zun came out. "I trust you rested well."

"I slept fine," Zun said, confused at the way he was being spoken to. "I understand you'll be wanting to see the sunrise, and then be departing for the Gate down the slope. I'll have some tisane and cakes ready for you for the sunrise, out on the observation deck."

Expecting further instructions from each of them, he quickly reminded himself of who each of them were. Ghenii, the man with ruddy complexion and kind smile. Simon, brown skin, blue eyes, and disdainful air. Amarel, cool and distant with night-black skin and hair. Koshka, tawny skinned, and bright energy. And Charestiz, warm and golden in hair and eyes. They were the one coming directly to him, surely about to give him further orders.

"We've already fetched our breakfast, thank you," Charestiz said. They gestured to the six sets of cups and plates on a tray.

"Did your sixth Traveler arrive in the night?" Zun asked.

"No," Simon snapped.

"We were not expecting anyone else to arrive," Amarel added quickly.

Koshka said, "We were thinking, as we prepared this, that you would relish the sunrise on the deck with us."

"That is… very kind," Zun said. "I don't know if it's appropriate."

"It's appropriate if we say it is, and we do," Charestiz said. "Right?" They glared at Amarel and Simon.

"Yes, we do," Simon said.

"Indeed," Amarel added, as if the words caused her pain.

"It's settled. Come, Zun. Enjoy the glorious sunrise with us."

"As you wish," Zun said.

He had only ever gone up on the deck to make sure it was tidy. He had been told it was sacred to the Travelers, not a place for him. In here, there were six chairs and a wide, curved window that brought the whole stunning panorama of the horizon into sharp focus. It somehow made the astounding view even grander, more majestic, allowing one to see not merely more, but further and deeper. As they took their seats, Zun took the last one, still feeling like he was intruding.

The horizon was particularly clear that morning, and as the sun came up, the Esceri Ocean was more visible than ever, the light dancing off the water as it reflected on the snow-capped mountains.

"Are you all right?" Koshka, who had been sitting next to him, asked, and he realized he had been weeping.

"Sorry, I just… I've never seen the ocean, not really. It's… it's a blessing to get to see something as wondrous as this. Thank you for sharing it with me."

"Absolutely," she said, getting up. "Now, come, time is of essence."

"Come?" he asked. "Oh, yes, to the sled run. You're all heading there now? You need me to come with you?"

"We absolutely do," Ghenii said. "It's been decided."

This must have been part of his duties that he hadn't been properly briefed on, but it made perfect sense. They would go down to the sled run so they could get to their next gate, and they would leave the furs and other clothes behind, so it made sense that he would gather them, retrieve the sled, and get things back to their proper state for the next Travelers.

He should have expected that.

Dressed to trek the snowy trail, he led them down to the sled run. He had checked the track every day, of course, made sure everything was in working order. He had tested it yesterday, like every day, and the sled had run down the track to the ledge perfectly.

"Here you are," he said, as he prepared a small fire in the pit near the top of the track. "Let me know if I can be of further assistance."

"You can, Zun," Charestiz said and they took off their furs and packed them in the bin next to the top of the sled. "In fact we need you."

"I'm here to serve," Zun said.

"You were right when we arrived," Ghenii said. "This particular journey we're on, the one that starts here with this sunrise? It needs six people."

"But our sixth got sick—" Simon snarled.

"Caught Indinarin fever in the Slonyt marshes—" continued Amarel.

"And we couldn't delay. Timing is everything here, Zun," Ghenii said. "But, you see… it needs six."

"Specifically," Koshka said, coming up behind Zun. "This sled has six seats." She reached around his waist and pulled off his shirt.

"Really, it's quite brisk," Zun said, not sure what was happening.

"Six seats," Charestiz said. "And we need the weight and balance of six people for it to work." They said this while pulling off Zun's trousers.

"Why are you undressing me, gentles?" Zun asked. "What are you saying here?"

"We're saying we *jhuxutek* need you, boy!" Simon said, the one word he said apparently not translatable by their charms. "So get in the seat!"

Ghenii and Amarel all but lifted him up by the arms and guided him onto the sled, in the seat next to Charestiz. The rest got into the sled.

"No, this isn't right, I can't— I have a duty—"

Charestiz took his hand and squeezed. "It's all right. Your duty is to the Travelers, and we need you here. With you, we all journey on. Without you, it could go horribly wrong."

"Horribly—oh—oh I am not sure—" He had always understood the principle of the sled run here, though he never considered what it would mean to be in the sled. What it would entail.

"Here we go!" Koshka said, and she pulled the release on the sled.

The sled rocketed down the run, gaining velocity ever faster to the ledge. It needed speed, it needed weight—and Zun could even understand it needed balance, but he wasn't prepared for that to mean him as the wind rushed and the cold air bit into his skin and they went faster and faster to the end of the run and the ledge and beyond that nothing but nothing but open air as they hit the end of the run—

The sled itself hit the stop, exactly as it was supposed to, and the six of them went flying out of their seats, over the ledge, out into the open sky.

Their flight arced high, and for just a moment, one single astounding moment, they just floated as if nothing in the world could touch them.

And then they started to fall.

Not just fall. Plummet.

Hands grabbed Zun's—he wasn't even sure whose—and someone shouted "There!"

Zun looked, and there, floating in the sky amid the literally breathtaking view of the mountains and the valley, was the glow of the Gate. Just in the middle of the air, too far from the ledge for anyone to reach with a mere jump.

And now they were rushing toward the Gate, faster and faster and Zun had no idea what was happening and it was thrilling and astounding and terrifying and if the others weren't holding onto him he wouldn't know what to do.

Then their cluster of six clutching bodies entered the Gate. For another moment, Zun felt like he was nowhere and everywhere and nothing and everything and—

Their six bodies went rolling out onto soft, orange sand.

"Amazing!" Charestiz said.

"Am I dead?" Zun asked. Now, all of a sudden he was warm, a salty smell on the air as the sun peeked over the horizon of the wide ocean in front of him. "Is this the place of final reward?" He couldn't believe it was right there, the waves rolling up to him, water just kissing his fingers as they sunk into the sand. This astounding place could only be the promised next life.

"No, you're not dead," Ghenii said.

"Then where is this?"

"This," Charestiz said, "is Telo-Sre-Nava."

ZUN WAS IN A DAZE OF WONDER AS CHARESTIZ AND THE OTHERS LED him along: first to a trunk at the base of the portal—which had what appeared to be several warning signs surrounding it—where they retrieved robes and sandals. Then off the beach along a cobble path, then up steps to a high ridge, where he found himself in a vibrant and bustling city. Most of the folks around them were dressed in bright, vibrant colors, almost all of them dark mahogany skinned, darker than even Amarel.

Zun knew he was gawking and staring, just agog at being somewhere else in the world, somewhere other than his village or the lodge.

They led him to a building with a symbol embossed on the door similar to the tattoos on everyone's wrist. They knocked, whispered something to the porter—who eyed Zun oddly—and were admitted. After some further conversation with the porter, where Zun couldn't understand a word the porter was saying—but he was also far too stunned to properly pay attention—they were brought to a balcony and seated at a table that gave them an overlook view of the ocean. Cool drinks, bright fruits and sticky pastries were put in front of them, which the others all started eating.

"Go on, Zun," Ghenii encouraged him. "You really have to try it."

That cracked the reverie Zun had been in. "I'm sorry, but… what is happening? Where are we?"

"We told you," Simon said. "Telo-Sre-Nava."

"Which is what?"

"Amarel, you're the geographer."

She put down her drink. "It's a city on a large island, about, hmmm, several thousand miles south of your village. And a little west, of course. Which is why the sun has just come up now."

"You do know how the sun works, don't you?" Koshka asked.

"How the sun works?" Zun asked. "It's… it's the sun. It rises in the morning, it sets at dusk, and it comes back each day. I don't understand the question."

"And it moves to the west over the day, yes?" Koshka asked. "So here, west of your village and the lodge, when the sun rose there, it hadn't yet risen here. And when the sun will set at the lodge, it won't have set here yet. Get it?"

"Not at all!" Zun said.

"Don't worry about that," Charestiz said. The porter had brought them a box, which they placed on their lap and opened up. "The point is you'll be with us, and we know where we're going. You don't have to worry about the details. Just enjoy."

"If you say." Zun picked up a pastry and took a bite. Like nothing he had ever tasted in his life. He didn't even have the words to describe it.

"But," Charestiz said. "We'll want to make your journey a little easier. This might sting."

They took his hand and pulled it toward them, exposing his wrist. Then they clamped a strange object around his wrist. His skin burnt with searing pain, like nothing Zun had ever experienced before. He screamed in absolute terror.

"Is everything all right, sir?" the porter said, approaching.

"No it's not all right, that was very—"

"Nothing to worry about," Ghenii said. "It's always a little jarring."

"Jarring? Sting?" Zun shouted. "That was—"

The object—which resembled a bracelet or a shackle—released his wrist and fell into Charestiz's hand. They put it back in the box and handed it to the porter.

"Thank you for this, Tg'ich. Log this under my account."

"As you wish, *mixten*," the porter said, taking it away.

"What was all that?" Zun asked. "And… wait, I can understand him now? Did he start speaking like you or—"

"None of us speak the same language," Simon said. "We're all from different parts of the world, if that wasn't obvious."

"But I… but you…"

Charestiz took Zun's hand and turned it over. On his wrist was the same tattoo that they had: the compass over the sunset.

"No, no," Zun said. "I'm not a Traveler, I'm just a warden of the lodge…"

"Today you are," Ghenii said. "And that has the translation charm in it, so you can understand everyone, and everyone can understand you. It'll make it easier."

"But, no, I have a duty—"

Koshka reached over and touched Zun on the shoulder. "Think of it as just for today. Join us until the sun sets."

"Just today?"

"One day," Charestiz said. "Then you can decide what to do next."

Zun looked around at the others, who all gave him approving looks. Even Simon and Amarel.

"If you all approve, then I suppose it's all right," he said. "One day."

"Then eat up," Koshka said. "Because the Summer Soar Festival is beginning!"

***

Zun didn't understand how it was summer. Amarel did try to explain it with a few pieces of fruit, but the explanation was beyond him. What did matter was the Summer Soar, in which the people of Telo-Sre-Nava sang and danced in the streets, and more importantly, flew all manner of kites.

Kites were not a thing in Zun's village, but seeing the sky filled with the flying streams of cloth and color, seeing these people's joy, getting to hold onto a kite's cord and feel the wind pull him… it was like nothing he had ever known.

He had been learning a dance from some of the locals when Ghenii tapped him on the shoulder.

"Come, it's time."

"Time?"

"For the next adventure."

They all piled into a carriage pulled by a pair of stout young men, who ran them through the city to a building that looked almost like a temple. They pushed through the doors, and then past a short line of people. Simon held up his wrist to an officiant, saying, "Sorry, have to claim privilege here."

"We have a schedule, sir," the officiant said.

"Sunchase," Koshka said firmly. She then whispered something in the officiant's ear.

"Very well," the officiant said. "Traveler's Privilege, let them through."

They were let through a doorway, past the waiting line who scowled at them, to a wide room with another portal shimmering in front of them.

"Come on!" Charestiz said, taking off their robe and sandals, leaving them in a cabinet near the portal. Zun did the same, realizing that it was the first time he was undressing himself in front of them all. But in this moment, with them all doing it as well, it felt… nowhere near as unnatural as he had presumed it would have.

"All at once," Amarel said, and they linked arms and stepped through the portal.

This one wasn't as jarring or disorienting, but still Zun felt himself —if ever so briefly—to be everywhere and nowhere all at once—before stepping out into a room that was warm and inviting, with lit candles and flowing, colorful drapes. It was also an occupied room.

"Oh, hello!" an old woman with bright white hair said, beaming at the six of them. A group of other people—also in their later years, were behind her, all undressing out of sets of fine clothing. "In from Telo-Sre-Nava? How is it?"

"Glorious," Amarel said. She held up her tattooed arm, and the old woman showed the same one on her arm. "Can we exchange?" Amarel asked.

"Of course," the old woman said, handing Amarel her richly embroidered coat as she removed it. "Good weather there?"

"Clear and bright," Simon said, taking the pants offered by one of the others in their groups.

"Are you sunchasing?" another old woman asked. Zun noticed these folks, they were covered in tattoos. He wondered what kind of story, what kind of journey, they all told.

"Started with the sunrise at Midpoint," Ghenii said. "Just on our third stop."

"Oh, that's a young person's game," the first woman said. "I did three sunchases in my youth. Longest I made it was seven stops. Rhojirin may have the record!"

The tiny-framed, wild-haired old man who gave Zun his tunic and skirt chuckled. "Once made fourteen stops, after I drank a mug of *yestua* root tisane in J'Ki'nak! Don't recommend it though! My heart was never the same!"

"We're planning for eight," Simon said. The six of them were now all dressed in the fine clothing of the elder Travelers, who waved as they entered the Gate.

"Where are we?" Zun asked.

"Gottinsholmikkaster," Charestiz said. "In the kingdom of Sjalstinat."

That meant nothing to Zun, but as they emerged from the receiving room, a group of officials looked them over, confirmed their tattoos, recorded their names in ledgers, inspected the inside of their mouths and ears, and then let them out into the city. The sun was bright in the crisp, cool air, and Zun was again in wonder as they were led first to a lodge. A flash of their tattoos and a whispered word from Charestiz granted them entrance, and they were fed smoked fish and simmered eggs and salty drinks before they were loaded onto a carriage and brought out of town.

Their destination, which they reached when the sun was high in the sky, was a violet lake, where hundreds of grand, elegant looking birds with orange and pink feathers gathered in an enormous flock. With a whistled call from Ghenii, the flock all took flight, almost choking the sky with their majestic wings. They loaded into the carriage and followed the flight of birds until they reached a town, where they checked in with a gatehouse official who took their names and marked their departure. They left their fine clothes in a wardrobe and jumped into the next Gate.

The Gate brought them to a Traveler Clubhouse in Hakelinak. Their credentials—tattoos and a whispered word from Charestiz—granted them silk robes and access to the house, and they went to the rooftop. They were served hot drinks that were both bitter and sweet at once, and they sat in the hot, dry air as the sun rose above them.

The next Gate brought them to Lollochfan, where the only clothes they were given were burlap sacks. But that was perfect, as they emerged from the Gate customhouse to find a morning downpour had just hit, and the locals—all also in their burlap sacks—were celebrating and carousing in the mud-filled streets. They all covered themselves in mud, threw it at each other while laughing and shouting, and ran through the streets with the townsfolk until they reached a great mud pit, which everyone dove into.

The next Gate—which they emerged from completely clean despite entering coated in mud—took them to Andexinadi. The locals—after confirming they were authentic travelers with their tattoos and Charestiz whispering the passcode—fed them smoked meats that were incredibly spicy, and then told them the day was the Festival of the Givalesa. The *givalesa*, it turned out, were great goat-like animals that they let loose into the streets, and then chased into a stampeding herd that thundered through the city. After the running of the *givalesa*, there was a raucous celebration in the city square, where all the local folks in *givalesa* masks ran through the crowd demanding kisses from every random stranger.

"It's considered rude to deny them a kiss," Koshka told Zun, and the six of them proved to be anything but rude, all giving kisses to several of the masked revelers.

Zun was wondering what that would lead to when they dashed off to a fountain on the edge of town, diving into the next Gate.

Bringing them to Rescinal, where they emerged in the center of town. The Rescinali people in the town square gave an excited cheer to see them, dressing the Travelers by giving them some of their own clothing. They were escorted to a great hall—embossed with the Travelers' symbol over the door—where they were brought plates after plates of the most incredible food Zun had ever tasted. On the stage in front of them, the Rescinali performed a vibrant opera, with elaborate dances and glorious costumes, which seemed to be a story of praise and worship of the Travelers. Zun had also been assured that this was the penultimate career performance of the grandest diva of the Rescinali stage, Glyneth Blackthorne Koromov, before her glorious retirement.

Somewhere during this performance, Zun realized it was still daylight.

It had been daylight since they left Midpoint Lodge.

But it had been—he had no idea how long it had been.

"How is that possible?" he asked Charestiz when the performance ended.

"Because that's what we're doing. We're sunchasing. When the sun sets in one part of the world, it rises in another. We keep going to a new place where the sun is just coming up, stretching out the day as long as we can stand. How are you holding up?"

"I have no idea," Zun said. He felt he should be exhausted, yet he wanted to keep seeing things, keep doing things. "You said I should stay with you for the day, and this has been the longest day of my life, and… I don't want it to end."

"Sooner or later, we have to surrender to sleep, of course," Ghenii said. "This particular chase, we planned for eight stops. And we timed it, of course, so we would see the Summer Soar, and the Mud Gala, and the Givalesa, this performance by Koromov, and—oh, we should move!"

And they ran to another Gate, giving their clothes back to the Rescinali who had gifted them, and dove through to arrive in Al'inaset-kuu. There—after a thorough inspection at a customs point that involved examination of every inch of their bodies—they found themselves dressed in riding uniforms and put on camels. They raced across the desert—and it was actually a race, a point Zun didn't realize at first—until they reached the city of Yafi'naq. They had apparently done very well in the race, as Zun was given a purse filled with more silver coins than he had ever seen in his life.

"You can't take that through the Gate, remember," Simon said, gently but pointedly.

Zun understood, and gave coins to every beggar and child and mother they passed on the way to the gatehouse.

They came through that Gate to Salocin, a city in Griasta, where it seemed to be a lazy, quiet day. The Griastans gave them cordial regard as they wound their way through the curving streets, down past the stonework houses to the beach, after stopping at a Traveler chapterhouse where Charestiz's whispered word yielded them a handful of local currency. On the beach, they all sat in the sand, and a vendor brought them succulent grilled meats on skewers, and they ate quietly while watching the sun set into the ocean.

Simon, Amarel, and Koshka had all fallen asleep in the sand, their bodies curled up with each other. Ghenii had stripped out of his clothes and went into the water to swim.

"So," Charestiz said to Zun. "That was your day with us. What do you want to do now?"

"I have to get back to the lodge, right?" Zun said.

"Is that what you want?"

"I mean, I have a duty. The Trav—that is, all of you—the village will be punished if I'm not there to mind it."

"Is going back what *you* want?" Charestiz's golden eyes seemed to bore into him with this question.

Zun thought for a moment. "I've tasted more of the world than I ever dreamed possible. And yet, I—" He hesitated, not sure if he could say what he was feeling. Not sure if he was allowed to even feel it, let alone put it to words.

Seeming to sense his hesitance, Charestiz spoke further. "Let me tell you something, Zun. Five years ago, by my reckoning, I was hired to mind a Traveler chapterhouse in my home city. And I watched these grand, fine people who came and went, telling these incredible stories of majestic places, and I realized... why shouldn't I also have that? Why can't I do that?"

"So you joined the Travelers?"

"No, Zun. I decided to be one." They moved closer, speaking in a whisper, and it was clear to Zun that he was being told an intimate secret. "I marked my wrist as I had seen it done and went through a Gate to wherever it would take me. Simon, Amarel, Koshka, Ghenii—all of us were the same as you, hired or assigned—or sentenced—to tend to Traveler's spaces, and we each realized that wasn't what we wanted. We wanted to see everything instead of being a caretaker to a single space.

So we… simply chose to. And we all found each other. And today…we found you." Their voice broke as they said this, and Zun realized this meant as much—if not more—to them as it did to him.

It was impossible, though.

"But if I don't go back, my village will be punished—"

"Not really," Charestiz said, patting his shoulder. "The Traveler's agents will talk a rough talk for a bit and then issue a warning and insist a new caretaker needs to go to the lodge, but they won't actually punish or sanction the village. They're never that cruel or capricious. Nothing will happen to them if you don't return. But if you want to, I can give you directions to a Gate that will bring you to a town about three days' ride from your village. You can go home, if you want."

"I want…" Zun said, tears streaming from the pure relief of just letting himself say it. He had never before truly let himself say what he wanted. He had never before in his life felt like he was allowed. Charestiz was the first person who had ever even asked him. "I want to see it all. I want to go everywhere. I want to be one of you."

"Then welcome, Traveler," Charestiz said. "You're one of us."

"Just like that?" he asked.

"You decided. That's all it takes."

"So…no ceremony or induction?"

"Oh, you'll want to go to the chapterhouse, read through the journals, and learn the navigation maps, so you can make your own journeys." They tapped the tattoo on his wrist. "That is your pass to every part of the world, and all the resources and credit that goes with the Travelers."

"And I need to learn the passcodes," he said. "I imagine there are quite a lot."

Charestiz laughed. "Do you want to know the biggest secret of the Travelers? The passcode is *nerifalio*."

"For the Midpoint Lodge."

"For *everywhere*," Charestiz said. "It really is that simple, Zun."

Zun laughed at the utter absurdity of it, that the key to unlock the whole world was just that easy, and he had had it all this time. And that unlocked another thought, which was now so obvious to him.

"Zunichar," he said. "After all this, I feel like I have fulfilled a sacrament of some sort, and that should be marked with more syllables to my name. So if you don't mind, it's tradition—"

"To incorporate part of the name of one who aided you," Charestiz said. "I'm beyond honored, Zunichar."

Zunichar laid back in the sand, looking up at the near infinite stars spread across the glorious black of night, and dreamed of the possibilities ahead of him.

SCHEMES, FACTIONS, AND CULTURE

NON-FICTION ESSAY BY
MICHAEL R. UNDERWOOD

Cultural worldbuilding informs plotting, characterization, and more. How do you build cultures and societies that set you up for political storytelling? What other tools can you use to make it easier to put together faction conflict and worldbuilding that embeds a character in overlapping and conflicting groups?

Content note: Because this is an essay about power and politics, it discusses sensitive topics such as systems of oppression and ways that people and groups accumulate and wield power; how power is used against marginalized people; and related issues of racism, nationalism, and religion.

Overview/what to expect:

- Power, broadly: the ability to make people do things or make things happen. This essay describes how it manifests in cultures and perpetuates itself, and also explores the interests of those that hold it.
- Politics: the use of power to organize or control groups and direct their actions, and how people negotiate its uses
- Worldbuilding: mostly cultural vs. physical/geographical/cosmological

- Plotting tools from role-playing games (RPGs), especially with regard to faction interactions and building plot from worldbuilding

Power and Politics

Good storytelling requires conflict, and identifying power—its sources, history, and imbalance—creates built-in conflict that can help a world feel lived in and relatable.

WHAT ARE THE TYPES AND SOURCES OF POWER IN A CULTURE OR GROUP?

- Force (military, police, magic)
- Systems (bureaucracy, money, influence)
- Ideology (faith, nationalism)

WHAT ARE THE POWER CENTERS IN YOUR PROJECT'S SETTING?

- How do they relate to one another, compete with one another, or overlap?
- Is the monarch also the head priest?
- Does the general of the army wish to overthrow the peace-loving prime minister?

CONSIDER THE FOLLOWING QUESTIONS ABOUT HOW POWER IS ACQUIRED and used in your story:

- How is power enforced? The threat of power being used is often enough to get what you want, but when power is challenged, coercion and/or violence may be used to punish dissent and reinscribe authority.

- How are your characters attempting to accumulate or wield power? Methods might include accessing institutional power or individual power, gaining power within a majority group or official system, or engaging with a system that is outside of what is approved
- Unapproved power sources might include revolutionary or opposition groups, a minority or oppressed group, a system or group unknown to the mainstream powers).
- How has the balance of power changed recently and over the past few years or decades?
- What generational projects are underway from what factions or groups, using what methods, and who is responding? *Interesting stories often happen at times of change, but big change usually follows small, slow change.*
- Is power applied overtly or covertly? Covert uses of power might include cryptocracy and corruption as opposed to overt use such as open oligarchy. Racist dog whistles and stochastic terrorism would be covert, whereas a white supremacist coup would be overt.

Popular Culture and Folklore in Worldbuilding

Few cultural elements are created in a vacuum. Folklore about medical practice likely developed alongside folklore about agricultural practice, for example. How are they interconnected? How do the hero legends of the culture reflect its ideas about what heroism means and what important technologies/blessings the culture needed to become who they are?

The Greeks tell the story of Prometheus stealing fire, an essential blessing, from the gods and giving it to humanity. But they also tell of Prometheus facing eternal punishment for that theft. What does that say about how the ancient Greeks viewed humanity's relationship with the gods?

Thinking about what elements of culture should resonate with one another and which elements make sense to be in tension can help develop a world that feels real. How does a civilization's popular culture reflect or challenge the ideology being propagated from power centers?

The following comparisons and questions provide some guided exploration:

- Compare the nationalism/jingoism themes in the television show *24* or the 2014 film *American Sniper* to the anti-imperialism themes in the Marvel films *Black Panther* and *Thor: Ragnarok*. Both types are huge pop culture phenomena but with different orientations.
- Compare these Marvel movies to outsider/independent films even more critical of imperialism because they're not commercially beholden to majority culture/large corporations. How much did being made as part of a multinational corporate media company influence the execution and/or reception of the work?
- In your setting, is theater a site of rebellion, a site of contestation, or a place where ideology is baked into cultural production? If all three, how do they interact? Are they performed in different places, different times? Are both revolutionary/subversive works and propaganda written by the same people? Are there works that are both at the same time, and how does that tension play out in your story?
- How do systems of power capture and defang revolutionary/reform movements to ensure that not that much really changes and the powerful stay in power? What token concessions do they make in order to disperse the pressure that might otherwise lead to widespread revolutionary action?
- How do the powerful exert soft control without violence/coercion? Through patronage and propaganda? Through overt control via censorship?
- How do sports in your story reflect the culture's history of warfare and/or martial traditions? Are they tied to one another like they are in the USA (e.g., through shared rhetoric, training for nationalism, honoring the military during/before NFL games in paid partnerships with the US military).

. . .

EXERCISE #1

- Apply the elements of this section to one of your works directly. Pick a protagonist or a faction in your story/setting and answer the following questions: How are your characters attempting to accumulate or wield power?
- Why do they seek power and what will they do with it?
- How has the balance of power changed recently and over the past few years/decades?
- Is power exercised overtly or covertly?

Deep Worldbuilding

Deep worldbuilding describes work that holds up to interrogation. It's more than surface level and is believably coherent. A creator who did deep worldbuilding would be able to respond to very specific questions such as the following:

- How does your version of fantasy Japan have enough hard metal and the population to be able to outfit a 10,000-person army with mecha-suits in a steampunk version of the 1800s?
- If only women are allowed to read in your kingdom, why is it still a patriarchy with patrilineal inheritance?

Some readers won't interrogate a setting in this way and don't care whether the worldbuilding is deep, preferring breadth over depth. Some worldbuilding choices are believable for one person and not for another. And sometimes you're not trying to get that much out of the worldbuilding. But as with all things, be conscious in your choices.

All that said, you don't have to be overly strict when trying for believability. Wonder Woman's invisible jet is an example of one of those things that are there because they're awesome/fun, and how/why they work doesn't matter. It's okay to follow the rule of cool. If something is set dressing, the reasoning for it probably doesn't have to be as rigorous, because it's not load-bearing. Rule of cool is a fine guiding star, just be deliberate and understand what audience you're writing for and how to set and then meet those expectations.

When deciding how deep is deep enough, keep the Scalzi Rule (associated with author John Scalzi) in mind: Ask why twice, and have an answer for each layer that's satisfying. For example:

Q1 – Why do the supernatural beings not outright take over the world?

A1 – There aren't enough of them to keep or maintain direct control in the modern age.

Q2 – Why?

A2 – Because it takes X many humans to support a vampire and here's some math that limits the number of vampires. Also, vampires are susceptible to guns, UV lights, and other limits on their power.

ANOTHER EXAMPLE:

Q1 – Why don't the supernatural beings take over?

A1 – I don't want them to be in charge.

Q2 – Okay, why don't *they* want to be in charge, or what is keeping the ones that do want to be in charge from assuming power?

A2 – They prefer shadow influence over direct control. Vlad tried open rule, but it didn't work out very well.

NOT EVERYTHING NEEDS TO HAVE DEEP WORLDBUILDING. MY background leads me to want deep worldbuilding with regard to culture, but let me repeat: Not every part of your worldbuilding needs to be rigorous. It's nearly impossible to rigorously describe or display every single aspect of a culture, especially if your focus as a storyteller is elsewhere. No one in our world knows everything about every culture and place on Earth.

Another thing to keep in mind: Different subgenres have different expectations of rigor for various parts of worldbuilding. Consider audience expectations in, say, space opera vs. hard SF (i.e., physical science–focused SF with high focus on plausible future technology.

. . .

EXERCISE #2

Apply the Scalzi Rule to a central element of your worldbuilding and ask a question that challenges its assumptions or believability. Then when you've answered that, ask yourself a follow-up question questioning the assumptions of *that* answer.

Are you satisfied with your second answer? If not, consider what interactions and assumptions you may want to adjust to feel confident that this central pillar of your worldbuilding holds up to interrogation in the way you want it to.

You might then ask a third question since the answer to the second question might not be rigorous enough for your own satisfaction even if it's true and a valid choice as a storyteller.

Tools for Worldbuilding Schemes and Factions

So, say you have your protagonists, they have a group, and they're seeking to wield power and undermine other systems of power. How do you show what the other factions are doing in a world/setting with political intrigue? Some possible solutions:

- Show them spying on those factions, getting glimpses via POV characters.
- Cut away to other characters to show movement in the shadows or more directly.
- Have characters see part of the story but not the whole picture.
- Let alliances and double-crosses show the control of information.

There's a broad overlap between the creative work of building a setting and a plot for a work of fiction and doing so for a table-top role-playing game (TTRPG) campaign or one-shot as the game master (GM). Therefore, game tools for creating believable factions or group conflicts can help you devise similar worldbuilding elements for your story.

A great source for inspiration and structure for developing schemes/plots is *Apocalypse World* (Vincent and Meguey Baker;

www.apocalypse-world.com), a post-apocalyptic game heavy on improvisation, role-playing, and the potential for player-versus-player conflict. Its fronts system helps GMs construct scenarios where different types of threats come at the protagonists from different directions.

Here's how it works: If there's a physical external threat, such as a marauding gang coming for the protagonist's town, the GM complements that with a social internal threat, such as a nascent religious movement challenging local leadership.

Every threat has its own clock representing the beats of what will happen if the protagonists don't intervene. *Apocalypse World* has clocks representing stages of a threat vector's plan: 3pm, 6pm, 9pm, 10pm, 11pm, midnight. There is a snowball effect from 9pm to midnight, during which things move faster, it's very hard to fully stop the threat, and major damage will be inflicted.

To use this clock system, write out several steps of a plan and think about how the plan advances at certain points (e.g., the times) if the protagonist doesn't intercede.

Develop different types of antagonism to deploy in order to challenge the protagonists along different axes and keep the story from being too repetitive or two-dimensional (e.g., all fight scenes, all the time). To accomplish that, consider the following questions:

- How do the different fronts interact?
- Does the growth of the religious movement undermine the local power and make it easier for the warlord to succeed?
- Does the growth of the religious movement bring in pilgrims that then provide new recruits for the city watch that make it *harder* for the warlord to take over?
- Do the protagonists pit the two against one another? Do they make a deal with the religious leader for short-term benefit, understanding or not knowing that they're laying the groundwork for the religious leader to exert more influence in the city?
- Were the religious leader and the warlord working together the whole time?

This framework is also useful for making the antagonist feel like the protagonist of their own story, though it's likely the protagonist and antagonist will be one another's greatest challenges.

How would other forces/systems—such as a religious movement versus a warlord, as in the example—get in the antagonist's way even if the protagonist does not?

EXERCISE #3

Pick a villain or faction in your story and write out several steps of their plan and think about it will advance at certain points of the story if the protagonist or someone else doesn't intercede.

EXAMPLE #1: MARAUDERS

Here's an example countdown clock for several threats, from the inciting incident through midnight (total victory for the antagonist)

3pm: The marauders strike a convoy bringing supplies to a community.

6pm: The warlord sends an infiltrator, posing as a survivor from the convoy, to bring down the community's defenses.

9pm: The warlord's infiltrator learns the community's defenses.

10pm: The infiltrator poisons the guards as the warlord's crew attacks at night.

11pm: The warlord kills or destroys anyone that could stop him from controlling the community.

Midnight: The warlord is the unchallenged tyrant of the community.

EXAMPLE #2: CULT

3pm: A charismatic outsider arrives in the community, claiming to be able to heal the sick.

6pm: The outsider heals a member of the community and gains acclaim for their miracle.

9pm: The outsider attracts a following as more people get sick—because the outsider's power just re-distributes the disease.

10pm: The community comes to doubt their leader as the disease spreads despite the increasingly-beloved efforts.

11pm: The outsider promises he can save everyone, but only if he can operate unchallenged. The outsider's zealots depose the community's leader.

Midnight: Now in complete control of the community, the cult leader sends his diseased followers to spread the good news of his power.

OTHER OPTIONS TO VARY THE VECTORS OF ANTAGONISM WOULD BE A food shortage, a natural disease, or a power struggle between existing factions in the community. If all of the vectors of antagonism are along the same axis (external and violent or interpersonal within the community) then your story may feel flatter and not give you the opportunity to round out your setting.

For greater dramatic texture, think about how the threats coming at characters or a group along several fronts of antagonism might interconnect and support or interfere with one another. Does the cult leader's undermining of the community make it easier for the warlord's infiltrator to poison the guards, or does the infiltrator get swayed by the cult leader and abandon his mission, prompting the warlord to take more desperate action? When and how do the protagonists interfere with these plans and how do the respective antagonists respond?

Of course, even a great scheme system won't work if you don't populate it with compelling factions. The game *Blades in the Dark* (John Harper; www.evilhat.com/product/blades-in-the-dark/) offers some good tools for building a web of factions.

Blades in the Dark is set in the industrial fantasy city of Duskwall, where you play as a brand-new gang trying to carve out territory, get rich, or die trying. Because every block is claimed as someone's turf, your gang can't advance without stealing turf from other factions. This means that faction relationships are very important. Here are some ways the game mechanizes this that I think can be stolen and implemented.

Rather than detailing every member of a faction, write one or two sentences describing the faction's identity/their deal. Give them an immediate or top priority, a leader or front-person character that represents what the faction is about, and then a couple of that faction's goals that they are actively working toward.

Factions in *Blades in the Dark* also have a tier rating, representing their relative scale and power. Tiers range from 0 to V (using Roman numerals). A Tier IV faction will likely be much broader in their reach and their ambitions than a Tier I gang just getting their footing.

Blades in the Dark represents this with a clock, but for our purposes, you could spell it out as a front and write the timeline to have your story beats determined. You can use different clocks of different sizes to represent simpler or more complicated projects (an *Apocalypse World* front clock has a 6-step clock, or 6-clock in Blades' terminology).

As you build your faction list, you also note faction alliances, including relationships up and down the city's hierarchy (e.g., small gangs allied against bigger gangs).

In play, the players' gang will gain and lose status with other factions, which will then move against or assist the player faction. Think about what factions could be allies to your main characters and which are opposed. How will the faction relationships change throughout the story?

In a political story, this type of efficient but interconnected faction design can help move the story along and help generate and structure side-plots. And the faction structure can be adjusted for any number of settings from a personal, Regency story of manners, to high school cliques in a YA novel, to various squadrons/units in a war story, and so on.

EXAMPLE FACTION: THE FORGOTTEN (TIER I)

Description: The Forgotten are the last survivors of an Imperial battalion betrayed by the Immortal Emperor in the last days of the conquest of Skovlan

Goals: Interrogate Baron VanTaeb (8-step clock), locate other betrayed veterans and recruit them (6-step clock)

Turf: A flophouse frequented by veterans down on their luck, a dingy bar in a flooded cellar

Prominent members: Ring Dalmore (they/them), a sergeant haunted by the memory of their fallen squadron (*determined, connected, compassionate*).

Notable assets: Several braces of rifles, military-grade ghost-hunting gear (gas masks, lightning hooks, spirit charms), gas grenades, trenching tools, maps of Skovlan.

Quirks: Several of the Forgotten are undocumented, listed as killed in action. Most are literally haunted by ghosts that returned to the city with them when they smuggled themselves back into Duskwall. They're all skilled fighters, more than a match one-on-one for most cops or street toughs.

Allies: The Strange Friends are allies of Ring's; the Red Sashes count many veterans in their number and respect the Forgotten's martial prowess.

Enemies: Ulf Irnborn seeks vengeance for the Forgotten's crimes against Skovlan during the war.

Situation: The Forgotten have procured the blueprints for the mansion of Baron VanTaeb, who gave the order that obliterated the battalion. The Forgotten are planning to break in and interrogate the Baron for evidence or a confession. But first, they need to swell their ranks to the point where they can overcome the Baron's sizable house guard.

EXERCISE #4

Detail three factions that will play a major role in your story using the framework given above: goals, turf, assets, prominent members, quirks, allies, enemies, current situation.

Create a front countdown clock for each faction representing one of their goals or plans. Decide on a combined timeline for the events. Think about how their respective plots would sync up or interfere with one another.

Example

The Red Ravens, the Gray Geese, and the Blue Bears are three factions. The Red Ravens want to install a loyal city council member, the Gray Geese want to blackmail the mayor, and the Blue Bears want to ally with a religious faction that seeks to control the city.

Combined timeline:

Blue Bears make regular tithes to the church.

Red Ravens gather intel on candidates for the city council election.

Gray Geese tail the mayor's staff, trying to figure out his schedule for leads.

Red Ravens arrange a meeting with a likely council candidate aligned with the local church who has, unbeknownst to them, already been bought by the Blue Bears.

Gray Geese hear about the Red Ravens' meeting through gossip among the mayor's staff and launch a plan to spoil the meeting and frame the Blue Bears for it.

And so on.

As you play *Blades in the Dark*, your gang will gain and lose status with other factions, which will then move against or assist your player faction.

RATHER THAN FEELING LIKE YOU NEED TO DETAIL EVERY MEMBER OF A faction, sketch out every line of their ledger. *Blades in the Dark* provides tools for building a spare but functional web of interconnected factions with competing agendas, which can help you tell a rich and sophisticated political story of alliances, betrayals, and opportunistic bids for power.

Depending on the scale of your story, it may only take a handful of factions to give your story the thickly-interwoven web of allegiance and antagonism needed to keep your story rolling.

I especially recommend thinking about factions and their plots in response to the protagonist's and/or antagonists' plans during the middle of a story—what's happening off-screen as the action follows the point-of-view characters. This middle is where many authors stall out trying to figure out what happens before an Act II reversal or the last twist that sets up the story's climax. If other characters or groups are active agents and the world is moving on as the characters act, it makes for a more dynamic setting and may provide opportunities for rising action, developing a subplot, and so on.

ACKNOWLEDGMENTS

When we launched the Worldbuilding for Masochists podcast, a key component we intended from the beginning was collaboratively building a world together, on air, inviting our guests to contribute. Just how collaborative, and just how much each interaction we had with each other and with guests and listeners would impact that world perhaps shouldn't have been surprising, but we're constantly amazed and humbled by the power of cooperative imagination!

This anthology would not have been possible without that cooperative imagination. First, a huge thanks to every collaborator we've had on the podcast—every suggestion, question, and "what if" has built a world and, more importantly, an ethos to guide building a world. You're too numerous to list here, but we've loved our talks with every one of you.

Our listeners have been the best group of nerds you could find from the beginning, and we're so grateful for your support as we've undertaken this anthology. For spreading the word, for social media shares, for enthusiasm—thanks. An especial thanks to those who supported us via Kickstarter, of course; without you this anthology literally would not have been possible:

Kristen R, Isabela, Jaiden Turner, Rook Riley, Miri Baker, D, Winifred Yost, Mary Morris, Paul Weimer, Victor Manibo, Haviva Avirom, Julia F, Clever By Half Productions, Solomon Stone Romney, Justin, Isaac Rudich, Susan Hance, D Franklin, Just_Eleanora, K.B Wagers, Natalia, mgshurst@yahoo.ca, kempfgd, Cara M, Angela Strong, Jamie Siglar, Nerdhogg, Johnny Lavinus, Xander Holdwine, Jaana, Luke White,

Korri Van Pelt, Melissa Shumake, Victoria Roman, constance, Ellie Pyle, Elizabeth Trzebiatowski, Robert Woods Tienken, Ceillie Simkiss, Heather Simmons, Henry Washington, Michael McCollum, Anne Morgan, Katharine Paljug, Laura Frantz, Lexie Hall, Sue Mosher, Myja Smith, Jacki Moffa, Elijah, CykoticArtist, Sam Bowne, Brian Moody, Danny Ray Smith Iii, George Neves, Erica Roberts, AJ Wentz, Michelle Oriolo, Dakota, Glorimar Medina, Julia Pillard, Jessi.halligan@gmail.-com, Annie Muirhead, Teresa McDonald, Ricardo Monascal, Stacy, Jessica Willson, Emmaline Conover, rooftophavoc, KateQ, Lian Duan, Miriam, Julia & Ken @SixthMoonPress, DNAPL, Thanasis Kinias, Kelly, Charles Gatlin, Abby Roberts, Chris McLaren, Matthew Nevers, George Stankow, Puck Malamud, Christine Hanolsy, d mayo-wells, Kim Woods, Austin Crabtree, Robert Suran, Edmund Schweppe, Jeff K, Stephen Rubino, Nina Mulligan, Nastasha LaBrake, Robert Czerwinski, MrDemolicious, penguinonstrike, eddi vulic, Stephaine Jacobson, William Ledbetter, Whalley Thomas, Abigail Fine, Alyssa Palombo, miyako, N. Frances Moritz, Elaewin, Kris Wiegand, Ruthan, Dan, Christina, Cathy Green, Jake Miller, Valentina, Rebecca, Jarel Reyes, Brooks Moses, Bill Frank, Caitlin Roberts, GeorgeZ, Colleen Feeney, Bethany Jezerey, Jeremy Brett, Dominique Reed, Caleb Jud, Jane Lowers, V, Michelle Matel, Andrew Bohata, K Parker, Oliver Stirland, Gary Davis, Becca Freeman, J.K., Neraven, Brendan Coffey, SinCity Minion, Lee, Bruce Arthurs, Steven Schend, Theaxofwar, Dawn P. Robinson, Mike Fatum, Eric, Tosha Crow-Walker, Jessica Wallace, L. M. Miller, Andrea Tatjana, Daniel Cormier, Charleson Mambo, Catherine Bascle, Kristina Downs, Mark Finn, Deborah, Stina Leicht, Eren Christenson, Lindsey Carmichael, Maureen McDonnell, Zoe, Denman Glober, Eddie A. van Dijk, Sofia Lindström, Erik DeBill, Dene Stareczek, Jacob Neal Sarvela, Sarah A. Macklin, Aleksandra, Mayken Brünings, Catherine Sharp, Elizabeth E Rowe, James Phillips, Kevin James, Sidsel Pedersen, Robert Paxton, Tom Hickerson, Emma Adams, Aura Lily V, Adrienne Haik, katastrophe, Rebecca Wilcox, Kieran Pritchard, Jack Finch, Kate Heartfield, elizabeth, Constance Wilde, Glynn Stewart, Noel Rappin, Thomas Bull, Akeisha Heard, myshade1973, pintofbovril, Sarah Ramsey, Jonathan, Craig Reynolds, Wazzull, Shadow, Mary Ellen Gilson, Cristina Bikanga Ada, Freyja

Andersdottir, Larisa LaBrant, Natalie, Sarah, Kelly Snyder, Jenni Calvert, Kayra, Adam Rajski, Edgar Governo, Ruth de Haas, Lilly Ibelo, Susanne Schörner, Joseph Procopio, Robert Claney, Adron Buske, James Olsen, Brynn, Amy, Eric Altmyer, Raf Bressel, Victoria Buckland, Omar Kooheji, Pearl, Agnes Metanomski, smercer, Carol Guess, Richard Halstead, clauclauclaudia, Elaine Brennan, Antennenwels, Elyse M Grasso, Patrice Sarath, Barbara Becc, Mark Zand, Adrienne Joy, Rhys Howell, E. Reed, Bona Books, kamalloy, Owen Blacker, Brenda N, Michael Feinberg, Miles Cormican, Margaret Hanson-Clarke, A. McGurer, Gerlinde F., Outi Aalto, paulcd2000, David 'slick' Sellers, Gas, Kolache, and Dramatic Skies, Marci, Andrew Zammit Montebello, Tibs, Todd Radford, Jason Kuroshima, Brent Lambert, Emily Gray, Nadia Graham, Dana Carson, Corey Fisk, Tim, Carina, Michael Lebowitz, Brendan Pease, Zeb L. West, Paige Kimble, Angus McIntyre, KJ, Ashara T., James Maher, JT, Dantzel Cherry, Becky seidel, Jeremy Talumin, Timandra, David Holden, John Card II, Christopher Dean Hagmann, Andrea Horbinski, Gerard-Jan, Vanessa, H Rae, Charlotte E. English, Alyc Helms, Aleksandra Żukowicz, Matt Knepper, Jakub, Ada Joy Kerman, Sietel & the Gene Queens, Ellis Kaye, Sarah Kaplan, Alana Joli Foster Abbott, Sergey Kochergan, Karawynn Long.

Thank you to each of our contributors—as you read these stories, you'll see why they deserve praise for breadth and depth of storytelling. As the anthology came together, a couple of additional collaborators deserve special mention. Our copyeditor, Viven Jackson, was a consummate professional and supported the clarity and vision of our writers immensely. Natania Barron, our cover designer, deserves kudos not only for a lovely and artistic design but for taking on the challenge of "a cover featuring the magical nude gate but not accidentally porn-y" and delivering in spades.

And finally, thank you as always to our families and friends for putting up with us and our weird niche interest (dare we say obsession?). Your love and support are appreciated more than you know.

ABOUT THE AUTHORS

NATANIA BARRON

The award-winning fantasy author of *Queen of None*, Natania Barron is preoccupied with mythology, monsters, mayhem, and magic. From medieval tales to Regency fantasy romance, her often historically-inspired novels are lush with description and vibrant characters. Of her first novel, *Pilgrim of the Sky*, *Library Journal* wrote: "Barron's debut is an sf adventure that mixes high action with exquisitely detailed depictions of everyday existence in these alternate worlds."

MARIE BRENNAN

Marie Brennan is a former anthropologist and folklorist who shamelessly leans on her academic fields for inspiration. She is the author of more than twenty novels and eighty short stories, and her work has been nominated for the Hugo, Nebula, and World Fantasy Awards. As half of M.A. Carrick, she has also written

the Rook and Rose epic fantasy trilogy, beginning with *The Mask of Mirrors*.

LINDSEY CARMICHAEL

Lindsey Carmichael (she/her) is a queer disabled writer whose fiction and poetry has appeared in *Analecta* and *Hothouse*. A mutant by birth and a cyborg by science, she multiclassed as a hedgewitch and two-time Paralympian. She set a world record in archery in 2004 and won a bronze medal in 2008. As of the Tokyo Games, she remains the only US woman to win an Olympic or Paralympic archery medal in singles since 1996.

MIKE CHEN

Mike Chen is the New York Times bestselling author of *Star Wars: Brotherhood, Here and Now and Then, A Quantum Love Story*, and other novels, as well as Star Trek: Deep Space Nine comics. He has covered geek culture for sites such as Nerdist and The Mary Sue, and in a different life, he's covered the NHL. A member of SFWA, Mike lives in the Bay Area with his wife, daughter, and many rescue animals.

KATE ELLIOTT

Kate Elliott has been publishing science fiction and fantasy novels and stories for over 30 years with a particular focus in immersive world building and epic stories of adventure & transformative cultural change. Her work has been nominated for the Nebula,  World Fantasy, Norton, and Locus Awards. *Black Wolves* won the 2015 RT Reviewers' Choice Award for Best Epic Fantasy. She lives in Hawaii.

VICTOR MANIBO

Victor Manibo is a Filipino novelist living in New York. A 2022 Lambda Literary Emerging Voices Fellow, he is the author of the science fiction novels *The Sleepless* and *Escape Velocity* from Erewhon Books. Find him online at victormanibo.com and on most social media platforms @victormanibo. 

MARSHALL RYAN MARESCA

Marshall Ryan Maresca is a fantasy and science-fiction writer, author of sixteen novels, most of which are part of the Maradaine Saga: Four braided series set amid the bustling streets and crime-ridden districts of the exotic city called Maradaine, which includes *The Thorn of Dentonhill*, *A Murder of Mages*, *The Holver Alley Crew* and *The Way of the Shield*. He is also the author of the stand-alone dieselpunk fantasy, *The Velocity of Revolution*. He is a four-time Hugo finalist the co-host of the podcast Worldbuilding for Masochists, and has been a playwright, an actor and an amateur chef. He lives in Austin, Texas with his family.

ROWENNA MILLER

Rowenna Miller is the author of the Unraveled Kingdom trilogy and *The Fairy Bargains of Prospect Hill*, as well as short fiction. She is also an English professor and a fairly handy seamstress. She lives in Indiana with her husband, two daughters, four cats, two goats, and an ever-growing flock of chickens. When she isn't inventing fantasy worlds, she teaches writing, trespasses while hiking, and gets into trouble with her sewing machine.

CASS MORRIS

Cass Morris lives her life at the intersection of storytelling, performance, and education as a writer and editor of novels, short fiction, and immersive experiences. Her novels, The Aven Cycle, are Roman-flavored historical fantasy. She is also one-third of the team behind the four-time Hugo Award Finalist podcast Worldbuilding for Masochists. Cass works as Story Editor at Mythik Camps, providing writing and developmental editing for the mythology-

themed summer camps' interactive theatrical experiences, as well as other programming and media projects. Previously, she worked in the education department at the American Shakespeare Center in Staunton, VA. She holds a Master of Letters in Shakespeare studies from Mary Baldwin University and a BA in English and History from the College of William and Mary. Find her online at linktr.ee/cassrmorris.

J.C. PILLARD

J.C. Pillard is a former academic who grew up wandering the forests of the Rocky Mountains. Her short fiction has appeared in *Abyss & Apex*, *Metaphorosis*, *Penumbric*, and elsewhere. When she's not reading or writing speculative fiction, J.C. spends time knitting and playing a frankly unhealthy amount of D&D. She lives in Colorado with her partner and dog. Find her at www.jcpillard.com.

MICHAEL R. UNDERWOOD

Michael R. Underwood is an author, game designer, and actual play producer. Their books include space opera *Annihilation Aria*, the Ree Reyes *Geekomancy* books, the Stabby Award finalist *Genrenauts* series, and *Born to the Blade* (written with Malka Older, Cassandra Khaw, and Marie Brennan). He's been a bookseller, sales representative, and was the North American Sales & Marketing Manager for Angry Robot

Books. They have been a co-host of the actual play show Speculate! and a guest host on the Hugo Award-finalist The Skiffy and Fanty Show. Mike lives in Baltimore with his wife, their dog, and an ever-growing library. He also loves geeking out with games and making pizzas from scratch.

VALERIE VALDES

Valerie Valdes is co-editor of the award-winning *Escape Pod* science fiction podcast. Her debut novel *Chilling Effect* was shortlisted for the Arthur C. Clarke Award, and her latest novel, *Where Peace Is Lost*, was named a 2024 Reading List Council honor title. Her short fiction and poetry have appeared in *Uncanny Magazine*, *Fit for the Gods*, *Magic: the Gathering* and several anthologies. She lives in Georgia with her husband, children and cats.

WORLDBUILDING FOR MASOCHISTS

Tide charts—a stack of books on constellation mythology—an elaborately sketched map—a bulletin board covered in illustrations of obsolete technology—research on textiles, naming conventions, architecture and a dozen ways to cook lentils—what could it all mean?

It means worldbuilding. Big worldbuilding. Elaborate worldbuilding. Obsessive worldbuilding. Dare we say… masochistic world building?

Play along with fantasy authors Marshall Ryan Maresca, Cass Morris, and Natania Barron as we delve into the intricacies of building a fantasy world from the ground up. Make that from the molten core out, because this is a worldbuilding deep dive. With new episodes every other Wednesday, guest authors, the occasional expletive, and a follow-along wiki as we build a new fantasy world together, we explore history, culture, science, and more as we learn new and exciting ways to *choose* the shape of our invented worlds, rather than merely repeating the presumptions of common tropes.